Ilona picked up her dagger and steeled herself for pain. Carefully, she opened the cut further and put her lips to her wrist, draining the wound of any venom that might have been injected, then spat into the grass, wishing she had a bandage for her wound.

A distant howl made Ilona stiffen. She jumped to her feet. The wind had picked up and roared louder through the leaves, carrying a musty, suffocating aroma. Shapes shifted between the trees, weaving in and out of the shadows.

"Who's there?" It took all of Ilona's courage to raise her voice, but if someone was there it would be better to feign bravado. "Show yourselves."

The sound of footsteps crushing rotting branches echoed in Ilona's ears. The shapes moved closer.

"There is somebody here." A low guffaw. "You were right, Varco."

In the Serpent's Coils

By Venom's Sweet Sting

Between Golden Jaws

Maiden of the Wolf

Queen of the Masquerade
August 2008

Oracle of the Morrigan
September 2008

The Marsh King's Daughter
March 2009

Snake Dancer
May 2009

Redemption
November 2009

Ouroborus Undone
Spring 2010

HALLOWMERE™

Volume Four

Maiden of the Wolf

Tiffany Trent & Angelika Ranger

MIRRORSTONE™

Hallowmere™
Maiden of the Wolf

©2008 Wizards of the Coast, Inc.

All characters, with the exception of the actual historical figures portrayed in this book, are fictitious and any resemblance to actual persons, living or dead, is purely coincidental.

This book is protected under the copyright laws of the United States of America. Any reproduction or unauthorized use of the material or artwork contained herein is prohibited without the express written permission of Wizards of the Coast, Inc.

Published by Wizards of the Coast, Inc. Hallowmere, Mirrorstone, and their respective logos are trademarks of Wizards of the Coast, Inc., in the U.S.A. and other countries.

All Wizards of the Coast characters, character names, and the distinctive likenesses thereof are property of Wizards of the Coast, Inc.

Printed in the U.S.A.

Cover design by Trish Yochum
Cover Art © Image Source/image100/Corbis
First Printing: May 2008

9 8 7 6 5 4 3 2 1

ISBN: 978-0-7869-4851-2
620-21719740-001-EN

Library of Congress Cataloging-in-Publication Data

Trent, Tiffany, 1973-
  Maiden of the wolf / Tiffany Trent & Angelika Ranger.
    p. cm. -- (Hallowmere ; v. 4)
  Summary: When Ilona is sent to an unfamiliar world to search for its
rathstone, she finds a chance at love that may cost her the mission to
protect Hallowmere.
  ISBN 978-0-7869-4851-2
  [1. Magic--Fiction. 2. Fairies--Fiction. 3.
Hungary--History--1000-1699--Fiction. 4. Fantasy.] I. Ranger, Angelika.
II. Title.
  PZ7.T314Mai 2008
  [Fic]--dc22
                                                                    2007050351

U.S., CANADA,
ASIA, PACIFIC, & LATIN AMERICA
Wizards of the Coast, Inc.
P.O. Box 707
Renton, WA 98057-0707
+1-800-324-6496

EUROPEAN HEADQUARTERS
Hasbro UK Ltd
Caswell Way
Newport, Gwent NP9 0YH
GREAT BRITAIN
Save this address for your records.

Visit our Web site at www.mirrorstonebooks.com

To my husband, who believed in me from the start.

—A.R.

PROLOGUE

[Translation note: Bottom of letter shredded as though by teeth or claws.]

August 1373

To Frater Ferenc, from Frater Gregorius, greetings. My dearest brother—

Of late, the Council has learned of a dark rumor in your country, new creatures that, it seems, now serve our Enemy. Some unholy union has taken place between man and wolf, most likely at the Prince's instigation, and now a breed of wolfmen, fierce in their bloodlust, roam the dark Eastern forests.

Beware them. They are devious and cruel, and it is the Council's belief that they are elite warriors among the Unhallowed. Keep your maidens well-guarded, for these wolfmen delight in nothing so much as carrying them off for their Lord's foul devices . . .

$\mathcal{T}$HE MOONLIGHT GLEAMED ON THE WOLF'S SILVER *coat. Ilona wasn't sure where he'd come from, but his cat-like amber eyes deepened in recognition even in the shadows. His ears pricked up, and his sudden howl echoed through the silent valley. He dashed up a hill and she followed, low to the ground. Her sense of smell had increased tenfold. The intense aromas of the forest distracted her: sweet wild poppies, a badger hole somewhere between the oaks, and a wolf's paw prints in the soft mud. Nose to the ground, she followed him. He waited for her on the peak. Together, they ran through the forest, branches flying by on each side. It was their time to roam and hunt, to be wild and free. Then a fog rose and separated them. The woods shifted, tilted. And the wolf was gone, taking his familiar scent with him.*

Once more, Ilona was alone.

Ilona took a few tentative steps across the unfamiliar forest clearing, trying to get her bearings. A wolf howled in the distance beyond the thin gray mist that hung low over the ground like cobwebs. She swiped at the musky air as though she could clear it.

She had no idea where she was. She wasn't even sure if she'd landed in the right place. She thought she'd end up somewhere she could fight her way to the rathstone, not in the middle of nowhere. She'd been wandering for perhaps an hour now but had found no sign of civilization. Just a forest thick with rotting undergrowth. Even the bark on the surrounding tree trunks was rotting, blackened and peeling off. The wind whispered through the gnarled branches, which cast eerie dancing shadows from the silvery moonlight.

Though she was disguised as a boy, wearing comfortable trousers instead of a full getup of dress, corset, and pinafore, she still tripped on a small rock as she rounded a boulder. With an unladylike curse Miss Brown would very much have disapproved of, Ilona pushed herself back up. *But Miss Brown can't hear me now.* She cursed again, enjoying her newfound freedom. Finally she was on her own, without anyone watching her, criticizing her, making her live by uncomfortable social rules.

Or helping her.

How will I ever find the rathstone here? Ilona wondered. She didn't know what it looked like, exactly, or who held it. Retrieving all rathstones from the Unhallowed was a tall order for the Council, but the mortal world's only hope.

How would the Unhallowed treat her? Wouldn't they see right through her, know her as an outsider, flung here from a world so different?

She straightened her spine and squared her shoulders. As much as the thought of encountering Fey made her insides squirm, she would not let them see her fear. *This is my chance to avenge the girls the Unhallowed stole. I can do this.*

The clouds parted and the moonlight cut through the fog, bouncing off the stones nearly hidden in the dense, weedy grass. Stones half-crumbled, half-covered by snaking green vines. Stones in neat rows. *A graveyard.*

Shivering at the possible symbolism of her first glimpse

of human life in this rath, Ilona walked to the nearest slab of rock, which sat in a mound of freshly turned earth, a bit apart from the older, untended graves. Its rough limestone surface gleamed dimly in the pale light. Underneath bloomed a single red azalea nestled in its dark foliage. *Someone cared enough to plant it here,* Ilona thought. *A caring soul in Unhallowed land.*

Curious, Ilona traced the inscription on the tombstone with her finger. Her heart beat faster. This wasn't English. It wasn't her mother tongue, Hungarian, either. Yet it brought her images from her childhood.

Her village classroom. Mrs. Kertész walked around, slapping her palm with a long ruler, her hawk eyes fixed on the children's small chalkboards. Benedek, in his seat behind Ilona, kept throwing pieces of chalk at her back. He should have known better. Even though he was two years ahead of Ilona, she'd pummel him outside at lunchtime, when their teacher wasn't looking. In class, she was content to turn around and stick her tongue out at him. Mrs. Kertész whacked her ruler on Ilona's desk. "Concentrate on your runes," she hissed. "They won't write themselves."

The Székely script—ancient Hungarian runes. How strange to see them once again. Recalling her primary school lessons, Ilona slowly deciphered a name and two numbers. Sofia Molnar, 1588–1604. *She was only sixteen when she died,* Ilona thought with a pang of sympathy. *This grave is fresh, so I must be in Hungary in the year 1604. Or some Unhallowed version of it.*

Snapping branches and a whistle somewhere off to her left made Ilona jump to her feet. She should have been more observant of her surroundings—her training had taught her nothing if not that. Her gaze flittered around, trying to penetrate the shrouding mist. *It's nothing,* she told herself, but still she hunkered down a little, hoping for what little cover the gravestone could offer.

A cool gust of wind made the hairs on her arms stand on edge. She had left Scotland in June, but it appeared to be autumn in this rath. Pulling her short jacket tighter around herself, Ilona hoped Corrine, Mara, Siobhan, and Christina fared well, wherever they had ended up. She especially worried about Christina. That girl could not take care of herself, that was sure. Ilona shouldn't have kept Christina's secret for so long, but she knew she would have lost Christina entirely had she not shielded her dealings with Rory from the Council's eyes. Now that they were separated, Christina's well-being vexed Ilona more than ever. She couldn't protect her now.

A long, slim shape, weaving through tufts of dry grass, caught her attention. This must have been the source of the noise, she figured, though she still held her breath as the green head of a snake rose toward her. The creature's golden eyes—so alien, so cold—locked with Ilona's. She didn't dare move a muscle. *There's nothing to fear,* she told herself. Vipers were the only poisonous snakes in Eastern Europe, and this wasn't a viper—it looked more like a little garden snake.

Yet beads of sweat formed on her forehead. Something was strange about this snake, otherworldly. It shouldn't have been out this late in the year; it shouldn't have been able to move this fast in the chill autumn air. Its skin was too smooth, too shiny.

The snake hissed, its pink tongue flickering in and out. The flat head undulated as though following a tune she couldn't hear. Mesmerized, Ilona held out her hand.

The snake slithered forward and coiled around Ilona's wrist, rubbing its cold belly on her skin. Then it slid back to the ground, wound in a circle three times on the rocky terrain, and took off into the grass.

Ilona glanced around the graveyard with a sigh of relief. She felt ill prepared to encounter strange wild animals in a Fey rath. Was the snake an ally of the Unhallowed? Her hand slid toward the little iron dagger tied to her belt. Perhaps she should have killed it.

With a soft hiss, the snake's head reappeared behind a gravestone. It flashed across the ground and wound around Ilona's left boot. The golden eyes beckoned and the tongue flickered in and out of the open mouth. *Hiss. Hiss. Hiss.*

Ilona unsheathed her dagger, tightening her fingers around the hilt. *I'm not taking any chances. This creature might be a messenger of the Prince himself.* She raised her hand to strike, but with a lightning-quick movement the snake slipped off her boot and into the foggy clearing. It shot into the grass, then stopped. It lifted its impassive head and glanced back at Ilona.

It wants me to follow, Ilona realized. *But that can't be right, can it? It's only a snake.*

The snake returned to Ilona's boot, circled her foot as before, then slithered back into the grass. Ilona took a few uncertain steps toward it. "Do you want me to come with you?" she whispered, immediately feeling ridiculous for speaking to a reptile. Still clenching her dagger, she walked on. When she had almost caught up with the snake, it slithered along for a few yards before it stopped again and swiveled its head back toward Ilona.

Branches crackled on her right. Her head whipped toward the sound and she squinted into the dense under-brush. Amber canine eyes stared back. The eyes turned orange, then hellhound red. They burned into her mind and glared into her soul, exposing her innermost secrets. Time slowed and she didn't breathe, couldn't move.

An owl hooted behind Ilona. She blinked. The eyes

had disappeared. Had they ever really been there? Or were they just a figment of her imagination? She stared hard into the trees.

The snake returned to Ilona's side and coiled around her boot once more. Ilona glared down in sudden disgust. *It's a trap.*

She thrust her dagger downward, but the snake was faster, and Ilona only grazed its tail. Cursing, she repeated the motion. But before her weapon could strike, the flat head darted forward and its yellow fangs dug deep into her wrist.

A sharp, searing pain ignited her arm. Ilona gasped but kept striking at the snake. No matter how quick she was, though, the snake was always quicker. The creature finally flinched and withdrew, hissing. The soft earth shook, and a hole opened up below the snake as wide as Ilona's fist. Head first, the snake slithered into the crack and disappeared.

Ilona bent down to peer into the hole, but it had already closed. Her hand fumbled on the hard, rocky ground, not finding any evidence of a recent opening.

Ilona examined her throbbing wrist, her entire body trembling. Two rust-rimmed puncture wounds had broken her skin. Twin rivulets of blood ran down her arm and dripped onto the ground. What if the snake had been venomous? Viper or not, how could she be sure in this strange Fey world?

Ilona picked up her dagger and steeled herself for pain. Carefully, she opened the cut further and put her lips to her wrist, draining the wound of any venom that might have been injected, then spat into the grass. She wished she had a bandage for her wound.

A distant howl made Ilona stiffen. She jumped to her

feet. The wind had picked up and roared louder through the leaves, carrying a musty, suffocating aroma. Shapes shifted between the trees, weaving in and out of the shadows.

"Who's there?" Ilona said in Hungarian. It took all of her courage to raise her voice, but if someone was there it would be better to feign bravado. "Show yourselves."

The sound of footsteps crushing rotting branches echoed in Ilona's ears. The shapes moved closer.

"There *is* somebody here." A low guffaw. "You were right, Varco."

Ilona backed away a few steps, her blood racing. Calling out had been the worse possible action. She knew better than that. What other creatures might she meet in an Unhallowed rath? She considered dashing into the woods, hiding between the black-barked trees. But they had seen her already. Swallowing her fear, she stood still.

"Hello." Her voice was small and raspy, so she cleared her throat and tried again. To keep up her disguise as a boy, she lowered her voice as much as possible. "Hi. I'm lost. Could you point me toward the next village?"

The men stepped into the moonlit clearing. There were six of them, tall, with square, sneering faces. From first appearances, they looked human. For a moment Ilona was relieved, but that didn't last long. Without Corrine's and Mara's magical abilities, how could she know if any of them wore a glamour?

The men's thick hair hung long and unkempt down to their shoulders. Some of them wore scraggily beards. Swords hung from their hips, and several carried longbows on their backs. Hunters. Her brothers loved hunting. She hoped against reason that these men were as harmless as her brothers.

"Catch anything?" Ilona forced a conspiratorial smile.

"We caught you, didn't we?" The man called Varco grinned darkly. His way of enunciating the Hungarian words reminded Ilona of her great-grandmother. He stepped closer, sniffing the air.

His gaze scanned her outline as thoroughly as if he had used his hands. "You don't look like a boy. And you don't *smell* like a boy." With a quick forward leap, he pushed her tweed newsboy cap off her short hair.

Ilona sprung back. She cursed the development of her female curves. Even last month in London, she'd mostly gotten by undetected. But she'd had to wear her shirt entirely too loose this time.

Her eyes darted from one man to the next. It was too late to run, but she had been trained to fight. Euan had once told her that every group has a weakest member. *That's your first aim,* he'd said. She unsheathed her dagger and held it out before her.

These men were all equally tall and strong-looking. *Men*—why weren't they Fey? Ilona hadn't expected to encounter humans in an Unhallowed rath. Her dagger trembled as doubt crept in. Varco knocked it out of her hand with his bare fist.

"Oops!" He sneered, then bent over the dagger in the grass and sniffed it. "Iron." He pulled a dirt-streaked handkerchief from his pocket and wrapped her dagger in it. Then he straightened up and glared at her. "Where did you get this weapon?"

Lips pressed together tightly, Ilona shook her head.

Varco stashed the wrapped dagger in his jacket as his men advanced, forming a tight half-circle around her. They withdrew their swords, the silver blades of which gleamed a deep sapphire blue in the moonlight, as though lit from within.

"Zador, Farkas!" At Varco's nod, the two tallest of the men dashed at her with unearthly speed.

Ilona ducked under their swords and slammed herself sideways into one of them, knocking his air out. She knotted her hands together and clubbed the other man's back. When his sword hit the ground, Ilona dived for it.

"Watch out, men. She's fast." A snap of Varco's fingers, and his other three men drew closer. Standing, Ilona clutched the sword with both hands. She retreated a few steps into the trees, keeping all the men in her sight. Sweat streamed down the sides of her face. She had trained mostly with a foil and sometimes with short swords, but never with a man's heavy broadsword. *Never with a Fey sword.* Already its weight dragged at her weary arms. Strangely, the blade did not glow when she held it.

Two of them came at her with swords raised high, growling. She parried their attack with one smooth movement.

"Aa-i-i-i-aa!" The sound escaping her mouth surprised her. Gripping the hilt more forcefully, she drove the blade forward to attack. She aimed for a shoulder, but the man moved and she struck only empty air.

A whistling arrow split the air above her head, missing her scalp by inches. Ilona had to move faster if she wanted to stay alive. She dodged a blow to her right, then skipped backward, dancing on her toes. Another arrow shot into the tree trunk next to her. Were they just toying with her? She should be dead by now.

Ilona drew a deep breath and pushed every ounce of strength into her aching arms. With a loud yell, she drove the men backward, attacking their limbs, swinging her heavy sword, swinging, swinging.

"Enough. We don't have all night." Their leader pushed forward, sword drawn.

With synchronized movements, the men advanced from all sides. Ilona cried out. Crashing metal knocked the sword from her hand, leaving her defenseless.

Varco faced her with a lopsided grin, running his tongue over unusually long canines. His brown eyes sparked with amusement.

Ilona scowled. "Must have been such a challenge for you, six against one."

He shrugged and motioned to the man whose face was graced by a long, puckered scar. "Farkas, pass me those shackles." He grabbed Ilona's left wrist and snapped on silver shackles.

Anger simmered to a boil inside Ilona. She balled her hands into fists. It had been such an unfair fight.

"You're not from this *grófság*, are you? Where did you come from?" He attached the other end of the silver chain to his own arm.

Ilona remained silent. She couldn't tell him she came through a portal from the human world, and she wouldn't tell him her mission here at any cost.

"If I have to make you talk, I will." Varco raised his sword to her throat, eyes narrowing. "Again: What is your name and where are you from?"

Ilona's thoughts raced. If she gave them the name of her Hungarian hometown, they would not gain any useful knowledge about her. But she loathed giving him her name; it seemed dangerous to do so.

"Well?" His blade scraped against her skin, drawing blood.

Ilona swallowed hard. Staying alive was more important than keeping her identity secret.

"My name is Ilona Takar. I'm from Battonya, in the county of Békés. It's a small town; you might not have heard of it."

Varco took his sword off her throat and sheathed it. "I know it. It's a couple days' ride south." In the pale light he looked young, not much older than Ilona herself; twenty years at the most. His eyes narrowed. "What are you doing so far from home, all by yourself?"

"Are you my mother?" Ilona snapped, against the advice of her pounding heart.

He laughed. Dark hair fell into his eyes and he swiped at it with an absentminded gesture. With a whistle at his men, he set out into the forest at a jog, pulling Ilona along.

The woods were dense and gloomy. Ilona squinted to make out the path, but there didn't seem to be one. The men spread out, finding their own ways through the thick undergrowth. Her captor never hesitated, pushing on as though he could see clearly through the surrounding darkness. Ilona asked several times where he was taking her and why, but Varco ignored all her questions.

Long after her feet grew sore and tired, they reached the edge of the forest. A village stretched below them in a night-gray valley, nestled between half-harvested fields. Little houses spilled haphazardly onto both sides of the rutted path that wound through the town. Dull straw covered the rooftops of ramshackle huts. Vines and brush crept from the forest's edge, reaching as far as the houses, as if the forest was attempting to swallow them whole. The village appeared abandoned.

The dark man by her side nudged her. "That's Cachtice village. It's not far now."

Not far to where?

Varco waited for all his men to assemble, then gave the signal for them to dash down the hill into the village. He pushed Ilona to her limits to keep up, yanking on her wrist so hard her shoulder joint screamed in pain. Ilona was glad for her trousers. She couldn't imagine having to run like this in an ankle-length dress, never mind the corset.

They slowed once they reached the first hut. The house lay silent, dark windows gazing blindly. The entire village was eerily quiet. The man with the bushy red hair walked up to the entrance and knocked. It was a hollow sound.

"Anybody home?" He kicked the door and laughed. "Any pretty girls in there?"

"Come on, Zador," Varco snarled. "You know this town is dead. And we already rescued a pretty maiden." He winked at Ilona.

Her cheeks grew hot with anger. She didn't need *his* compliments. And he certainly hadn't rescued her—what was that all about? Avoiding his looks, she glanced around the village. The houses were small and crooked, as though blown here by the wind. *Cachtice village.* Ilona tried to recall the map of northern Hungary, but geography had never been her strong suit.

A human settlement, she thought. How strange. The Council had told her that the rath would be entirely populated by Fey. So what were all these mortals doing here? And what else had the Council gotten wrong?

Varco's men snuck around the houses, peering into windows and sniffing at the doors. Ilona grew uneasy watching them. Their odd behavior chilled her more than the autumn breeze blowing from the north.

"I think I found one." The one with the gray hair and

scraggly beard—the oldest-looking of the marauders—leaned against the front door of a tiny shack. He pressed his ear against the wood and grinned. "Aye. I heard a giggle."

All the others except Varco, who was still tethered to Ilona, trotted toward the house. Boards covered the windows, but the men ran into the door as a pack. It crumpled like paper on their second attempt. All five men jostled through the opening.

A high scream pierced the night air, followed by a pleading cry. Ilona glanced at Varco. He idly played with the silver chain of the shackles linking them together, looking about the town with unconcern.

Soon the men returned, two of them gripping a slender girl between them.

"Well done, boys," Varco said. "Hurry now, we have to get back."

The girl trembled. Her eyes were wide; they dominated her pale, delicate face. Thin and dressed in a simple, dirty-white shift, she didn't look a day over twelve.

Behind them an older woman, stout and wrapped in a dark shawl, cowered in the doorway. She stretched out her wrinkled hand for the girl and wailed.

The last man to leave the hut laid a hand on her shoulder. "Don't cry, woman. You know that your girl will have a better life in Castle Cachtice than you could ever provide for her."

The old woman wiped her tears and nodded. "God bless the countess," she said. "God bless our *táltos*."

"Mama!" the young girl cried out. She tried to twist out of the men's grasp. Her left hand slipped free, but the other man laughed and wrapped both of his hairy arms around her.

"Didn't you hear? You'll be a fine maiden of the countess, sleeping on silk and eating bonbons all day. Be grateful!" He buried his ugly, scarred face in her chestnut hair, sniffing and growling. "Give Farkas a kiss."

Ilona's stomach tightened. She swallowed her rising fear and stepped forward as much as her shackles allowed. "You're scaring her. Let her go!"

Farkas raised his head and grinned. "Or what?" His grip on the girl tightened.

Ilona raised her voice. "You're a coward. If I had a sword, I'd put you in your place." She strained against her binding and kicked up dust toward the scarred man.

Varco pulled her back. "Enough." He turned to Farkas. "Stop fooling around. Bind the girl and come along."

Farkas nuzzled the shrieking girl's neck. For a moment, Ilona thought she glimpsed fangs behind his snarl. "I caught her." He narrowed his eyes at Varco. "I can have some fun with her if I like."

"You follow my command," Varco said in a sharper tone. "And that's all."

Farkas pushed the girl into the redhead's arms and pulled his sword from his hip. "Is that so?" He lunged forward and thrust the glowing blue tip of his sword against Varco's throat. Farkas's putrid breath enveloped Ilona and made her gag.

The next moment, she realized how much in the way she was. The silver band around her wrist tied her to Varco's right arm. As he reached for his weapon, he yanked her hand down, then back up as he whacked Farkas's sword away from his neck.

Farkas smirked. "I see you have a little handicap. Don't you know better than to tie up your sword arm?"

Varco threw Ilona a sidelong glance. "She's my secret weapon."

His arm shot forward, attacking Farkas. Ilona was propelled along, fighting hard to keep her balance. If she fell, Varco would be unable to block Farkas's higher blows.

Farkas parried, dancing around Varco, aiming for his unprotected left. But Varco deftly switched hands and managed to ward off his assault. Ilona kept as much to the side as she could, trying to stay clear of the sharp, swinging blades.

The other men watched the fight, yelling encouragement to Varco. But none of them made an attempt to help their young leader. Ilona gave them an angry scowl as she sought to keep her balance without interfering with Varco's fight.

A metallic clank caught Ilona's attention, and she swiveled back to the fight. Varco's sword tumbled through the air and landed on the ground.

Varco dived for his sword, yanking Ilona down with him. A wrenching pain seared through her arm as she stumbled and fell. Farkas kicked the sword away and stomped on Varco's neck.

When Ilona twisted away, she spotted Varco's sword next to her. Instinctively, her hand shot out and gripped the handle. With a yell, she slashed sideways into Farkas's calves.

A long howl echoed in her ears. Ilona sliced once more before Varco pulled her up and wrestled the sword out of her hands. For a moment, their eyes met.

He leaned forward as though to embrace her. "Thank you." The words were almost imperceptible, mumbled into her hair.

Farkas crouched in the dust. Dark stains widened on

his green pantlegs. He gave Ilona a hateful look out of eyes that glowed orange in the moonlight. Her knees quivered, and the world spun. Varco steadied her with his arm.

"Let's go," he said to his men. He gave a nod in Farkas's direction. "Get up. You're not badly hurt."

Two of his men tied the new girl with ropes. She had stopped crying and looked at Ilona with sad, stunned eyes, as though begging for help.

Ilona tugged at Varco's arm. He had shown a sliver of mercy earlier. "Can't you let her go?" she asked in a low voice. "She's so young—what do you want with her?"

Varco shook his head slowly. "It's not my call. She's for the countess."

Without further explanation, Varco rushed his men down the road. Ilona jogged by his side to keep up.

As they hurried past, the door of a small house opened, and a stooped, gray-haired man stepped out. He shook a pitchfork at the men. Ilona suppressed the thought of crying out for help. What good was one pitchfork against six swords?

"Be gone," the man yelled, in an oddly high-pitched voice. "Be gone, creatures of darkness!" He held something with shaking hands. Ilona had to squint to make it out. A wreath of some kind. Made of onions? No, garlic. Then the Unhallowed couldn't be far off.

Ilona's captors chuckled and sneered at the old man.

"Go back to sleep," Varco said. "We have no interest in you."

The group of marauders followed the path out of the village. Ilona and Varco brought up the rear. She turned her head to glance back. The man still stood on his threshold, the wreath of garlic now around his neck.

"I shall pray for your lost souls," he called after them.

"You're welcome to," Varco muttered. "Pray for all of us." His brown eyes took on a troubled expression and the tip of his boot kicked a rock on the path. Then he shook himself and yanked on Ilona's chain.

"So, your name is Ilona Takar. Ilona means beautiful—how fitting." He laughed. "I'm Lieutenant Varco."

Ilona glared at him. "Aren't you a little young to be a lieutenant?" She kicked at his shins, but he leaped sideways just in time.

"Whoa. Still itching for a fight? You did a decent job earlier, but it's over now, you know?"

The genuineness of his smile irritated her. Ilona didn't want to like him. Pointedly, she looked the other way. They were passing the last of the village houses, a tilted, ramshackle building with several aimless chickens running near the path. Their excited clucks caught Varco's attention. He licked his lips. Then he frowned.

"We should get back to the castle. Dawn is near."

A strip of orange marked the horizon in the east. Darkness of night receded fast. Varco pulled on Ilona's shackles. "Come on. We're almost there."

On weary feet, Ilona stumbled along beside him. A growl made her turn and glance back once more.

A huge black wolf stood in the middle of the path. It clutched a chicken in its fangs. Blood dripped down its muzzle onto the sandy ground and its glowing red eyes bored into Ilona. Ilona turned her head away as the wolf dropped the dead chicken and held it down with one large paw, using its sharp teeth to rip it apart.

~ Two ~

THE BAND OF MARAUDERS HURRIED UP THE SLOPE OF A grassy hill as the rising sun tinged the clouds orange and pink. Sickly brown weeds grew into the path, and sharp rocks dug through the thin soles of Ilona's shoes. A swarm of bats circled low overhead, letting out heart-stopping shrieks before fluttering off into the horizon.

Goose bumps prickled over Ilona's skin and her wheezing breath became irregular. She would have preferred a calmer pace, but her captor tugged at her shackles whenever she showed signs of slowing down. Her shackled wrist throbbed as much as the snake-bitten one, and Ilona wondered whether her skin looked as raw as it felt.

Her eyes on the rocky ground, Ilona rushed on, trying hard to appear strong. Finally Varco paused, yanking her to a standstill.

He pointed up ahead. "Your new home." His sneer mocked his words. "Castle Cachtice."

Around the bend, behind a line of scraggly pine trees, rose the black outline of a castle. Its massive walls loomed tall and impenetrable, overgrown with lush emerald ivy. Screeching bats dived in and out of the arched windows of high towers that stood black against the pre-dawn sky.

Varco jerked on her shackles again to get her moving. The agony in Ilona's wrist sharpened and she bit her lip to keep from crying out.

His dark eyes scanned the brightening horizon. "I want to get back before dawn," he said. "Keep moving."

What's wrong with dawn? Ilona wondered. But her mind was too exhausted for further questions.

The twisted path became steeper and dense with vegetation. Willow branches snatched at Ilona's ankles as though trying to stop her from walking on. She shivered as she brushed them aside.

Ahead, the men came to a halt before an eight-foot wall. A huge wooden door reinforced with bronze blocked the entrance. Varco pushed to the front, pulling Ilona along with him.

She glanced at the pale girl slung over the shoulder of the younger redhead that Varco had called Zador. Her eyes were closed; she had either passed out or fallen asleep.

Varco took a brass key out of his pocket and turned it in the lock. With the squeal of neglected hinges, the door swung open. As they entered the castle courtyard, Ilona tripped over something soft and, with a cry of surprise, fell into Varco's back. A black shape arched its back and yowled. Green eyes glowed in the dim light. The creature dashed through the open door and disappeared down the path.

"Hey! Watch it!" Varco yanked Ilona back to her feet and kicked the door shut with a curse. "Damn cats. I can't stand them. They're always underfoot."

Ilona glared at him. "Get your hands off me. I can walk by myself." Her eyes darted around the courtyard. If she was going to be a prisoner, she might as well continue her work looking for the rathstone. This was as good a place to start as any.

"Whose castle is this?" she asked Varco. If she was to survive in this rath, she desperately needed more information than the Council had given her. "Who do you work for?"

Varco raised a finger to his lips. "The countess will be the one asking you questions, not the other way around. Hush now." He turned to his troop. "Good job, everyone. Get some sleep." He motioned toward a cluster of sheds at the far side of the yard.

Farkas turned to Zador, who still carried the girl. "Give her to me," he demanded. *"I'll* deliver her to the countess."

The redhead hesitated and gave Varco a quizzical look. Varco stepped between them, holding up his left hand.

"I don't think so, Farkas," he said. "You're dismissed."

Farkas thrust his head forward. A threatening growl came from deep in his throat.

Varco reached for his sword. As her wrist was yanked along, Ilona groaned inwardly. Not another sword fight with her in the middle!

Farkas glared at Varco, his eyes ablaze. Ilona was sure he would pull his sword, but he abruptly swiveled and ran after the other men toward the sheds.

She stared at his receding figure, an odd feeling of foreboding bubbling in her stomach.

Zador waited until the door of the shed banged shut behind Farkas, then he turned to Varco.

"You better watch out for Farkas. He'll take you down if you don't pay attention."

Varco shrugged, but his eyes darkened. "You're watching my back, right, Zador? I'm not worried."

"He might try to turn some of the others against you." Zador shifted the girl on his shoulder.

The two men led the way across the cobblestone yard toward the main entrance. They'd entered through a side gate where rotten food littered the ground—Ilona guessed that this must be the kitchen door and the rotten food the midden heap. She held her breath against the stench as they crossed a small green plot and walked up a grand cobblestone drive to a marble entryway.

Varco banged on the door with his fist, ignoring the skull-shaped knocker. An elaborate gas lamp dangled above them from an ornate brass pole. It threw a dim pool of light on the threshold. Varco had raised his hand to knock again when the door opened. He shuffled his feet.

A young girl peeked out. Wide brown eyes dominated her pinched face. She wore the plain dress and long apron of a maid and motioned the men inside with a nod.

"You're home late tonight." The girl held the door for them as they entered the hall.

Zador pushed past her with a wide grin spreading on his face. "Did you miss me, Anci?" He attempted to smack the girl's bottom, but she quickly danced out of reach. "I'd take you out to the Black Bear for a drink sometime, but Varco makes me work night after night." Zador made a show of rolling his eyes at his lieutenant.

"We all have our loads to bear," Anci replied. With red, chapped hands, she tucked a stray strand of her mousy hair behind her ear. She didn't smile, but the way she cocked her head and stood a fraction too close to Zador gave Ilona the impression that she wouldn't have turned down his invitation.

"Will you be so kind as to fetch Madame Joo?" Varco's

polite words clashed with the impatience of his tone. "It's not getting any earlier."

"Yes, sir." Anci curtsied with a mocking smile and ambled out of the hall.

"No rush," Varco mumbled at her back. Turning to the redhead, he added, "I don't know what you see in her, Zador."

"Nah." Zador scratched the thin stubble on his chin. "Anci's as charming as a rabid bat. But at least she's still got some spirit." He heaved the blond girl onto his other shoulder without waking her. "Unlike this dead load."

Ilona glanced around the entrance hall, a large, oval room with passageways leading off to all sides. She shuddered at the thought of that soldier's attention directed toward the young girl he carried. Before her, a grand staircase swept up to a gallery. Massive cherry wood beams held up the vaulted ceiling from which a huge chandelier with brightly glowing candles dangled. She blew on her hands and massaged them. It wasn't much warmer in here than outside.

Varco kept staring at her, his gaze as hot and penetrating as a blast of fire. "You're cold?" He wrapped his hands around hers. An unnatural heat radiated from his palm and warmed her hand almost instantly. Ilona sighed as her fingers thawed. Then she quickly withdrew her hand from his.

"I'm fine."

Varco bent his knees and dipped his head, trying to catch her eye. She stared at the torch beyond his shoulder.

"So, who taught you to use a sword?"

Ilona glared at him. *The Fey Prince himself, as a matter of fact.* But that was a fact that this kidnapper would never learn from her. She couldn't trust anyone, and if the

Prince found out she was here . . . she shuddered at the thought.

"Come on. You can't tell me you used a sword for the first time today!" He nudged her with his foot. "I've never seen a girl with such quick reflexes."

Ilona let her long bangs fall into her eyes and avoided his gaze. "I don't know what you're talking about. No one would teach a girl to fight."

"Maybe she's not a girl." Zador chuckled.

Ilona's shoulders rose and fell. "Maybe I'm not."

Varco grinned. "I believe there's a way of finding out."

Ilona's fist reeled back. "Try it."

At the creaking of a door, the men spun around. An older woman entered the hall, shoulders square and back ramrod straight. The iron-gray hair piled on top of her head gave her the illusion of height.

Both Varco and Zador bowed low. "Madame Joo." Varco straightened. "We *rescued* two girls tonight." He motioned to Ilona and the other girl, who still lay motionless across Zador's shoulder.

"Only two? You're not having a good week, Varco." Madame Joo shook her head and clucked her tongue.

The lieutenant mumbled an apology.

"Bring them into the parlor." Madame Joo walked ahead of them through a doorway.

Ilona exhaled in a long hiss of relief. She had expected some Unhallowed monster to inhabit this castle. Madame Joo was probably only a mean, withered spinster, and Ilona would be able to deal with her just fine, once she got her fingers on another sword. And then she could get on with her mission—finding the rathstone.

At a tug on her wrist, Ilona followed Varco. He ducked

under an arch to enter a small sitting room. A fire crackled in the stone hearth, more warm-looking and welcoming than she expected from such a severe woman, and candle-light threw shadows at the paneled walls. But despite the fire it was still freezing in this room. Zador dumped the girl into a plush armchair in the corner. Her head lolled back, and her arms dangled over the armrests.

Varco produced a tiny silver key and removed Ilona's shackles. Ilona winced at the sight of her raw, crimson wrist. At least the bite marks of the snake had closed on her other wrist, and the swelling had gone down.

Varco turned to Madame Joo with a wide grin. "The one dressed like a boy is Ilona Takar, from Békés county. She's a handful."

Madame Joo shot Ilona a narrow-eyed look and waved her hand at the men. "Thank you. You're dismissed."

Varco hesitated with a glance at Ilona. Then he nodded at his redhead companion and walked toward the door. When he brushed past Ilona, he pressed her arm and whispered, "You'll be all right."

The night's cold had lodged deep into her bones, and Varco took the last of the warmth with him. Ilona inched toward the fireplace, hands outstretched. The flames leaped and the logs crackled, but the hearth didn't throw any proper heat. Like a mere image of fire, it couldn't warm her body.

Madame Joo approached Ilona. Deep creases lined her skin and the black hairs on her chin trembled as she spoke. "So, your name is Ilona Takar?" She lightly jabbed Ilona with her finger. "Ilona is *my* given name. How dare you waltz in here with my name?"

Ilona had never heard such absurdity before. "Ilona"

was such a common name in Hungary. And in any case, her name was not her fault.

"And look at your hair! The countess loathes short hair! Have you chopped it off yourself?" Madame Joo reached out a wrinkly hand.

"Don't touch me!" With a quick movement, Ilona pulled back. She had cut her hair off herself, first in her grief over the disappearance of her best friend Jeanette, that awful spring when the Unhallowed Fey had taken her. Then Mara had cut it once more to disguise Ilona as a boy for her secret Council missions on the streets of London.

The girl in the armchair stirred and groaned. Wiping her golden hair out of her face, she opened her eyes. Her gaze fell on Madame Joo and she gasped.

"Good morning, my pretty. Have you slept well?" Madame Joo smirked.

The girl hid her face in her hands and began to sob quietly.

The old woman approached the chair. Sitting on an armrest, she stroked the girl's long locks with slow, deliberate movements. "So soft," she muttered. She pried the girl's hand away from her face. "The countess will be pleased. What is your name, child?"

"Katalin." Tears streamed down her rosy cheeks.

"How sweet. And how old are you, Katalin?"

"I'm twelve years old, ma'am."

Madame Joo's thin lips stretched into a smile. "Perfect. I will show you to your new bedchamber in a moment."

"No!" Katalin's voice rose. "Let me go home. I want to live with my family. Oh, please, let me go!"

"Quiet down." Madame Joo patted Katalin's shoulder.

"You are very lucky to be chosen to live at Castle Cachtice. Your family will be proud."

Without thinking, Ilona stepped forward.

"Can't you see she's frightened?" She glared at Madame Joo, tightening her fists. She didn't have her dagger, but she had grown strong over the last year. She would defend this girl even against a seemingly harmless old woman.

Madame Joo regarded her coldly. "You are a stranger in our *grófság.* This does not concern you. Little Katalin is here for her own good. The village peasants are poor and cannot provide the luxuries of Castle Cachtice." She waved at the lavish draperies and plush couches of the room, as if to indicate the kind of care Katalin would receive, then went to the bronze stand by the hearth. She took the fire poker and jabbed it at the logs.

Ilona couldn't imagine that being ripped out of her home could be good for Katalin, even if she came to live in the finest of castles. She put her hand on Katalin's shoulder. "Hush, don't cry. I'll keep you safe."

Katalin's sobs quieted. A shimmer of hope returned to her large eyes. She leaned her head against Ilona. "I knew I shouldn't have killed that big spider in my bedroom," she whispered. "It's such bad luck."

Growing up as an educated merchant's daughter, Ilona had been taught little of common peasant superstitions of old, but she knew a few from her uncle's servants on his estate. This was one she hadn't heard before, and she wondered how many times she'd brought down bad luck upon herself cavalierly killing spiders for her more squeamish friends. If it were true, of course. She kept stroking Katalin's hand, wondering what else to do. It did seem like a nice place to live, though colder than it ought to be. Madame Joo was not the nicest person, but the castle was very beautiful, and perhaps Katalin really would be safe here. It reminded her of Falston, though—fine furnishings didn't necessarily make a good home.

Still, she had to be careful not to draw too much attention here. Perhaps cunning would be required more than action at this moment. She studied Madame Joo, who still stood tending the fire. Then Madame Joo turned around to face Ilona. In the low light, her shadow on the wall grew taller and taller, spreading across the ceiling. Her ugly face stretched into a long visage with hungry red eyes. Her fingers reached for Ilona's hair, turning into blood-encrusted claws. A snake-like hiss escaped from the narrow line of her lips, bringing with it the pungent reek of decay. Ilona gagged and turned her head away from the creature before her. Chills arced down her spine, but she couldn't move. She closed her eyes.

For a moment, Ilona's mind returned to the church at St. Fillan's, to Corrine and Mara inside the circle, holding on to the rathstones while they opened the gates. She envisioned her friends: Christina, Corrine, Mara, Siobhan. Each one of them had left the safety of their world to enter an Unhallowed rath, even the terrified maid Siobhan. Ilona shook her head and opened her eyes. She couldn't see through glamours like Corrine could, but there was something about this Madame Joo that told Ilona that this was the place to begin her search. Whatever she had just seen, it had been the sign she needed. She would go along with whatever this woman required—for now. Until the moment was right.

The candles lit in a flash, and the shadows receded. Once again, Madame Joo was an ugly, elderly woman, no creature of the night. Ilona blinked rapidly and exhaled in relief.

Madame Joo glanced at the flickering candles in surprise. Then she narrowed her eyes at Ilona. "I see you're not an ordinary farm girl. I don't think you belong here at all." Madame Joo's voice lowered to a whisper. "Where are you really from? And how did you get here?"

Ilona swallowed hard as her heart raced. Above all, she had to keep her quest for the rathstone hidden. Or she'd surely fail the Council.

After a long moment of silence, Madame Joo spoke again. "No matter. Keep your secrets, then, *Ilona*." Madame Joo sneered. "The mistress won't be pleased. I wonder what she'll do with you."

Ilona's head hurt. Too much had happened in one night. Then Madame Joo's words hit home. "The mistress? Aren't you the mistress of this castle?"

Madame Joo cackled. "Me? Mistress of Castle Cachtice? But haven't you heard of Countess Bathory?"

Ilona mutely shook her head. Even if it confirmed she was a stranger in these lands, she couldn't pretend to be familiar with the name. She lacked the knowledge to back it. "Should I have?"

"No matter," Madame Joo repeated. "You'll get to know her soon enough." She rubbed a mole enfolded in the sagging flesh of her neck. "I believe those are her footsteps on the stairs."

THREE

*A*N ICY DRAFT ACCOMPANIED THE TALL WOMAN WHO SWEPT into the parlor. Her features were clear—beautiful, Ilona would call her, far more beautiful than anyone she'd ever met—and her raven hair undulated in waves over her indigo silk dress. Her finery matched the finery of the castle, as though she were the jewel of the crown. The fire flickered and flared as though bowing to her presence. The woman's eyes seemed to pull Ilona closer. As black as swamp water, they were equally ancient and knowing, two dark orbs glowing in her smooth white face. Her smile could have been taken for welcoming, had Ilona not already been suspicious.

She's one of them. The realization struck Ilona in the thump of a single heartbeat. *She must be Unhallowed. This is why I'm here.*

"My lady." Madame Joo bowed her head. "We have two new arrivals. One of them is quite lovely."

With a gait so graceful she seemed to be gliding, the countess moved closer. Ilona restrained herself from grasping for a weapon. She must remain cool, and not alert this creature to her true origins. *Just go along, be a normal girl for a little while.*

The countess's cold stare skimmed from Ilona to Madame Joo. "You don't mean this one, I hope?" Her merry laugh stung Ilona more than she would have liked to admit.

She knew she was no beauty, but did the countess have to be so forthright about it? Normally Ilona valued straight talk, but she didn't need reminding that she was no ordinary girl.

"No, of course not." Madame Joo motioned toward Katalin sitting wide-eyed in the armchair. "I was speaking of this maiden here. I believe she would be a perfect addition to your entourage."

The countess approached Katalin with a sigh. "You are right, Joo. She *is* beautiful. Look at that golden hair—and the fair skin!" The countess ran a long finger down Katalin's pale cheek. "You will be so happy and content to live here. Your family is lucky we found you."

Ilona watched the exchange with puzzled curiosity. "What could you offer Katalin that was so much better than the love of her own family?" she couldn't help but let slip out.

Madame Joo puffed up her gray cheeks. "This one's audacious. Your men found her outside the village. What sort of girl sneaks through the woods in the middle of the night wearing boys' clothes?"

"Indeed." The countess glided closer.

Ilona fought the urge to back away. No matter what she suspected, she couldn't let on that she knew any more than she'd already given away.

"Her clothes fit her well, though, don't they?" The countess strode around Ilona, regarding her from all sides. "The dirt on her pants matches the calluses on those huge hands. Say, *girl*, do you embroider with those hands?"

Ilona narrowed her eyes and took a deep breath to control her anger. "Not willingly."

The countess turned to Madame Joo. "Take the pretty one to the maidens' chambers and settle her in. I'll have a closer look at her later." The raspberry tip of her tongue flickered over her open lips.

Madame Joo took Katalin's arm and led her to the door. The girl whimpered softly but didn't struggle.

The countess patted Ilona's shoulder with a long, slender hand, a gesture that might have seemed motherly coming from Miss Brown. "You, my dear. We really must get you better clothes. Perhaps then your looks will improve. You may not be the right sort for my entourage, but perhaps we might find a good use for you."

The countess waved at her clothes, and Ilona suddenly realized what she was implying. She shook her head vehemently. "I'm not taking my clothes off!"

The countess shifted closer, bending down until the dark pools of her eyes were only inches from Ilona's. She touched Ilona's cheek. "We mustn't get off on the wrong foot, now, must we? I can do great things for you if you let me, but I have no need for a stubborn girl who will not obey me."

Again Ilona reminded herself that if she got thrown out—or worse, killed—it would do her cause no good. Perhaps it would be better to humiliate herself for a few moments to get a place in the countess's household. It would afford her some sort of freedom to move about without having to break in past the soldiers and servants, not to mention Madame Joo.

A hot jolt of sparkling fire snapped Ilona's attention back to the countess's light touch. Suppressing her urge to fight back, Ilona feigned her best impression of Siobhan, stuttering and nodding. "Yes, my lady," she said as she slid out of her clothes and stood shivering in her thin undergarments. It took all her effort to keep her eyes dry and clear. She never cried. She wouldn't start now. "Happy now?" she grunted.

The little shockwaves of pain returned when the countess ran her fingers up and down Ilona's arms. Ilona fought a sudden nausea and the impulse to pull away and run.

"Muscles; firm, thick flesh. You're as much a girl as my soldiers outside!" Disgust laced Countess Bathory's voice. She shoved Ilona away.

The abrupt absence of pain made Ilona dizzy. She tried to calm her breath and steady her swimming vision. Out of the corner of her eye, she saw Madame Joo return to the parlor.

"Tell the soldiers not to bring me any more like her," the countess commanded. "I like my girls soft and supple."

Holding on to the wall for support, Ilona sighed. *Thank the heavens.* The countess didn't want her. That could only be good news. But she did need to stay here, somehow. She was becoming increasingly aware that infiltrating this castle might be the most important part of her mission here in this rath.

"I understand." Madame Joo rubbed her hands. The rust-red stains on her fingers gleamed in the fire light. "Perhaps it would please my lady to place her into my charge? I could think of many ways to amuse myself with her."

The countess gave her a weary glance. "She looks strong enough to do the work of two. Put her in the kitchen, where she'll be of some use. If she proves troublesome, you may get a chance yet to try out your devices on her." Before

Madame Joo could reply, the countess left the room.

A kitchen maid? The countess had just given Ilona the keys to the kingdom, as far as she was concerned. That would be the perfect position to gather more information about the rath and its ways, perhaps even find out where the rathstone was hidden. Ilona reached for the bundle of clothes by her feet.

"Leave that," Madame Joo said in a sharp tone. "From now on, you'll wear the dress of a maid."

The floors and walls of the laundry room gleamed, though Ilona could smell faint traces of mildew coming from somewhere. The simple old-fashioned chemise and kirtle Madame Joo grabbed from a rack of neatly folded extras was as clean as the outfit the girl Anci had been wearing when she answered the front door. So cold she couldn't keep her hands from trembling, Ilona pulled on the plain brown kirtle, but she was unable to lace it up on her own.

Madame Joo led Ilona half-dressed, carrying apron and head scarf, through the great entrance hall to the kitchen. "Anci," she screeched. "Anci, where are you?" The same maid who had opened the door hurried from the hearth toward Madame Joo, wiping her hands on her apron.

"Yes, ma'am. I'm here." Anci's brown eyes shone dim in the warm light. Her face didn't betray any emotion.

"Where's your *basma?*" Madame Joo barked.

Several strands of loose hair slipped from Anci's neat chignon as she fumbled inside her apron pocket and pulled out a soiled headscarf. "It fell into the goulash, ma'am."

"Then wash it." Madam Joo yanked Ilona forward by her sleeve. "Here's a new kitchen girl for you. Lace her up and teach her the chores—but watch out! She seems to be particularly stubborn and devious."

Anci gently turned Ilona around and tied up her laces, then helped tie the long apron cords. It didn't fit well, but at least the multiple layers made it warm and serviceable. Ilona tied on the old embroidered headscarf, tucking her short hair underneath.

While they were arranging Ilona's clothes, Madame Joo sniffed the fragrant air. "Do I smell omelets? Hurry up and serve the breakfast for the countess and me in the green parlor."

Anci curtsied deep and low until Madame Joo left the room. Then she spat on the floor. At Ilona's raised eyebrows, she replied in a hushed voice, "Madame Joo bears the *rontás.*"

"The evil eye?" Ilona asked. "That's just a—" She stopped herself. If the Unhallowed were real, who was to say that anything Ilona used to dismiss as superstition weren't possible?

"Spitting will ward it off. Quick, do it now, while she's not here to see you."

At Anci's imploring look, Ilona spat onto the floor, sure that as the new girl she would be the one to get floor-cleaning duty later. *What a disgusting habit,* she thought.

Anci pushed her shirt's cuff up and revealed a red ribbon tied around her forearm. "I also wear this, night and day. In my home village of Alsoberecki we use this to protect small children from the evil eye, but since I'm an unmarried maiden, I hope it will help me as well." Anci eyed Ilona with a calculating look. "What's your name? Have you been in service before?"

"Of course not," shot out of Ilona's mouth before she had a chance to think. She couldn't tell this girl that she was the daughter of a wealthy merchant and used to having her own servants. Anci wouldn't believe it anyhow.

Ilona thrust out her hand in greeting. "I'm Ilona."

After hesitating for a second, Anci took her hand and laughed. "Anci." Then she grew serious. "Welcome to Castle Cachtice. I know it's supposed to be an honor working for the countess, but I wish for your sake that her soldiers hadn't caught you."

"Why is it supposed to be an honor?" Ilona asked. "Forgive my ignorance, but I'm a stranger in these parts."

Anci looked surprised. "You must be, if you don't know. Countess Bathory is our *táltos*—our benevolent protector. She uses her special shaman powers to look after all the people living in her domain's farms and villages. In return, the peasants show their respect by offering sacrifices in the form of food and servants."

Ilona had felt the countess's witch powers on her own body and didn't believe for one moment that the countess ever used her powers for the good of the people. *But if she's the strongest Unhallowed in this rath, she is bound to hold the rathstone. I've come to the right place. Now I only have to find a way to get out of the kitchen and explore the grounds.*

A clock chimed somewhere in the distance. Anci flinched. "We'd better hurry. We have so much work to do. Can you make porridge?"

Ilona groaned. She was prepared to fight the Unhallowed with a sword, but make porridge? "Doesn't Countess Bathory have a cook?"

"Oh, yes, Polly serves the countess and her friends during the night. The countess can stay up quite late. And the soldiers, of course. They eat a lot. I do the cooking during the day."

Anci showed Ilona the long wooden tables set along the kitchen walls for food preparation and the racks of silver or bronze utensils and chopping knives. A basket of round, raisin-studded buns gave off a fragrant smell and Ilona's hand reached for one before her mouth could form a request.

Anci slapped her hand away. "Don't! The buns are for the countess's maidens."

"Her maidens?" Ilona asked with raised eyebrows.

"Yes. The maidens who live in the east wing chambers. It is part of our job to serve them their meals."

Before Ilona had a chance to ask anything else about the maidens, several other girls wearing *basmas* and long aprons appeared in the kitchen. Anci introduced Ilona, and each girl replied with a small curtsy and their own name, before going about their chores without another glance in her direction.

"We can't be caught chatting," Anci explained with an apologetic shrug. "Madame Joo won't have it."

Evike, a thin girl with a harelip, left with two rusty buckets and returned with water. Dorika took the buckets from Evike, heated the water in a large cauldron above the fire, then filled the sink and began to scrub the crusty dishes. Gizi, her long nose red-tipped by the cold draft in the kitchen, cut up leeks and roots on the counter.

"What can I do?" Ilona asked. "I'm not a good cook."

Anci gave her a long look.

"You could chop some firewood," she suggested at last. "It's the soldiers' job, but they always forget. And I don't like reminding them." Anci frowned at her toes, and Ilona wondered if the soldiers were in the habit of giving the maids a hard time.

"I'll be glad to." Ilona stretched her arms. She could use the exercise.

Anci led Ilona through a small door into the kitchen yard. A cold blanket of night frost covered the herb garden, and the ground crunched under Ilona's boots.

A black cat meowed on the nearby castle wall. Anci shooed it away with both hands. "Black cats are a bad omen," she said with a worried look on her face. "This one keeps showing up and it makes me nervous."

How complicated all these pagan superstitions make their life, Ilona thought. But perhaps they helped the peasant girls survive living in an Unhallowed castle.

They reached a small shed behind the herb garden. Hundreds of logs had been piled against the castle wall and an axe stuck in the nearby chopping block. Ilona pulled it out and weighed it in her hands. Her finger slid along the sharp blade. She gave Anci a questioning look.

"It's made from silver? How can it chop properly? Silver isn't strong enough."

"Hush." Anci glanced around the deserted yard. Then she leaned forward and whispered, "Iron weapons aren't allowed in the castle. It weakens the *táltos*'s powers. And this sort of silver is much stronger than any iron I've ever seen. It must have a shaman spell on it."

Ilona remembered the strange glow of the soldiers' weapons and nodded. She knew from Corrine that iron hurt the Fey, so it made sense that they wouldn't use it in their tools or weapons.

She took one of the birch logs from the supply and placed it on the block.

"Don't cut your hand off." Anci wrapped her arms around her shivering frame and eyed Ilona with an expectant expression.

"I won't." Ilona held the shaft of the axe firmly with

both hands and raised the blade high over her shoulder. With a whoosh of air, the axe came down and split the log precisely in two. A few more strokes provided Anci with an armful of kindling.

"You're strong." Anci smiled up at Ilona. "Chop as much as you can."

Ilona watched Anci trudging back toward the kitchen, wondering whether the look in Anci's eyes had been true admiration or only gratitude for the firewood. Ilona hoped she would find friends among the servants. She could use their help in finding the rathstone.

Ilona chopped log after log, dead on her feet after an exhausting night. The exertion and the rising sun soon warmed her. She kept an eye out for the soldiers who had captured her the night before, but the yard remained deserted. Only sparrows kept her company, hopping around the cobblestones pecking for crumbs and flittering into the sky with each strike of her axe. The black cat kept its distance, eyeing her from the castle wall.

When the sun stood high overhead, Ilona began to worry that she *would* chop her own hand off in her blurry fatigue. Her hands ached with new blisters forming atop her old fencing calluses, and her muscles quivered. She put down the axe and rejoined the other maids in the kitchen.

Anci crouched in front of the cold hearth, cleaning out the ashes with a brush.

"I'm famished," Ilona said. "Isn't it time for lunch?"

Anci swept a strand of brown hair from her brow, smearing soot across her pale skin. She didn't look up from her chore. "There is fresh bread in the box. And some dried meat." She waved a dirty hand toward the counter. "Help yourself."

Ilona slunk to the bread box and peeked in. There was a warm loaf and a side of salted pork. She cut herself a large slice of each, then halted, remembering how Christina had nearly died after eating a piece of Unhallowed fruit. It made her wonder if she should eat at all while she was in this rath. But how would she manage even a day without food? She was *always* hungry, and she hadn't eaten since they'd left Fearnan for St. Fillan's kirk. And the kitchen maids didn't look like they were starving.

"Is the food safe to eat?" Ilona asked Anci. "I mean, does it ever make you sick?"

Anci frowned. "We get our supplies from the surrounding farms. They always send their very best to please the countess. You won't go hungry here."

Leaning against a table and taking a big bite of her bread, Ilona watched Anci work. "Do you ever think about escaping from the castle?"

Anci gave a strangled sound. She dropped her brush into the ashes and covered her face in her hands.

Ilona flew to her side and gently touched Anci's shoulder. "What is it?"

A shudder went through Anci. Then she wiped her dry eyes and swallowed audibly. "I did once. I bribed the soldiers with kisses and ran home to my family," she whispered.

Her voice was so low that Ilona leaned in closer to hear. "And?"

Anci looked around, careful to see that no one else was in earshot, and cleared her throat. "My father strapped me to his cart like cattle and brought me back to the castle. He was too scared of the countess to hide me from her." Anci began to cry. Thick tears streamed down her cheeks, washing lines through the ash that smudged her cheeks.

The kitchen door flew open, and Madame Joo charged in, clutching Dorika by her long braid.

"I found this little hussy in the bedchamber, lounging about like there's no work to be done. Anci, you have failed me again. Will I have to remove you from your position? Do I have to punish both of you?"

"It won't happen again." Anci stopped crying, but trembled all over, her hands twined firmly into the folds of her apron.

Madame Joo narrowed her eyes. Her gaze fell on Ilona. "I fear your behavior will give the new maid wrong notions. I would like to impress on her what happens when you lot defy me."

All emotion drained from Anci's face. No muscle moved in her body, as though time had come to an end.

"No, ma'am, that's not necessary. Please. We'll be good. She won't give you any trouble."

Madame Joo's lips twisted into a malicious smile, and she hooked Dorika's arm in her claw-like hand. "No, she won't. I will make sure of that."

~ Four ~

*I*LONA STARTED TO FOLLOW MADAME JOO AND DORIKA OUT the door, fists clenched, but Anci stopped her.

"If you follow her, you will only get punished, and make it worse for Dorika, too," she said. "We can't help her. We can only try not to gain Madame Joo's attention again."

Ilona looked around the kitchen at the other girls, who studiously avoided her eyes. Gizi struggled to light a fire with flint and tinder in the large, wide hearth, and Evike picked up the buckets to haul more water. Anci touched Ilona's arm tentatively, saying, "All we can do is wait. And care for Dorika when she returns."

"What will she do to her?" Ilona asked. Shame and help-lessness compounded her anger and her deep disappoint-ment at being unable to protect these girls from Madame Joo. But if she was to succeed in her mission to find the rathstone, she couldn't go charging in and get herself killed over one girl, even if that girl was being mistreated.

"I don't know," Anci said, moving to the table and wiping down the morning's leavings. She also avoided Ilona's eyes. "I try not to think about it. I've been to Madame Joo's room once, and I never want to speak of what I saw there."

Ilona couldn't get any more out of Anci after that.

Anci barked at the other girls, nearly on the verge of tears, ordering them to get the countess's lunch quickly to the green parlor. It wasn't long after Evike returned from that errand that Madame Joo returned, a stumbling Dorika in tow. She threw Dorika to the floor.

"Let that be a lesson to you, new *girl* with my name. No second chances." She gloated over them while Anci and Ilona rushed to aid Dorika. Her back was covered with welts, apparently from a whip. "Get her cleaned up and get back to work. Feed the maidens."

After Madame Joo left them, Ilona gave voice to her feelings. "How can you stand being treated like a slave? Isn't there anything we can do?" She gripped the handle of a silver knife and slashed it through the air. "We should give that woman a taste of her own medicine!"

Anci jumped to her feet with a startled look in her eyes and laid a hand on Ilona's arm. "Don't. You can't fight Madame Joo with a bread knife." She carefully slid the utensil out of Ilona's grasp and placed it back on the counter. "There is nothing we can do but obey her." Anci's dark eyes became tired and cold. "You'll get used to it." She jerked her chin up. "In time."

Ilona mutely shook her head. She wouldn't be here long enough to get used to anything. Already she was formulating a plan. She would have to wait until the right time to tell them, though—these girls had to be ready to stand up for themselves.

Anci helped Gizi start a blazing fire, and Evike secured the cauldron over the crackling flames. Ilona turned back to Dorika, who had dried her tears on her dirty apron. Only a slight tremble betrayed her pain and distress, but the back of her dress was ruined.

"I'm so sorry Madame Joo hurt you." Ilona clenched her hands into fists. "I'll get you a new dress."

"It was my own fault," Dorika mumbled. "I shouldn't have gone to the sleeping chamber during the day. But I was just so tired." Her eyes misted over. "I'm always tired. The howling of the wolves keeps me awake at night."

Ilona didn't know how to respond. After not having slept all night herself, she could understand the impulse to lie down and nap during the day.

When she returned from the laundry room with a new chemise and kirtle for Dorika, Anci banged a spoon on a pot to get the girls' attention. "Back to work. No time for chatter." She squinted when something small and sparkling buzzed through the window. A creature the size of a dragonfly spun cartwheels through the air and finally alighted on Anci's arm.

Curious, Ilona approached Anci for a closer look. She had heard Corrine's stories about pixies and pillywiggins, but so far hadn't seen any for herself.

The creature on Anci's arm was a tiny girl—a fairy, with iridescent green wings and hair the color of polished pewter. Ilona gaped at her. Only a short while ago, she hadn't believed in the existence of any sort of Fey, but since then she had become so entangled in the Council's problems that she had slowly accepted fairies as real. Yet the sight of the minuscule girl in a rustling dress the colors of autumn made her breath hitch.

The pixie whispered into Anci's ear, hands gesturing.

Anci paled and nodded. She shook the fairy off her arm, who gave a little squeal before fluttering her wings and darting out of the window. Ilona wondered how such a pretty thing could be serving the Unhallowed Fey. But perhaps the pixie wasn't here by choice, either.

Anci touched Ilona's elbow. "That was the fairy Vanillina. She is our *táltos's* messenger. The countess is calling for me. I have to go and see what she wants." Anci's eyes appeared even darker rimmed by the paper white of her face.

Ilona regarded her with new respect. Where did Anci find the power and courage to battle down her fear and face her evil mistress day after day?

"We'll work on the kitchen chores without you." She squeezed Anci's arm. "What needs to get done?"

Anci shrugged, already moving toward the door. "You should prepare the food for the countess's maidens and deliver it to the east wing. There's plenty of meat and fish in the pantry."

After Anci left, the girls assembled several trays, piling them high with such delicacies as deer meat, rainbow trout, cakes, custards, cheeses, and pungent fall apples. Ilona's mouth watered, but the apples had a strange, waxy shine to them. They put her in mind of the Unhallowed fruit that had made Christina deathly ill.

The door to the kitchen garden flew open with a bang, and Varco stepped over the threshold, bearing a load of firewood. He dropped the logs by the hearth.

"We didn't need those today," Evike told him, turning her nose up. "Ilona chopped wood already."

Varco turned to Ilona. His eyes sparkled. "Are you doing my chores? That's sweet of you."

Ilona shrugged. She had meant to make Anci's life easier, not *his*.

Varco leaped to the trays on the counter and swiped off a chicken leg. He chewed it up, bones cracking between his teeth. "Delicious," he mumbled with his mouth full. He reached for a tart, but Ilona stepped forward, holding up her hand.

"For the countess's maidens," she said. "Not you."

Varco laughed. "Forgive me, fair Ilona." His gaze swept over her, and Ilona became painfully conscious of her silly, untidy kitchen maid attire. She'd been up to her elbows in food and hadn't really paid attention to where stains might form. She straightened her apron and glared at him.

"Looks tempting, though, doesn't it?" Varco pointed at the platters. When Ilona nodded, his grin disappeared. He gripped her arm and lowered his voice.

"Don't eat any of the fruit, Ilona. Not ever. And don't drink the maidens' wine."

Ilona yanked free. "I won't. Why would I?"

Varco gave Ilona a searching look, then bowed mockingly to the other maids. "I shall take my leave, then, my beauties." With a bounding step, he disappeared through the exit to the gardens.

Gizi bolted the door after him with a sigh and glanced at the girls. "Whose turn is it to deliver?" she asked. "I went last time."

The maids fell silent, cautiously peeking at each other. Ilona's thoughts raced ahead. She'd learn nothing new by staying in the kitchen. Exploring the castle at any opportunity was the best way for her to collect more information about this rath. Her hand shot up.

"I'll go."

Evike's eyes widened. "You will?" She exchanged surprised glances with the other maids. "I'll go with you, then. We can each carry two trays."

Gizi hung leather flasks around Ilona and Evike's necks.

"Mulled wine," she explained. "Fill each maiden's goblet."

Carefully holding the full platters, Evike and Ilona walked through the door, which Gizi held open. Dorika made the sign of the cross over them as they passed and Gizi mumbled something that sounded like a good-luck chant.

Flickering torches cast shadows along the maze of narrow, drafty corridors. For a fortress that looked so well-kept, Ilona couldn't figure out where the cold was coming from. Perhaps it was just the nature of a building so big. It had to be hard to heat with just a fireplace in each room.

"The east wing is this way." Evike balanced both trays on one arm and knocked on a wooden door. "The guards that protect the countess's maidens are . . . rough," she whispered. "But if you show no fear, they won't hurt you."

The door grated open to the dark face of a hulking man peering out at them.

Evike shrank back. She raised her full tray. "We bring the maidens' meals."

Ilona shuddered inwardly as they passed the grunting guard. He loomed over her in a horned helmet fashioned from black metal that failed to hide his uneven features. He looked as if he'd been in one fight too many, with a nose that must have been broken once. Yellowed teeth protruded from wide lips—apparently he took no care for his dental hygiene as Miss Brown had taught the Falston girls to strictly observe. His body odor was overpowering but unfamiliar. *Farmyard,* Ilona thought. *Or maybe graveyard?*

The guard led the way along another dark corridor. He wasn't tall—in fact, he was a couple of inches shorter than Ilona. But his shoulders were massive and his legs as thick as tree trunks. He carried a short sword on his belt and wore chain-mail armor across his torso.

I could take him down, Ilona thought. *With the right weapon, at the right time.*

They entered a great parlor with a fire crackling merrily in the grate. Two more guards, with the same hefty build and unpleasant faces as the first, sat at an ornate table that seemed intended for something far more elegant than the game of chance being played upon it. A leather cup and several gaudy-colored game rocks sat upon the glossy surface, a game Ilona wasn't familiar with. One of the men was extremely hairy, with tufts of chest hair sticking out from his tunic, and the third man was small compared to his two comrades.

" 'Tis feeding time," the guard with the horned helmet growled. The two men at the table went back to their game, ignoring the girls. Ilona glanced around the large, sparsely furnished parlor. Two doorways curtained off by faded velvet drapes led out of the room.

"Where are the maidens?" Ilona wondered if she would see Katalin among them, hoping that the young girl had fared better than Ilona herself had.

"They share two bedchambers," Evike said. "If you take the left, I shall take the right." She motioned toward the curtains.

Reluctantly, Ilona stepped through and entered a hall the size of a small ballroom, filled with a long row of plush four-poster beds. The room was cast in darkness; the tall windows lay hidden behind elaborate black drapes. Flickering lanterns atop a nightstand by each bed provided the only light. Slim shapes sprawled on top of the beds or in the plush chairs beside them. *The countess's maidens.*

The carpet under Ilona's feet was woven so thick that it felt like walking on a mossy forest floor. Ilona approached the first bed and placed her trays on the silken bedspread. A slender girl of about fourteen huddled against her thick pillows. She wore a cobalt blue housecoat over a lacy nightdress and curly red hair shimmered down her back.

"Are you hungry, miss?" Ilona indicated her tray. "I have whatever your heart desires."

"Whatever your heart desires," echoed the girl in a singsong tone. Her vacant gaze was not quite rooted in the present. It was as though she had just woken from a dream that hadn't yet released its grasp on her.

The girl's fingers slid from the salted meat to the raisin tarts, then sped toward the apples. "Desires." She polished the apple on her dressing gown and bit into it, breaking the skin with a crack.

Ilona cleared her throat. The girl's deportment unsettled her, although she couldn't quite say why. Her gaze fell on an empty bronze cup next to the lantern. She opened her flask and poured a measure into the glass. An aromatic smell of cloves, cinnamon, and nutmeg rose up, taking her back to Christmases at her father's estate, to pleasant evenings by the fire after a long sleigh ride.

With a sigh, Ilona held the cup to her nose, inhaling the scent of the wine like the sweetest perfume. Before she knew what she was doing, she had raised the goblet to her lips, closed her eyes, and taken a sip of the rich wine. The sweet taste of honey and spices glazed her lips and tingled on her tongue. Ilona had never tasted anything this delicious in her life. *A little more won't hurt,* she decided, lifting the cup again.

No~o~o~o~o~o!

A long, agonized cry, like the howl of a tortured soul, startled Ilona. Spilling wine over her hand, she quickly put down the goblet and glanced around the quiet chamber. What had she done?

A soft breeze stroked her cheek and Ilona stumbled forward as her vision wavered like water in a pond. She grasped for a flash of blinding white light but only caught air. A sigh whistled into her ear and chilled her skin, then broke off abruptly.

Suddenly coming to herself again, Ilona shook her head. A sound like bells ringing in the distance made her stand still and listen, but then that was gone, too. Breathing fast and shallow, Ilona glared at the damp plaster on the walls. A girl in an adjacent bed moaned softly.

Ilona regarded her wine-stained fingers with disgust and wiped them on her apron. *I shouldn't have drunk that wine,* she thought. *What will it do to me?*

Still shaking, she picked up her trays and walked toward the next bed. At the sight of the girl lounging on her side in a ruffled cotton gown, she almost dropped the food.

"Jeanette!" She sat her trays down and took the girl's hands. "Is it really you? I thought I'd never see you again!" Even in the dim light, there was no doubt that she had indeed found her best friend, the one the Unhallowed Fey had stolen from Falston. From her.

"Oh, Jeanette! Are you all right?" She peered into Jeanette's face, squeezing her hand for a response, but her friend stared with unseeing eyes at some point over Ilona's shoulder. She hummed softly to an inaudible tune. But her soft brown curls shone as though freshly brushed, and her skin had a healthy pink glow. She didn't look harmed, only disoriented.

"Can you hear me? Jeanette?" Ilona rubbed the girl's arm, hoping for some spark of recognition. "It's me, Ilona." She lowered her voice to a whisper. "From Falston. Remember Falston? Christina and Miss Brown?" Speaking Christina's name hurt Ilona's throat and spread warmth and longing through her. Gone for only one day, it seemed as though she hadn't seen her in ages. Would she be all right? Who would protect her, all alone in an Unhallowed rath where anything could happen?

But Christina wasn't here and Jeanette was. Ilona could do something for her now. She stroked Jeanette's hair. "Are you hungry? You should eat something." Ilona handed her a sweet roll from a platter. Jeanette absently began to chew.

With shaking hands, Ilona refilled the cup on Jeanette's nightstand. Why did the countess keep these girls here in such a state of oblivion? Why did she bother feeding them delicious foods and giving them clean sheets to sleep on?

A shiver raced across Ilona's skin as the truth revealed itself to her in the pink glow of Jeanette's plump cheeks. "She's fattening you like a Christmas goose, isn't she?" Ilona's voice rasped over her suddenly tight throat.

"I'll get you out of here," she whispered to the softly humming figure beside her. "Soon." First she had to find the rathstone. And she still had no clue to its presence. But Jeanette would be safe here for a while longer. At least she wasn't starving and wasn't made to do harsh, humiliating chores. Wasn't beaten with a whip.

Ilona kissed the top of Jeanette's head and picked up her trays. "It'll be all right. I promise."

~ FIVE ~

$\mathcal{E}$VIKE AND ILONA SILENTLY FOLLOWED THE GUARD BACK TO the locked door, carrying their empty trays and flasks. Ilona's heart was heavy as she thought of Jeanette, so strangely quiet and unaware of her surroundings. The guard looked different than he had on the way in. Ilona couldn't put her finger on it, but he looked more *gray* somehow. Not quite human.

At the door, he twisted a large silver key in the lock and let them out.

Alone in the hallway, Ilona turned to Evike. "So—I've seen fairies. And whatever those guards were, they weren't human, were they? Who else works for the countess?"

Evike shrugged. "I don't know. And I don't want to know." She gripped her trays tighter and hurried along the stone floor. "This place is part of the Fey Prince's realm. All kinds of wicked creatures live here. There are rumors, but I try not to think of them." She quickly spat on the ground, turned around on her toes three times, and chanted something Ilona couldn't quite understand. Perhaps she was speaking in the ancient Hungarian in which the gravestone scripts had been written.

Ilona sucked in a long breath. Part of her wanted to

confide in Evike and tell her about her reunion with Jeanette. But that might lead to questions about Ilona's reason for coming to the rath, and she wasn't ready to reveal her mission to anybody. Especially not these meek maids, who could so easily be cowed by Madame Joo and the countess.

She glanced at Evike's tired face. "I wonder if we could help the countess's maidens, somehow. You know, try to release them."

Evike stumbled, lost her balance and hit the wall. The empty trays clattered to the ground. She pressed her hand to her chest, eyes wide. "No. You cannot do that."

"Why not? There are only three guards, and they would let us inside if we pretended to bring food."

Evike, recovered from her shock, picked up her platters. She shook her head vigorously. "Don't be so thick. Those guards—you're right, they're not human. They use an evil magic, a glamour that most people can't see through, that's what they say. But you really want to know what everyone says they are? They're trolls. The kind that wait underneath bridges and steal little girls. And they have swords, and besides, we'd still have to leave Castle Cachtice. And that's impossible. The *grófság* soldiers guard the yard and all the gates."

Ilona nodded, deep in thought. *Yes, the soldiers. But they're just men, not Fey. It must be possible to defeat them.*

Back in the kitchen, more chores awaited the girls. Ilona peeled a barrel of potatoes for the soldiers' evening meal, drew pail after pail of water from the well in the kitchen yard, and chopped sweet-smelling peppers until her fingers ached and her stomach growled with hunger. While doing her tasks, she spoke in low tones to the other girls whenever she could, trying to find out how they had come into the rath. Their stories saddened Ilona. Each had been ripped from her home in the middle of the night by the countess's soldiers. Each left behind her family, her peaceful village life, and found herself in the nightmare of Cachtice castle.

However, none of the girls mentioned the rathstone, and Ilona didn't dare ask them straight out. *How am I supposed to find the stone, stuck in the kitchen as a maid? I wish I had Corrine's magical power of detecting it,* Ilona thought. *I don't even know for sure if it is the countess who's holding it.* But nobody else in this rath seemed to wield as much control as Countess Bathory did, and her power must come from somewhere. No, Ilona was almost certain that she had come to the right place.

She had to be very careful. If the countess or Madame Joo grew suspicious of her . . .

After the kitchen maids worked a full day of scrubbing dishes and cooking for the countess, Madame Joo dismissed them to their bedchamber. A heavily-armored soldier—another troll, Ilona realized, making out his bulky misshapen shape underneath a thinning glamour—guarded the door, but at Madame Joo's command, he produced a ring of keys and opened the chamber. Ilona walked past the troll with her chin up, although she detested having one of *them* so close to her bedside.

The bedchamber was as cold and drafty as the rest of the castle. Unlike the rest of the castle though, the veneer was far too thin in this room. Only two candles splashed puddles of orange light on the dirt floor. Box beds filled with straw covered with graying sheets full of holes provided bedding for the girls. *Ghastly,* Ilona thought. In

Falston, she hadn't slept on down pillows, either, but the sheets had always been clean and mended.

Madame Joo assigned her the only available bed space, in a corner under a tiny, barred window. The thick tail of a rat disappeared behind it in a scurry.

"Pleasant dreams," Madame Joo snarled, her thin lips drawn downward. As the old woman walked out of the room, Ilona made faces at her receding back, her fists clenched into tight balls. She felt as powerless as a child. *In a sword fight, she wouldn't stand a chance against me. How much longer do I have to be her maid?* The answer was easy: Until she found the rathstone. But how could she find a stone as small as an average pebble? It could be anywhere, hidden under a loose floorboard or in the eye of a statue. She had hoped to sneak out at night to look, but with a troll guarding their bedchambers that opportunity was far from her reach.

With a noisy crunch, the guard troll locked in the kitchen maids. Ilona glared at the door in dismay. To explore the castle and to find the rathstone, she would need help. If there were only someone she could trust.

A single rusty bucket filled with icy water from the well served as a washbasin for all seven maids sharing the room. Ilona lined up behind the other maids to wash.

Evike turned around and smiled at Ilona. "It's your first night in the castle. You should count the corners!"

"I beg your pardon?" Ilona rubbed her tired eyes. Sometimes the maids did not make any sense.

"You know. If you sleep in a new place where you've never slept before, you ought to count the corners of the bedchamber, and your dream will come true."

Another silly superstition. Ilona yawned. "I don't have to count. All rooms have four corners."

Evike *tsked* and pointed at the ceiling.

"All right. Eight corners, then." *And I hope I dream of finding that bloody rathstone and taking Jeanette home with me.*

After washing, she stretched her aching limbs out under the rough sheet, which smelled like boiled cabbage and onions. The dim light and the quiet chatter of the girls made Ilona sleepy.

I'm only going to rest my eyes for a moment, she thought. *Then I'll think of the perfect plan.*

Ilona sped across the night-dark meadow, her paws padding along silently, her nose to the rocky ground. The moon had hidden behind dense clouds, but she found her way through the darkness by following the scents and sounds of the wild.

An owl hooted nearby, then swooped to snatch a squeaking field mouse. A deer flew across the short-cut grass and darted into the underbrush, followed by its mate.

Ilona sniffed the breeze. Damp fall leaves, frightened rabbits, a burping toad. But no sign of her pack. She shook her head in confusion. When had she gotten separated? How?

Must find them. Ilona ran on. A single wolf was worthless, in constant danger. Only with her pack she was safe.

She left the meadow and cautiously stepped onto a path. A multitude of smells, mostly human, assaulted her sensitive nose. A cold wind whooshed by her ears, carrying a strange, strangled sound. A long sigh, like someone's last breath. The breeze carried the stronger scent of old blood and decay.

Deep cartwheel ruts led north. Ilona ran along the path, following the new smell. A light blinked in the distance, glimmering like a group of dancing fireflies. It grew until it resembled a globe of witchlight, hovering over the exact point of the road crossing another. Ilona leaped toward it.

The witchlight bobbed and expanded, flowing outward in all directions.

When Ilona reached the crossroads, the glowing shape became a transparent girl. She wore a lacy nightdress and her hair flowed loosely down her back. Her pale feet didn't reach the ground. Ilona could detect no scent.

The girl stooped, put a white hand on Ilona's head and scratched behind her ears. The translucent hand felt surprisingly solid. Ilona closed her eyes and enjoyed the contact. Then she nudged the girl's knee with her nose.

Who are you? Ilona asked in her mind. Why are you here?

The girl straightened. She opened her mouth as if to speak, but only a trickle of a dark, viscous substance dripped out of her parted lips and stained her chin. She reached for the collar of her nightgown and pulled it down, exposing two small, circular wounds.

Did the countess hurt you?

The girl nodded. Then she held a hand out to Ilona. A stone the size of robin's egg lay nestled in her palm. A warm light pulsed inside it, like a heartbeat. It was at once beautiful and frightening. When Ilona pushed her nose against it, it disappeared.

The girl lifted her arm and pointed.

Ilona spun around. The black silhouette of the castle loomed above her.

Are you trying to tell me that the rathstone is inside the castle? Is the countess the one hiding it?

The girl's finger moved in a wide arc until it pointed at the dense woods. A warm wind bristled Ilona's fur, and then she was among the trees, alone. The branches swiped across the forest floor and the trees drew back to create a path. The moonlight bathed the trail in silver light. Ilona trotted forward. The path ended in front of an ancient oak with a trunk so broad a carriage could have driven through.

A crack in the bark widened until it created a large opening. Sniffing cautiously, she put a paw on the rim of the hole. She sensed no danger.

A howl in the distance made her ears prick up and stiffen. A second howl followed, much closer. Her pack! Forgetting the tree and the rathstone, Ilona leaped around and bounded down the path. At last she wasn't alone *any longer. Relief floated her upward like a dandelion seed, and when she ran down the hill, her feet didn't touch the ground.*

Ilona sat up, gasping for breath. *Where am I?* In her dream, she had been running through the forest and down a hill, running after the—

A howl outside startled Ilona. *The wolves. I was running with the wolves. And now I'm alone.* Sudden anguish and desolation cut through Ilona like a shard of glass. *I'm always alone.*

A narrow sliver of moonlight fell through the barred window, bathing the bedchamber in pale light. Ilona unclenched her fists, which had become tangled in the sheets. Tiny speckled pieces of eggshell rained from her sweaty palms. Ilona picked up the largest piece. *A robin's egg. The girl in my dream showed me one . . . but it was the rathstone, wasn't it?*

Confused, she swiped the broken shell off her bed. *It was only a dream.* Even though it had felt so real, real enough to leave a keepsake in her hands.

Outside, another howl cut through the night's silence. Ilona shivered.

"Loud, aren't they?"

Ilona's gaze spun to the source of the speech. She recognized Dorika, huddled on another bed in a thin nightgown.

"Every night, they howl and howl. I can't sleep."

"Right." Slowly Ilona disentangled herself from her strange dream. "You told me that yesterday. Are there lots of wolves around here, then?"

Dorika's large eyes gleamed in the near darkness. "I've never seen any."

Ilona got up on her bed, balancing on the box frame. Standing on tiptoes under the high window, she looked into the yard. She could make out the compost pile and the far end of the yard, where the soldiers milled about with their swords. Torchlight flickered, and snatches of their yelled conversations and laughter drifted up on the breeze.

She sank back down. "I can't see any wolves, either. Only the soldiers." She was half relieved, half disappointed. The wolves in her dream had seemed so real.

Dorika, arms wrapped around herself like a shawl, looked tired and lost.

"Don't give up hope." Ilona smiled, unsure if Dorika could see her face in the darkness. "We might still get out of here."

Dorika's eyes remained jaded. "You haven't been here that long. There is no hope for us. The countess . . . and the soldiers . . ." Dorika paused and when she resumed speaking, it was in a low, quavering voice. "There's something unnatural about them."

"What have you noticed?"

Dorika's eyes darted around the bedchamber, presumably checking for eavesdropping ghosts or fairies. "The soldiers' weapons gleam in the darkness as though forged out of moonlight. And Madam Joo has the evil eye." Dorika quickly crossed herself three times and spat on the floor. "I'm not complaining, though," she continued. "Every time I think of how hard my life is, I remember the countess's maidens."

"Why?" Ilona asked. "They are the countess's prisoners like us, but at least they are fed well and they may lounge on their soft beds all day. They are not lacking any essentials."

"Freedom is an essential," Dorika countered. "And so is life."

Ilona silently agreed. The girls were guarded "for their protection," Evike had said, but just as no one could get in, neither could they get out—and they were in no state to think as clearly as Ilona was, no matter the danger from Ilona Joo. With a sigh, she leaned back on her bed of straw. The howls outside had drifted farther and farther away.

"Go back to bed. You need your sleep," Ilona said. When Dorika didn't move, she lifted her sheet. "You can sleep here with me. I won't let the wolves get you."

A shy smile crept over Dorika's face as she readily took up Ilona's offer. "At home, I used to share a bed with my big sister," she whispered. "I miss her."

Ilona held Dorika until her breathing turned into the relaxed pattern of sleep. Then she lay on her back and looked through the window at the stars. The intermittent howls sounded far off now; their desperate sound called to something buried deep in her heart.

The sky was still dark when the guard troll unlocked the girls' bedchamber and led them to the kitchen, where Madame Joo assigned chores in her harsh voice. Ilona, only half awake, scrubbed a towering pile of dishes left from the soldiers' nightly meals.

Her thoughts revolved around the ghost girl in her dream. She was convinced that the ghost had been trying to help her find the rathstone. The robin's egg in her hand had been real enough. But why had the girl first pointed to the castle and then to the forest? The stone couldn't possibly be in both places.

Ilona groaned in frustration. She wasn't free to search the forest. And she could only explore Castle Cachtice if she could find an excuse to get out of the kitchen. But it seemed as though she would be stuck doing menial chores forever. Cursing, she swatted at something buzzing near her face.

"Watch out!" The voice was as small as the speaker. Vanillina buzzed around Ilona's head. "You almost hit me!"

"Get on, then. Leave me be." Ilona's hand sailed through the air, but the fairy's wings beat ferociously, and the small creature danced out of her reach.

"Won't you let me land?" Vanillina circled Ilona's head and tugged at her earlobe. "I have a message for you."

"For me?" Curious, Ilona held out her hand, palm turned upward.

The iridescent green wings slowed, and the pixie alighted. She danced a pirouette on the tips of her pointed silver shoes before giving Ilona a sly grin.

The minuscule girl in her palm weighed next to nothing, and Ilona felt tempted to poke her to ensure she was real. She lowered her voice, conscious of the other maids' stares.

"Are you Unhallowed?"

"Pah." Vanillina jerked her chin up and turned her eyes skyward. "Pixies aren't Unhallowed. Don't you know anything?"

"But you work for the countess," Ilona said. She didn't like the fairy's snooty attitude.

"As do you." A petite finger accused Ilona's nose. "Which reminds me. Countess Bathory requests tea in her purple dressing room. And you're the one to bring it." Without waiting for a reply, Vanillina spiraled up into the air and zoomed out of the open door.

Ilona stared after her as if enchanted. A hand on her arm startled her back into the reality of the smoky, chaotic kitchen. Anci stood before her with a sympathetic look on her face.

"An order from the countess?"

Ilona blew her long bangs out of her face and nodded.

"I'm to serve her tea. In the purple dressing room. Wherever that is."

Anci's voice rose above the din of the working girls. "The tea things. Hurry!" As though stung by bees, the girls raced around the kitchen. Dorika fetched a silver tray from a cupboard, Gizi placed a lacy handkerchief upon it, Evike brought out the china cup and saucer. Soon an elaborate tray with steaming hot tea sat on the counter.

"Remember, up two flights of stairs, turn left, the last door on your right." Anci peered at her from below her *basma*. "Don't forget to curtsy, and don't drop the tray. You'll be fine." With a firm hand on her shoulder, Anci steered Ilona out of the kitchen.

Ilona walked through the quiet castle, the only sound the pounding of her heart. She had been hoping for a chance to leave the kitchen, but now she was so nervous, she could barely keep the tea tray steady. Ilona remembered too vividly the cold stare of the countess's eyes, the pain her touch brought. It was clear that she was involved with the Unhallowed, either as a witch serving the Prince or perhaps as an Unhallowed Fey herself. She was no benevolent *táltos*, that much was certain. A shaman was supposed to protect and heal her community, and despite her "rescuing" of the maidens in her entourage, Ilona had seen no such healing.

But if she is hiding the rathstone in her castle, it might help to get close to her. Ilona squared her shoulders and hurried. In the deserted hall, Ilona passed beneath the chandelier and turned to the wide staircase leading to the upper floors. A scarlet carpet lined the stone steps, looking gorgeous and feeling soft to walk upon, but a moldy smell rose up and covered the fragrance of the tea. There was something more going on here that Ilona wished she had the power to see.

On the second floor landing, several portraits decorated the walls. The faces stared down with undisguised contempt, and their eyes seemed to be following Ilona. The idea made the hairs on the nape of her neck stand on end, and she stopped to glare at the faces in the portraits. *They're only paintings. Bad oil paintings, in obscene gilded frames. Don't be such a mouse.* The man in the portrait before her suddenly seemed to smile. Ilona leaned forward to read the plaque underneath. *Ferencz Nadasdy, 1555-1602. Beloved Husband of Elizabeth Bathory.*

The very notion of the countess loving someone was absurd. Ilona nearly laughed, but the tea tray's heaviness reminded her that the countess was waiting, and her amusement faded. She hurried down the dark corridor, searching for a purple room. "Last door to the right," Ilona muttered. Carefully balancing the tray on one hand, she knocked.

"Come in." The voice was frosty and commanding.

Ilona took a deep breath and threw the door open.

The countess sat on a high-backed chair in front of a vanity. Katalin stood behind her, combing the countess's long raven hair.

"Katalin!" Ilona blew out a long breath, glad to see Katalin safe and sound.

The countess spoke without glancing away from her mirror image. "I ordered my tea twenty minutes ago. What took you so long?"

Ilona approached. "I came as fast as I could, ma'am."

"I am *kékvéru*—nobility. You will address me as 'my lady' or 'your highness,'" the countess snapped, not looking at Ilona.

Ilona curtsied. "Of course, my lady. Here's your tea." The top of the vanity was covered with jewelry, hairpins, and combs made of pale ivory, leaving no room for the silver tray.

"Let me help." Katalin put down her brush and swept the clutter aside. Ilona was glad to see that Katalin didn't look as dazed and vacant as Jeanette and the other maidens.

Ilona quickly set down her tray before she could drop it. She grasped Katalin's small hands in her own. "I've been worried about you."

Countess Bathory turned to Ilona with a smile. "Why would you worry about a girl in my service? Do you not think me a kind mistress?" Her even face with the high cheekbones and big eyes epitomized beauty and implied the goodness of a kind *táltos*, and Ilona automatically nodded.

Her glance flew back to Katalin, who took up the brush once more and began to braid sections of the countess's black hair. She looked like someone who had just awakened from a nightmare. Her hands trembled and her eyes were haunted.

"Pour my tea, maid," Countess Bathory commanded. "And don't forget three lumps of sugar."

"Yes, my lady." Leaning forward, Ilona noticed a rust-brown stain on the bodice of the countess's nightdress. It provided an odd contrast to the intricate silver necklace around her throat and its striking blue sapphire. Ilona picked up the teapot and poured the steaming tea. She smiled weakly at the countess's reflection in the vanity's mirror. Then her pulse galloped.

The face of the woman in the glass slowly changed. Small lines appeared around her eyes and mouth. The flesh of her cheeks and neck sagged into mottled folds. Tendrils of hair framing the face turned gray, then white.

Sharp thorny teeth appeared, protruding from thinning lips in a snarl. Only the eyes remained the same, cold and piercing. The creature in the mirror hissed at Ilona, hissed with knowing hatred.

The teapot slipped from Ilona's hands and shattered on the stone floor. Hot tea splashed up and burned her legs. With a yelp, Ilona jumped backward, finally released from the mesmerizing image.

"You clumsy girl." Countess Bathory pointed a long, pale finger at the mess on the floor. "What are you waiting for? Clean it up!"

Ilona bent to collect the shards of broken china. Katalin joined her. Her darting hands found the small pieces in the cracks between the stones and placed them in her apron, until the countess yanked her upward by one of her blond braids.

"Who told you to help her? You are not finished with my hair yet." The countess's voice was low and calm, but Katalin immediately jumped to her feet and attended to her mistress's hair. Her whole body shook as she pulled a comb through the black mass.

"Ouch! You careless oaf!" The countess whirled around and snatched the comb out of Katalin's hand. A thick strand of hair had become entangled in the tines.

"My hair! Are you trying to rip it all out? Why am I surrounded by incompetence and stupidity?" Countess Bathory flung the comb into a corner. Before Ilona had a chance to step between them, she lunged at Katalin. Her long, painted fingernails raked the girl's soft cheeks. Blood seeped from the cuts in three long lines. Katalin stood wide-eyed and mute, like a bleeding statue.

"Leave her be." Ilona finally managed to find her voice.

She snatched up one of the bigger shards and held it up like a weapon.

The countess ignored her. She leaned close to Katalin and stroked her wounded cheek with the back of her hand.

"My sweet, my sweet." The words falling from the countess's lips were as seductive as the fragments of a melancholy song. She pulled her hand away and rubbed the blood into her own skin. "Beautiful. My skin. It's so soft . . ." A dreamy look replaced the countess's harsh appearance as she cocked her head to one side and gazed at her hand. Katalin stood by, shivering and weeping.

Ilona positioned herself in front of Katalin, gripping the sharp china piece in her sweaty hand.

"Let Katalin go home. You don't need her." Ilona hoped her voice sounded as tough as she intended. She knew she couldn't defeat the countess with a shard, but perhaps a strong stance was enough to dissuade the countess from doing Katalin any more harm.

Countess Bathory's eyes cleared. Her expression became hard as steel once more. Keeping Ilona in her gaze, she raised her hand to her mouth. Her tongue flicked over her bloody fingers.

Ilona watched with growing disgust. The countess's eyeteeth looked more like thorns in a hedge than human teeth.

The next instant, the countess struck Ilona's hand, sending the piece of pot flying. A circle of pain enveloped Ilona's wrist where the countess's cold hand gripped her tightly.

"Get out. Back to the kitchen with you, boy-girl."

The hissed command rang in Ilona's brain, and she wasn't sure the countess had spoken aloud. A hazy instant later, Ilona found herself back in the corridor, in front of a closed door. And she couldn't recall having walked out of the parlor.

She's not getting rid of me that easily. Ilona pushed down the door's curved handle. It was locked. With the full force of her body, Ilona slammed against the door. It didn't budge.

Her heart hammering, Ilona leaned against the wood. The sound of Katalin's high-pitched shrieks filled her eyes with hot, angry water. What was the wicked witch doing to her? Once more, Ilona raged against the wood of the door, banging and clawing at it. Her blood rushed between her ears as panic took hold. *I can't help her. Oh, God, I can't help her.*

Then the screams stopped. All Ilona could make out was a strange gurgling, slurping sound, and then a heart-freezing, empty silence. Again and again, Ilona threw herself against the door, bruising her shoulders and hips.

A hand on her arm startled Ilona into a shriek of her own. She spun around and faced Madame Joo. The old woman revealed her yellow teeth in a wicked grin.

"Do you want to be next?" She laughed, loud and cheerless. "Because I could arrange that for you."

Ilona pushed Madame Joo aside and darted down the corridor. Menacing laughter followed her all the way back to the kitchen.

~ Six ~

*T*HE NEXT COUPLE OF DAYS WENT BY IN A BLUR. THE STRANGE dream from her first night in the castle didn't repeat itself, and Ilona still wasn't sure what to believe. Had a ghost really tried to contact her? And if so, what exactly had the message been? Ilona also wondered if the moaning voice that had stopped her from drinking more of the Unhallowed wine was connected to her dream in some way. If only she could return to the maidens' chambers, she might be able to find out, but the countess did not call on her again. Stuck in her mind-numbing chores, Ilona cooked and cleaned as though she had never known a better life.

And what had the countess done to Katalin? Her screams had burned themselves deep into Ilona's mind. She remembered Kenneth, and how the Unhallowed had ripped his body apart. Poor Katalin had undoubtedly met with a similar end.

Three mornings after arriving in the rath, Ilona carried firewood from the yard into the kitchen and piled it next to the hearth. Straightening, she saw Anci leaping up with a squeal. With a few quick steps, Ilona was by her side.

"What is it?"

Without answering, Anci held out her hand. Vanillina danced down onto her palm. Silver and golden sparks flew up in tiny clouds each time she flapped her wings. Then the pixie sank down, smoothing her skirts made from colorful autumn leaves.

"Do you have a message for me?" Anci's voice was wary. "If so, spit it out. I don't have all day." Anci's eyes met Ilona's over the fairy's head. A smile tugged on Anci's mouth.

Ilona grinned back and made a clapping motion. *Kill the messenger.*

Vanillina jumped to her feet and whirled around, hands on hips.

"You!" she said. "My message is for you. Bring more food to the countess's maidens."

Ilona brought her face down to Vanillina's level. "I'd love to."

Vanillina spat into Ilona's eye. "Bah." She rose on flittering wings and zoomed out of the room.

Ilona rubbed her eye, still grinning. The tiny dewdrop felt like a grain of sand. *She'll never know that she did me a favor,* Ilona thought. *I can't wait to get out of the kitchen.*

This time, Anci helped carrying the silver trays.

"Are you afraid of the trolls?" Ilona asked.

Anci gave her a sidelong glance. "No."

"No?" Her answer surprised Ilona. All the other maids had a healthy portion of respect for the guarding Fey. "Why not?"

"The trolls never hurt me. It's the countess I'm scared of." They trudged on until they reached the entrance to the maiden's chambers in the east wing. After they knocked, the door popped open, and the guard troll with the horned helmet ushered them into the damp parlor. Instantly, the three trolls' pervasive body odor made Ilona nauseous. The hairy one lay in his chair with his head drooping backward. His clawed hand gripped an empty bronze goblet in his lap, and snores roared from his throat. The smallest one, sitting on the second chair, stared at them with beady black eyes.

Ilona couldn't be sure how she could see their sharp teeth and misshapen faces so much more clearly this time, and she didn't really want to examine that too closely. All she knew was that they went pretty quickly from being really ugly, smelly men to really ugly, smelly trolls.

With a parting nod, Anci disappeared through the curtains on the right. Eager to get away from the trolls, Ilona crossed the parlor and stepped through the curtains on the left.

Entering the dimly lit maidens' chamber, Ilona remembered the ethereal sound that had warned her not to drink the mulled wine. Perhaps she'd encounter the voice again today. If it belonged to the ghost girl of her dream, Ilona had so many questions she would like to ask. She peered into the shadowy recesses of the room, hoping for a glimpse of the translucent girl. But all she saw were dust and cobwebs.

Ilona hurried past the first girl toward Jeanette in the second bed. Her friend glanced at her with blank eyes, but she reached for a slice of rye bread and goat cheese.

With trembling hands, Ilona refilled Jeanette's cup with the dark wine. This time, she tried not to inhale the heady, compelling scent. *It's poison*, she reminded herself.

But on her last visit, tasting the Unhallowed drink

had brought out the strange, unearthly voice and she'd started seeing things she hadn't seen before. Perhaps the voice would cry out again? Ilona dipped her finger into the wine.

"This looks so delectable," she said loudly. "I cannot resist." She held her moist finger to her lips, waiting. The room remained silent, save for an occasional sigh from one of the drugged girls.

Ilona wiped her finger on her apron with a groan. Perhaps it was too much to expect a ghost from a dream to materialize. She smoothed Jeanette's hair back and placed a bunch of ripe purple grapes on her friend's lap.

"Don't worry," she whispered, although Jeanette looked untroubled. "You'll be home again soon."

Ilona went from bed to bed, dishing out cakes and fruit, dainty tomato sandwiches, and cold chicken legs. As she approached the last beds, Ilona's breath caught in her throat.

"Katalin!"

The young girl lay unmoving under a heavy linen blanket. Her blond hair surrounded her head on the pillow like spun gold.

"You're alive." Ilona put down her trays and peered into Katalin's pale face. The girl's chest rose and fell, but her eyes were closed, and a thin, bloodied line of spittle ran out of her mouth.

Ilona's chest tightened with renewed hope and worry. She took Katalin's wrist and felt for a pulse. It fluttered against Ilona's finger, weak and fragile like a small caged bird. Against all odds, the countess had not taken Katalin's life. At least not yet.

"I have to get you out of here." Ilona caressed Katalin's

white cheeks. Her gaze fell on two swollen marks on Katalin's neck. "What's this?"

Ilona ran a light hand along the twin holes. They had partially crusted over with brown scabs and oozed creamy pus. They reminded her of the snake bite on her own wrist, now completely healed. The mark of the Unhallowed.

Ilona imagined the countess bending over Katalin's neck, draining her blood from her body. It must have been terrifying.

Poor Katalin. Ilona paced the room, wondering what she could do to help the countess's maidens. She wanted to take them home with her, every single one. And not only the maidens, but the kitchen girls as well.

But first I need the rathstone, Ilona thought. *Without the rathstone, I cannot go home at all.* She sank onto the foot end of an empty bed in the very corner of the room, contemplating the faded rose pattern on the wall.

"How, oh how, can I find the rathstone?" she muttered.

The flame inside the lantern on the chipped nightstand flickered and died. A glimmering outline appeared next to Ilona, stretching and elongating until a translucent girl lay on the pillows.

Ilona froze and held her breath. It was the same girl she had encountered in her dream.

The girl folded her white hands over her chest and regarded Ilona out of sleet gray eyes. She remained still and silent until Ilona's patience broke.

"Hello." Ilona kept her voice low, expecting loud noises to scare the ghost away. "Are you here to help me find the rathstone?"

The pale girl nodded. Then she lifted her hand and pointed to the long velvet drapes.

Ilona jumped to her feet and pushed the drapes aside, letting in the bright noon sun. The ghost began to fade and became nearly invisible in the sunshine. Ilona pulled the drapes, in a hurry to hide the window once more.

"Don't leave me yet," she breathed, returning to the bed. "I still don't understand. Do you want me to go outside? Into the forest?"

The girl nodded once more. Relief washed over Ilona. Finally she had help.

"To that hollow tree you showed me in my dream?"

For the third time, the ghost girl nodded.

Ilona leaned forward in her eagerness. "Is that where the rathstone is hidden, then?"

Platters clanked in the distance. "Ilona," Anci called, sticking her head through the curtain-covered doorway. "It's time to go."

"In a moment." Ilona turned back to the bed, but it was empty. The ghost had disappeared into silence. Picking up her trays and muttering colorful curses, Ilona rushed out of the maidens' chamber.

Anci waited in the parlor, tapping her foot and glaring at the three trolls. The hairy one got up from his game to usher them out into the hallway and lock the door behind them.

In the damp corridors, Ilona pondered meeting her ghost. Too bad that Anci had interrupted them. Then Ilona remembered Katalin. She took Anci's arm.

"One of the girls in the maidens' chambers has been hurt by the countess. She looks deathly ill. Is there anything we can do for her?"

Anci sighed. "I'm afraid not. This happens every once in a while. Madame Joo takes a girl up to the countess and returns her in an altered state, with marks on her neck and an unhealthy pallor. They stop eating, and within a month, they pass on. There is nothing we can do to help."

"How horrible." *Poor Katalin. And Jeanette,* Ilona thought with a pang. How much longer until Madame Joo took her beloved friend to let the countess feed on her? If Ilona only knew the location of the rathstone, she'd take all the girls away from here *tonight.*

"But I do," she said, stopping in the middle of the hallway, earning a strange look from Anci. *I do know where the rathstone is. It's in a hollow tree in the forest. The ghost as good as told me.*

Excitement surged through Ilona. Finally she knew what to do. She would free the girls and lead them into the forest. They could all search together for the stone in the hollow tree.

"What is it?" Anci interrupted her thoughts. "What's on your mind?"

Ilona hesitated for a moment, looking around to be sure no one overheard. If she had Anci on her side, the other girls would certainly follow their lead. "I want to leave here tonight. And I want to take everyone with me: all kitchen girls as well as the countess's maidens."

"How? Do you have a plan?" Anci's face flushed and her eyes gleamed.

"Well." Ilona cleared her throat while her thoughts raced. "How many kitchen maids are there? Including the servants that work at night?"

"About a dozen," Anci said. "Enough to overpower three unsuspecting trolls. Well, four, counting our bedchamber guard. And we'll have surprise on our side."

Ilona grinned. She admired Anci's fighting spirit. "Yes,

we outnumber them. And we're not as defenseless as they might think. There are many knives and cleavers in the kitchen. And don't forget the axe outside."

Ilona wished she could teach the girls basic fighting skills, but there wasn't enough time during their hard daily routine. And the risk of Madame Joo noticing was too great.

"I don't know." Anci chewed on a strand of her mousy hair. "It's a bit chancy, don't you think? What about the soldiers? We might run into them on our way out."

Ilona remembered fighting Varco and his men. They were quick and experienced and had superior weapons. "I'm not worried about the soldiers," she lied. "We'll sneak past them somehow."

"You've got courage, Ilona. I like that." Anci smiled. "But what will we do once we make it out of the castle? Where would we go from there?"

Ilona bit her lip. She couldn't tell Anci about the rath-stone and a portal leading to another world, could she?

"If I said that I know of a way to forever escape the countess, would you trust me?"

Anci gave Ilona a long, searching look. Then she slowly nodded. "I guess so."

"Will you help me convince the other girls, then? They seem so . . ."

"Disheartened?"

Ilona nodded. Even worse, they appeared as though the life force had been drained out of them. They had resigned themselves to their fate a long time ago, and it might be hard to rouse them from their stupor.

Together, Anci and Ilona approached the other maids, explaining their scheme in hushed voices. To Ilona's surprise, all of the girls reacted with enthusiasm. Ilona recommended putting their plan into action the very same night, afraid that one of the maids would give their secret away to the countess or Madame Joo—either by accident or out of fear. Ilona was sure she hadn't been the only one caught by the effects of Countess Bathory's mesmerizing stare.

Evike suggested hiding their "weapons"—an assortment of carving knives, a wooden hammer and the axe—in an old coal chest near the kitchen. All afternoon the girls took turns sneaking out of the kitchen with a knife or two concealed in their apron pocket.

Ilona decided to take the axe herself, as it was the largest item and thus the most dangerous to convey. She found an empty potato sack and stuffed the axe inside. Only an inch of its handle showed. What else could she do to prepare? Ilona's eyes fell on a heavy, greasy casserole pan. With a quick movement, she stashed it in her sack as well.

"What do you want with that?" asked Gizi.

Ilona winked at her. "You'll see." Emboldened by the excitement of the impending battle, she ran all the way to the coal chest. Luck was on her side and she didn't meet anybody along the way.

She flipped up the worn lid of the cherry wood chest and surveyed their little hoard. *Yes, this will do,* she thought, stashing the axe. She closed the strongbox and ran to the maids' bedchamber, the casserole still in her sack smacking against her shins. The bare bedroom held no decent hiding places, so Ilona simply shoved the sack under her bed sheet.

Ready for battle.

Ilona straightened and smoothed down her apron. Then her breath caught in her throat. A softly glowing figure illuminated the open doorway, shimmering in the half-darkness of the bedchamber. A translucent girl floated toward her, stopping only a foot away from her. She cocked her head sideways and regarded Ilona with interest.

The ghost maiden. Ilona gasped and reached out, only to have her hands fall through the pale image. "Thank you for helping me find the rathstone," she whispered. "I'm taking all the girls out of the castle tonight to look for it in the forest. Will you guide us?"

The ghost girl didn't answer. She turned around and walked into the hallway, her feet never touching the floor. Ilona followed reluctantly. Madame Joo would miss her presence in the kitchen any minute, but she was determined not to let the ghost slip out of her sight again. No doubt it had reappeared for a reason.

Flickering in and out of focus, the ghost slid down the drafty corridors. As quietly as she could, Ilona followed, cautiously peeking around each bend, half expecting Madame Joo's sneering face. But they didn't encounter anyone on their way through the castle. A tightly coiled staircase brought them up to a small landing with a wooden door. The ghost motioned Ilona on with her hand, then floated through the closed door. Ilona tried the knob, but the door was locked.

"Psst," she hissed and gently knocked on the wood. "I can't get in. It's locked." She could barely keep herself from banging against the door. Had the ghost forgotten that mortals couldn't simply pass through walls?

Ilona rattled the knob again. It grew cold under her hands and its brass color turned gray. With another push, the door opened. The ghost waited on the other side of the threshold.

"Thank you." Ilona stepped inside the drafty chamber. Shivering, she looked around. The room was full of strange devices fashioned of bronze and silver. Some hung from hooks on the stone wall, others sat on the floor or on the workbench that stretched along the length of the room. A small, barred window just underneath the ceiling showed a glimpse of the darkening sky, and candles flickering inside staring skulls threw an orange glow. A hearth with a pile of cold ashes dominated the nearest wall. Next to it, several sets of shackles dangled from the walls and ceiling. The wooden floors underneath showed dark brown stains.

"Madame Joo's torture chamber," Ilona whispered. She gave the ghost a quizzical look. "Why are you showing me this?"

The girl floated through an arched doorway into the next room. A chair, studded with sharp points, sat in the middle. Thick straps encircled the chair's armrests, and a bar with a shackle at each end sat between the chair's legs. The ghost sat on the chair and slipped her arms and legs through the restraints. She threw her head back and closed her eyes. A horrible low moan escaped her pale lips.

"Is this where they tortured you?" Ilona asked, tears pricking the back of her eyes. "Is this how you died?"

The ghost girl's translucent form flickered and faded until only a vague outline of her was left. A moment later, that disappeared as well.

"Wait," Ilona groaned. "Don't leave me." But she was alone in the silent torture chamber.

Stepping closer, Ilona regarded the chair with morbid fascination. She grazed the studs with a careful palm and yanked her hand back when the tips shredded the topmost layer of her skin. A pearly drop of blood appeared on her hand. She quickly wiped it off on her apron. The studs and the shackles were iron, not bespelled silver, making Ilona wonder about Madame Joo. If iron didn't bother her, did it mean that she was human—not Fey? But she had some magic of her own, Ilona thought, remembering the strange mind trick Madame Joo had played on her when she had first entered the castle. *And humans can be as wicked as the Unhallowed,* she reflected. *Just as not all Fey are evil; some are Hallowed still.*

But there was no doubting Madame Joo's wickedness after encountering her torture chamber. Ilona scurried back to the kitchen before she could be found in that horrible forbidden room.

~ Seven ~

*A*T BEDTIME, THE GIRLS DOUSED THE LIGHTS AS ON ANY other night. Ilona and Anci had decided to wait until midnight to put their plan into action, to ensure that Madame Joo was soundly asleep. Before they had left the kitchen for the evening, they had conveyed their scheme to the night shift girls and persuaded them to come along as well.

When the church tower chimed twelve times in the distance, the other girls silently gathered around Ilona, waiting for her lead.

"How will we get past the troll in front of our door?" one girl whispered. "He has a sword."

Ilona had noticed the sword as well. It was short but broad, with a heavy bronze blade that looked like it could slice easily through flesh and bone.

"Anci will distract the troll, and I'll whack him with this." Ilona opened her sack and pulled out the smelly casserole dish.

Gizi stifled a giggle behind her hand. "With that? That's not a weapon!"

"Anything can become a weapon if you're desperate enough," Ilona said with a grim face. She hid behind the door and locked eyes with Anci. This was a crucial part in her plan. If Anci showed any sign of nerves and the troll got suspicious before Ilona had a chance to take him out, they wouldn't even get out of their bedchamber, let alone out of the castle.

Anci, however, seemed calm and collected. In the glow of the silver moonlight, Ilona gave Anci the signal to begin.

Anci knocked on the door and rattled the knob.

"Hello out there!" she called. "Are you interested in some friendly company tonight?"

The troll on the other side grunted something that sounded curiously like "ghoulish gardens."

"If you let me come out for a moment, I'll show you what I mean, Frundle."

Ilona froze at the flirtatious invitation, staring at Anci in disbelief. Anci waved away Ilona's concern.

A key ground in the lock, and the door opened a crack. Anci stepped over the threshold and out of sight.

"And how are you tonight?" Anci's voice was a sweet singsong.

Ilona tensed, the pan raised high over her head, ready to strike. She nudged the door open with her foot and swung the casserole dish down on the troll's head. The bone visor of his helmet shattered like porcelain, and Frundle collapsed.

"Quick, girls, pull him inside." Ilona lifted the thick legs, and Anci and Evike pushed his still torso into the bedchamber, where he lay like a heap of mottled cloth.

"Are you going to kill him?" Anci asked. The white in her eyes gleamed in the dim light.

Ilona crouched next to the unmoving troll, her breathing turning shallow to escape the stench of his stale body odor. She unbuckled his belt and slid the sheathed sword and the heavy key ring off. Frundle didn't make a sound, but they couldn't be certain that he would stay unconscious for long. It wouldn't do for him to alert Madame Joo.

Ilona slipped the blade out of its sheath. It was forged out of a dark, gleaming bronze. When Ilona ran her finger along its edge, it began to glow, first softly, then bright as a shooting star. *Detestable Unhallowed magic. It looks beautiful, though,* she thought begrudgingly.

She pointed the razor-sharp tip at Frundle's chest. *Frundle.* Why did it make a difference that she knew his name? That he *had* a name? A nameless troll she could have killed in an instant.

"Should I?" she asked Anci. In the long moment of silence that followed, the other girls crept out of their beds and re-lit the candles.

"Or we could simply lock him in," Anci finally said. "That would be easiest."

The girls slipped out of the bedchamber. Using Frundle's key, Ilona locked the chamber door behind them. Single file, they tiptoed down the drafty corridor to the kitchen. The night servants took the remaining knives and followed Ilona and Anci. Only Polly, the cook, had reservations.

"What if the countess or one of her soldiers comes into the kitchen and finds it empty?"

Ilona had considered the possibility. However, there was nothing she could do about it. "We'll just have to hurry."

Shivering, the girls ran down the hallway, as swift and stealthy as thieving rats. They stopped at the old coal chest to retrieve their weapons.

"You can have the axe," Ilona whispered to Anci. "I'll use the troll sword."

Ilona, followed by the other maids, approached the maidens' chambers in the east wing. Excitement and nervousness coursed through her veins. Ilona had no doubt that she could take on the trolls, even on her own, if necessary. Weeks and months of training had prepared her for this very moment.

At the entrance, Ilona banged hard against the wood. "Open up. By order of the countess." She winked at the girls huddled behind her. In their long nightgowns, holding their kitchen knives, they looked like startled housewives—the opposite of the army Ilona wished defended all the girls the Unhallowed had kidnapped.

Heavy footsteps approached and the door creaked open. The troll wearing the horned helmet appeared on the threshold. When he saw Ilona holding a sword, he stepped out into the corridor. Anci banged the door shut behind him.

"What's going on here?" The troll's piggy eyes slid over the cluster of girls and focused on Ilona.

She used his moment of confusion to thrust her sword forward. The blade sliced through his leather armguard and pierced his gray skin.

He jerked back and snarled, showing yellow fangs. He drew his sword. The girls gathered at the end of the corridor, spurring Ilona on in low, excited voices.

The harsh *clank* of reinforced bronze swords colliding echoed through the passageway as Ilona battled the troll. Drenched in sweat with the effort, she pushed the troll ahead of her farther and farther down the corridor. He was stronger, but his massive body wasn't as agile.

Finally she had maneuvered him into a corner. With a yell, Ilona sprang forward into a crouch and plunged her blade into the troll's unprotected thigh.

He cried out and stared at the black blood bubbling out of the fresh wound.

Ilona pulled her sword free and raised it for the next blow. The troll glared at her. Ilona hesitated, and that was her mistake. The troll used his greater weight to his advantage and shoved her across the hallway. Then he dashed around her and ran for the door to the maidens' chambers. He pushed Anci out of the way and disappeared behind the door.

"He's going to warn the others," Anci said.

"Then let's hurry." Ilona tried to open the door, but it was locked once more. Hoping that all trolls carried the same set, Ilona pulled out the keys she had taken from Frundle. The second key fit into the rusty lock. When Ilona opened the door, the girls behind her cheered.

Why she hadn't thought to use these keys before knocking and keep element of surprise to her favor, Ilona tried not to think about. Too many mistakes already. "Come on, everybody. Keep your knives ready!" Ilona rushed down the short hallway and entered the guards' parlor.

Ilona had expected the three trolls to wait for them with their weapons drawn, but they appeared to be arguing.

"They's only little girls," the hairy one huffed. "What d'ye mean, they's attacking?" He scowled at Ilona and the maids. "Where she get that sword?"

Ilona swung it over her head and jumped at the stunned troll, aiming for his throat.

He threw himself backward and finally reached for his own weapon. The one with the horned helmet and the smallest one followed suit, rushing toward the girls.

Ilona focused, drawing in a long breath. Her glowing blade clanked against the hairy troll's again and again. He wore armor made from leather and bronze plates, as well as his metal and bone helmet. Ilona tried for the soft flesh of his short neck, between chest plate and head.

Out of the corner of her eye, Ilona saw Dorika next to her, holding a long cleaver. With a shriek, Dorika slashed the hairy troll's hand. He dropped his sword and cursed.

Ilona raised her blade. *Now. For Jeanette.* Her arms swooped down, and the tip of the gleaming sword entered between collar and chin. The troll clutched her sword's edge, claws screeching over the smooth bronze. His eyes rolled back, yellow and bloodshot.

Ilona, gripping the handle with both sweaty hands, pushed it deeper, ignoring the horrible popping sound, the black blood around his wound. With a gurgle, his heavy, furry body tumbled to the ground. Frundle's sword still stuck obscenely out of his neck.

Over his still corpse, Ilona's eyes met the gaze of the smallest troll. With a careless motion of his thick sword arm, he whacked a bread knife out of Gizi's trembling hands. Then he leaped toward Ilona.

"I'll take him." Dorika wielded her cleaver once more, but the troll's bronze blade cut her knife clean in half. Dorika dropped the broken weapon and cowered on the floor.

Ilona positioned herself in front of her. There was no time to pull her sword out of the dead troll's neck. She was unarmed.

He's going to kill me. Ilona's eyes darted around, hoping to see something she could use to protect herself. *Anything.*

The troll lifted his broad sword and grinned at Ilona. "I gots you now." Then he collapsed with a grunt, an axe stuck in his back. Anci stared at Ilona with startled eyes.

"I got him!" She sounded surprised at her own daring.

"Well done." Ilona wrestled the troll's sword out of his limp hands. He wouldn't need it anymore. Anci's blow had slashed through the leather armor on his back and severed his spine.

"Watch out!" It was Gizi's voice, shrill and tense.

Too late. The troll with the hornet helmet grabbed Anci around her waist and dragged her backward. Ilona noted with some satisfaction that his wounded thigh dripped thick dark blood and made him limp. But now the tip of his dagger poked into Anci's throat, grazing the pale skin. He pulled her into a corner at the far side of the parlor.

"Drop the sword," he said to Ilona. His eyes flickered as though glowing coals burned inside his skull. "Drop it now, or she dies."

Heart pounding, Ilona glanced at the other girls. Most of them had lost their knives in the short battle. Many were bleeding—how badly they were injured was impossible to tell. Their faces showed defeat. It was up to Ilona.

Two trolls are dead already. He is the last one. He's all that stands between me and saving the girls. Ilona's hand tightened on the hilt of the Unhallowed sword. The magic in it weaved around the blade in golden shades. She carefully stepped closer to the pair across the room. *I can take him out.*

The troll raised his voice to a bellow. "Not another step! I says drop the sword *now!*" His blade dug into Anci's skin and a thin line of blood trickled onto her dress. Beads of sweat appeared on her brow.

Ilona calculated how long it would take her to sprint across the room. Too long. Anci would be dead before she reached the troll.

"Kill him, Ilona," Anci said. "You can do it. Kill him

and save the others." Her eyes pleaded with Ilona, saying, *Don't listen to him. Don't drop your sword.*

The troll roared. He shoved Anci to the floor and kicked her ribs. Then he raised his blade to strike.

"Wait!" Ilona dropped her sword. The sound of metal hitting stone reverberated through the parlor. "Let her go. We surrender."

The troll breathed out in a long puff. He glared at Anci, and for a second, Ilona thought her capitulation had been in vain, and he'd still kill her. Kill all of them perhaps. But then the troll grabbed Anci by her wrist and yanked her to her feet.

His sword still on Anci, the troll motioned to the other girls. "Everybody drop their knives and whatnots. And no trying no tricks on me, either, or your friend 'ere dies."

One by one, the girls released their puny weapons. Dorika sobbed quietly. Gizi and Evike held hands. The cook shook her head, muttering that she'd known it was a bad idea from the start.

Ilona stood frozen. Her plan had failed. Would Madame Joo torture her? Or worse, the countess would rip her apart. Now Corrine and the Council would wait forever for her triumphant return with the rathstone.

The troll held Anci for a moment longer, sniffing and growling at her neck and face. Then he pulled her closer and covered her mouth in a slobbery kiss. Anci didn't react. She lay in his arms like a lifeless doll.

Ilona slowly bent down. Kissing Anci distracted the troll. Maybe all was not lost yet. Carefully, carefully, her fingers inched toward the sword on the ground.

"Anci, move—now!" she yelled when her hand closed around the hilt.

Anci slipped through the troll's grasp and dropped on the ground. As quick as a cat, she rolled out of his reach.

"Enough!" The troll spun toward Ilona.

She gripped the sword tightly and straightened. Snarling, the troll aimed his weapon at Ilona. With slow steps, they circled each other.

The other girls pressed themselves tightly against the parlor walls. Ilona took a few deep breaths, her confidence returning fast. One on one, each working with an Unhallowed blade, Ilona had the advantage of speed and her extensive training. A smile crept across her face, and she attacked.

Her first blow grazed his upper arm but failed to cut through his armor. When he managed to parry her next two strikes, Ilona changed her approach. She lithely danced around him, then crouched low and stabbed her blade into his already wounded thigh. He yelped.

Ilona rolled out of his reach and soared to her feet, dancing toward his other side. His sword thundered down where she had been a moment before.

Ilona dropped onto her knees and stuck her sword straight through his good thigh. Then she twisted the blade.

The troll howled. Ilona pulled her sword out of his wound and flung herself backward, away from his fury. Again he slashed through empty air.

I'm almost there, Ilona thought. *He won't last much longer.* She leaped up, positioning herself for her next attack.

The troll's ears perked up, and then Ilona heard it, too. A banging door in the distance. The fall of footsteps on the stone floor.

The grin spreading across the troll's ugly face showed through the openings in his bone visor. He struggled to straighten himself, leaning against a wall. His sword pointed once more at Ilona.

No! Rage and disappointment surged through Ilona. She'd been so close to winning this battle. With aching muscles, she lifted the sword and brought it down hard against the troll's. His blade flew out of his hand. Her enemy stood before her unarmed. But it didn't matter anymore.

Six soldiers burst into the parlor. Ilona recognized the men as the ones who had brought her to Castle Cachtice. Varco skidded to a stop in front of Ilona. His eyes widened and a smile flickered over his face.

"You again?" He glanced around the room, taking in the two dead trolls, the overturned chairs and table. He shook his head, still looking more amused than upset. His gaze returned to Ilona.

"Are you going to surrender to me? Or would you like my men to disarm you *again*?"

His emphasis on the last word enraged Ilona even further. She stomped her foot and threw her bronze sword at his feet. It was useless. She couldn't win a fight against six of the countess's soldiers.

Her hands trembled with anger as Varco locked the silver shackles onto her wrist once more.

"You should execute her right 'ere and now," said the troll, sitting on the floor and poking at his wounded leg. "She killed two of my friends."

Varco hardly acknowledged him. His eyes were still on Ilona. "I don't think so. We'll take her up to Countess Bathory."

~ Eight ~

$\mathcal{V}$ARCO SNAPPED THE FREE END OF THE SILVER SHACKLES TO his own wrist. With a whistle at his men, he led his group out of the maidens' chambers. Ilona made him drag her along, digging in her heels and hanging on to doorframes. *I won't give up without a fight, no matter how meager.* Varco ignored her fussing and pulled her along as easily as though she were a stubborn puppy on a leash.

When they reached the grand curved staircase, Varco dismissed his men. During the climb up to the countess's chambers, Ilona's stomach began to twist with worry. What would the countess do to punish her?

Varco had to tug harder and harder on her chains as her feet grew heavier with each step.

"You're right to be afraid," he said with a sideways glance. "She'll rip your head off."

Ilona kept her chin up, but her heart fluttered like a bird. The graying portraits on the corridor walls smirked down at her. She closed her eyes. How would she get out of this mess?

Varco stopped in front of a fancy glass and silver door. His fist knocked so hard against the glass Ilona thought it would crack. The countess's deceptively warm voice ordered them to enter.

Countess Bathory sat on a velvet-cushioned chair with a high, gilded back. Her brocade dress spilled over the sides and to the parquet floor. On a small teak table beside her steamed a cup of brackish liquid, which she stirred with a tiny golden spoon.

"What's this, Varco?" She pulled her brows together and thin lines appeared on her forehead. "Why is my new kitchen maid in chains?"

Varco shifted from one foot to the other. He grinned, but his eyes became dark and serious. "Because she's quite the troublemaker, my lady. Earlier tonight, Frundle called me and my men to help him after he was attacked by the maids. We tracked them to the maidens' chambers, where we found this one fighting Marf. Groundlock and Firrs are both dead."

The countess looked from Varco to Ilona. She snapped her fingers. "Messenger!"

Ilona rubbed her sweaty hands together, pulling on her chain. Frundle would doubtlessly remember her—and not fondly. She glanced up when a shadow moved on the ceiling. A creature she hadn't noticed before stirred in the far corner. Eight legs pushed up a heavy, hairy body and scuttled across the ceiling. Stopping above the countess's chair, the creature dropped into her lap.

Her long, red-painted nails stroked the spider-being's back before she gave it a shove. "Get Frundle and Marf. And be quick about it."

Ilona shivered as the unholy being ran past her and through the open door. *A daoi,* she thought, remembering Corrine's stories. *Shadow creatures. Unhallowed spies and messengers.*

Countess Bathory addressed Varco again. "So you're

saying this girl has single-handedly slain two of my guard trolls? May I ask how she accomplished this?"

To Ilona's relief, she looked more amused than angry. The deep blue sapphire pendant on her silver necklace glittered as she bent to sip from her cup.

Varco shook his unkempt hair out of his face. "I don't know. Maybe she used her beauty to put an enchantment on them?" His long yellow teeth gleamed as he grinned at Ilona.

She narrowed her eyes at him, tempted to stick her tongue out, and squared her shoulders. "I used Frundle's sword," she admitted, her voice hoarse. While she was reluctant to take all the credit for defeating the trolls, it would be worse to indict her friends.

The daoi returned. Passing Ilona, it hissed and showed curved fangs around a strange, tubelike mouth. Then it climbed up the wall and was swallowed by the shadows.

Frundle and the troll Ilona had injured entered at a jog, sweaty and out of breath.

"Your highness." Both trolls took off their helmets and bent one knee to bow before the countess. Frundle helped the struggling Marf back to his feet.

Countess Bathory eyed the bandages around Marf's legs. "Lieutenant Varco told me an unlikely story about the kitchen maids attacking my trolls. What happened?"

Marf twirled his horned helmet in his large hands. Dark folds of gray flesh sagged under the troll's bloodshot eyes. He nodded at the countess before pointing a clawed finger at Ilona.

"It was that one, my lady, what led them on. They all come down to the east wing to make trouble. We didn't do nothin'."

Countess Bathory examined her perfect nails. "I suppose by 'they' you mean the kitchen servants? Are you telling me you were overpowered by unarmed girls?"

Marf shuffled in his boots. He gave Frundle a questioning look, but the other troll ignored him. "Well, my lady, they weren't unarmed. They's had these big knives and axes and all kinds of forks . . ." He glanced from the countess to Ilona. "And that one, she had a troll sword. She stabbed my legs."

Varco made a coughing sound and quickly hid his face behind his hand.

"And she whacked me over the 'ead with this big, heavy pan," Frundle chimed in. "Dangerous, that one." He rubbed his head and pouted.

The countess began to laugh. Warm peals of laughter rang through the ornate sitting room, bouncing off the paneled walls. Her glowing, flushed skin radiated health and good humor. *Such a contrast to her evil personality*, Ilona thought.

"You deserve your injuries, if you cannot defend yourself against my maids," she said, merriment twinkling in her eyes. "Now, what have you done with the other servant girls? I hope you haven't slain them all, or we will have to prepare our own breakfast in the morning."

Marf looked mortified. "No, your highness. I've sent them back to the kitchen."

"How very brave of you," the countess mocked. "Now get out of my sight."

Dismissed, Frundle and Marf turned and trudged out of the room. The countess regarded Ilona with cold eyes.

"So, you like to play with swords, do you? Just as I thought—there's not a single particle of girl within you.

How peculiar. And somehow very revolting." Countess Bathory's hand absently played with her necklace.

Ilona bit her bottom lip. She was *not* revolting! Then she quickly suppressed her anger. The conversation could have taken a worse course. The countess could have been furious at her, instead of merely disgusted. She could have turned her over to the "mercy" of Madame Joo—or worse. What if . . . ? An idea half formed in Ilona's mind, and the words rushed out before she could think them over.

"Perhaps I would serve your ladyship better as one of your soldiers, rather than as an incompetent maid," she began, trying to make it sound like a casual suggestion, but her voice trembled. If she could only get out of the confines of the kitchen, then she might finally be able to get into the forest and conduct a real search for the rathstone. And if she could gain access to weapons, all the better.

Countess Bathory gave Ilona a long, penetrating look from under her heavy eyelashes, icy fingers reaching deep into her soul. Ilona didn't dare breathe.

"If you want to hear my opinion, my lady," Varco said, stepping forward. "I think it's an excellent proposal. Why don't you put her under my command? I can always use another skilled fighter."

For a long moment, the countess glared at both of them. Then she sighed. "Why not? But she must wear regular soldiers' garb. After all, there's no use pretending she's a girl." She laughed again, a mean-spirited cackle this time, which distorted her fair features. "And she's to be watched at all times and may not exit the gates without your supervision."

Ilona's spirits fell into a bottomless pit. So much for her plans of hunting for the rathstone. Her disappointment was so great she could have sat down and cried, but Varco tugged on her chains.

"Come on," he whispered. "You're mine now."

He led Ilona out of the countess's chambers and trampled down the stairs, forcing Ilona to jog to keep up.

The countess's careless remarks still rang in her ears. *There's not a single particle of girl within you.* That wasn't true, was it? Certainly, fancy, frilly dresses held no interest for her. Neither did dancing or fine needlework. Things like bugs or dirt didn't bother her, and she never fainted at the sight of blood the way Christina always did. But did all that really make her less of a girl?

In the entrance hall, Varco kicked the heavy door open and yanked Ilona outside. The chill night air raced over her bare arms. Gusting autumn winds swept yellow leaves across the courtyard. In the light of a shuttered lantern, Varco guided Ilona toward the squat wooden buildings huddled between the castle and its outer walls—the soldiers' quarters.

They passed a row of targets, where several soldiers practiced their archery skills by torchlight. Men spilled out of the sheds, carrying swords and longbows. They nodded at Varco and gave Ilona curious glances.

"There are six buildings," Varco explained, pointing ahead. "One for each group of men. The Bats sleep in here." He motioned at the low shed near them. "In the next building, we have the Copperheads, then further on the Rats, the Hawks, and the Bears."

Ilona shrugged. She tried not to show her rising excitement. As a soldier, would she get to practice fighting with the men? She had always wanted to learn to shoot a bow.

"My group is called the Wolves." Varco pulled Ilona

toward the open doorway of an oblong structure. "And this is our den."

A zoo-like stench of dirty straw and animal waste overpowered Ilona's senses and made her gag. *This is worse than the drafty maids' chamber,* she thought. *I can't sleep here, with the men!*

Varco took Ilona's wrist in his hand and removed her shackles with his tiny silver key. "Don't worry," he said, still leaning over her hand. "You won't have to sleep in here."

Ilona's face snapped up, and she nearly banged her head against his. Had he read her mind?

His dark eyes gleamed with amusement. "Of course, you may sleep here, if you prefer. Or I can give you something more private."

Ilona rubbed her wrist and scowled. "I'll have my own bedroom, then."

With a chuckle, Varco walked to a plain wooden chest and rummaged through it. When he straightened up, he held a bundle of clothes in his arms. "Come along. I'll show you the stable."

Ilona followed him into the courtyard and across the cobblestones into the far reaches of the grounds. So she was to sleep with the animals? Well, it was better than to share with smelly, disgusting men.

At the entrance to the stable, Varco spun around and gave Ilona an apologetic smile. "It's small and not all that clean, I'm afraid. Countess Bathory's horse used to reside here." He opened the door and hung the lantern on a hook. He motioned her inside and handed her the small bundle.

"The horse's name was Thunder, a fine stallion." The shadows cast by the lantern flickered over Varco's dark face. "The countess rode him every day. But one night, after a bad cold spell, when the hunting was scarce, we got so hungry that we ate him." His broad grin revealed his long canines. "The countess was in a rage for days."

"Ah," Ilona said, for a lack of words. She glanced around the narrow stall. It smelled stale, but the straw didn't look any dirtier than the bedding in the maids' chamber. Varco handed her a rough horse blanket.

"I hope you'll be comfortable here. Let me know if you need anything else." Varco winked. "And always bolt your door before you sleep . . . if you don't want to end up like old Thunder!"

Ilona only smirked while Varco shook with laughter. She had no intention of letting the men into her stable. They'd be in for a surprise if they'd tried to pull anything on her.

"Well, get changed into your new clothes," Varco said, growing serious. "Then meet me in the yard. I'll have to assess your skills before we begin practice." The moment Varco left the stable, Ilona pushed the heavy beam across the door to bolt it shut. Then she slipped out of her dirty maid's uniform and into the clothes Varco had given her. The brown cotton pants fit perfectly over her slim hips, and the green belted top was soft and loose. Then she tied the long, empty sheath around her waist. A jade felt cap finished her outfit. Ilona stuffed her short, unruly hair under it, wishing she had a mirror. She imagined she looked just like a young soldier—not even her mother would suspect a girl underneath these clothes. Why did men get to wear such wonderfully comfortable garb while girls had to wear tight corsets and gowns that got in the way every time you turned around?

In the yard, Varco was waiting for her, holding a sword and a shield of the same luminous silver material. His eyes traveled up and down her frame, making Ilona glower at him in embarrassment. She doubted that he looked at his men like *that*.

"Is that mine?" She couldn't hide her eagerness and reached out for the shimmering blade.

"Just a moment." Varco held the sword high above her head. "First listen. I've seen that you possess skills with a sword and that you're not afraid to use these skills. However, now you're under my command. If you ever draw this blade against my men or any of the countess's servants, I'll have to kill you." He smiled when he said this, as though killing her would not trouble his soul for more than an instant.

Ilona groaned. Did he think she was that stupid? There must be at least thirty soldiers in the countess's service. If she attacked one, she would have to fight all of them. She'd last less than five minutes.

Varco raised his eyebrows, the sword still raised high.

"I promise," Ilona said, forcing contrition into her voice.

"All right." Varco lowered sword and shield into her outstretched hands.

The hilt fit into her palm perfectly, and when Ilona swished the sword through the night air, the blade began to glow.

Varco stopped her with a hard hand on her wrist. "Why didn't you listen to me?" he hissed.

"Pardon?" Ilona broke free and returned his glare. "I have no idea what you're talking about."

"The maidens' wine. You drank it, didn't you?"

A rush of blood warmed Ilona's cheeks. How had he guessed? "It was only a sip," she said. "I didn't mean to."

Varco kicked at a rock. "It would have been better if you had resisted the temptation."

"What did it do to me?" Ilona's heart hammered; she wasn't sure she wanted to hear the answer.

Varco, too, hesitated, shrugged. "I don't know, exactly. But our sword is reacting to you now. You saw it glow."

Ilona balled her fists. So that's why the troll's sword had been so easy to use. She had made a grave mistake when she let something of the Unhallowed touch her inside. Now she had to pay for it. Ilona imagined the wine turning into blood, circulating its evil in her body, and suppressed sudden nausea.

"Then your swords are really enchanted?" she asked, remembering what Anci had told her.

Varco nodded. "Our weapons are forged at the Prince's court. The silver blade is reinforced with magic, which makes the metal stronger than any human iron. Perhaps it is just as well that you now have the ability to command your weapon. You'll make a better soldier that way."

Yes, Ilona thought. *And perhaps being a better soldier will help my goal of defeating the countess.*

He loosened the leather straps of his chest armor and slipped it off. "I want you to wear my armor for tonight's practice. I'll try my best not to hurt you, but we don't need to take any risks."

Ilona let him slide the armor over her head and buckle the straps on her sides. The armor was large on her, covering not only her chest, but her entire torso. The front and back plates were fashioned out of the same gleaming silver as the sword and shield in her hands. It made her feel safe.

Varco positioned himself a few feet opposite Ilona and pulled his own sword from its sheath. "Ready?"

Ilona hesitated. She had trained with the Fey Prince; of course she was ready. But would it be wise to show Varco all she could do? Wouldn't her skills expose her as the spy she was?

Varco lowered his sword. "What is it—are you scared?"

The challenge in his eyes drove her caution away. "I'm ready," she barked.

Without further notice, he attacked. She parried, noting the impact of her blade against his. The strength of the magicked weapon flowed through her hand into her arm, giving her more power than she normally possessed.

It's magnificent! Ilona's amazement at her new weapon swiftly overrode her disgust with sharing some of the Unhallowed's powers. As she swung it around to strike, it zipped through the air as though it weighed no more than a pin. Varco lithely jumped backward, then attempted a quick blow from the side. She spun around and blocked with her shield.

From her training experience, Ilona realized that he began with an easy warm-up routine. Soon he was testing her for real, and her light soldiers' garb became drenched in sweat. Adapting from the fighting style she had learned from Euan—stabbing with a narrow foil—to slashing with the broader blade of a sword required all of Ilona's concentration. Somehow Varco had ignited her ambition, and she wanted desperately to impress him with her skills. So she kept up her focus and gave her all, blow after blow.

However, Varco didn't seem to tire, still going with full force when Ilona's arms had already jelled and her knees threatened to buckle with each step. Ilona was loath to ask for a break, but when her breath came in ragged gasps, Varco finally lowered his sword.

"Are you tired?" he asked.

Ilona shook her head. Hands on her knees, the courtyard spinning, she tried to catch her breath. "I'm fine."

Varco sat on the cobblestones, crossing his long legs. He invited her to follow suit with a pat on the ground. Reluctantly, Ilona sank down.

"You're better than I thought," Varco said. "Do you still claim that you had no formal training?"

Ilona took a deep gulp of chill air. "I had some training," she admitted.

He gave her a questioning look. "You're not from the area," he stated. "And even if it's true that you are from Battonya, you're not from this rath."

Ilona looked away from his penetrating eyes. Instead she watched the soldiers at their bow practice. Their arrows hit the targets with unusual precision.

"Where are you from, Ilona?" The tip of his sword tapped her leather boot.

"Nowhere." He'd be angry now, at her stubbornness and secrecy. To her surprise, he only laughed softly.

"Miss Nobody from Nowhere," he said. "How charming."

Ilona stretched her sore arms and yawned. It had been a long night after a long day. With the sudden fall in adrenaline came exhaustion as thick as a fog.

"Don't you ever sleep?" she asked.

Varco gave her a surprised look. "We sleep all day."

"Why?"

"Because we get tired." He laughed at his own joke. Then he became serious. "It's just more convenient for us to sleep during the day. We usually are out at night, on our raids. It's more effective if we attack at night, when the humans are asleep."

A cold shiver raced over Ilona's damp skin. The thrill of sword fighting had almost made her forget the dark reason behind the soldiers' employment. Had it been Varco and his men who invaded Falston to steal Jeanette?

Varco sprang to his feet and pulled Ilona up. "You can get some sleep now. It might take you a few days to adjust to our routine."

"Can I ask you something?" Ilona asked on the way back to the stable.

"Certainly." Varco gave her an expectant look.

"How is it that you are the Wolves' lieutenant? Aren't you the youngest of the group?" In Ilona's experience authority came with age and wisdom.

Varco laughed softly. "Actually, Dezso is the youngest, and Zador is not much older than I am. And not all of my men think it's for the best that I'm their leader. I only got the position recently, by defeating every one of them when Gyala, our last lieutenant, retired—if you must know."

They had reached the stable door. He put a hand on her shoulder. "I need my armor back. And I'll take that sword."

Indignant anger bubbled up in Ilona. *He doesn't trust me to keep the sword.* But maybe that would change in time. For some reason, she wanted to earn his trust along with his respect. Handing over her new weapon, she bid him good night.

"Sleep well," he said. "You'll need all the rest you can get. Tomorrow night, you'll join us on your first raid."

NINE

ALONE ON THE MEADOW, ILONA TILTED HER HEAD BACK AND howled. Then she waited for her pack to answer. But only darkness surrounded her, and a hushed, cold silence.

An iridescent light appeared in the distance, then was joined by another, and another. Soon a multitude of flickering orbs danced in the field, playful as puppies.

Ilona followed the swirling, glowing spheres. Underneath her paws, the meadow changed to a trodden path. The lights bobbed ahead of her, goading her on. When she got closer, they changed, becoming pale, floating maidens with sad faces.

On the crossroads, they waited for Ilona to catch up. They circled her, their immaterial bodies pressing close. When they smiled, blood oozed between their stained lips and trickled onto their white nightgowns. Then the maidens grasped each other's hands and moved around Ilona in an ever-tightening ring of rainbow light. The air rippled like water in a pond, and Ilona closed her eyes. Nose pointed up, she sniffed and listened. The air smelled of trees and wet leaves, of forest creatures. The night was curiously still.

When Ilona opened her eyes again, a thick mass of shadow maidens took up the path ahead, spilling onto the fields on both sides. So many girls—too many to count. Crowded together like rabbits in a warren, they pushed forward, toward the woods.

Ilona followed the procession, then dashed through them. An icy draft chilled her bones, made breathing difficult. Ilona hurried on, paws pounding the ground, until the maidens and the meadow blurred together.

Between the trees, she felt calmer. The hollow tree waited for her and opened when she pushed her paw against its crack. She leaped inside. Her vision swirled.

She sat on a tiny chair fashioned from woven branches and moss. Her long legs stretched in front of her and her hands held a thimble-sized cup. Carefully, she placed it on the small knobby piece of wood serving as a table.

"I already drank too much in this world," she said to the little man.

He crossed his stubby arms across a barrel chest. A green beard covered much of his face.

"It cannot be undone. You have changed." Ancient eyes squinted at her from a lined face. "Many trials are yet in store for you. But you are not alone."

"Thank you. I'm glad of it."

A howl rang out somewhere in the forest. Ilona tensed. "I have to go."

"Don't let the wolves distract you, Ilona," the little man said. "Find me. I can help."

A rap on the door woke Ilona from deep slumber. She wiped the sleep out of her eyes and sat up in her straw bed. *I have the strangest dreams in this rath,* she thought. *Who was that little man?*

"Get up, Ilona." Varco's voice rang through the thin door. "It's dark already."

Ilona pushed the horse blanket away and jumped out of bed. She had slept in her new clothes and only had to slip into her boots and jacket. After tucking her hair into the beret, she slid the bolt on the door. Varco stood on her threshold in the flickering torchlight.

Groggy from sleeping through the day and into the night, Ilona stumbled past him into the courtyard, where the soldiers were practicing their sword and bow skills. Her stomach rumbled, loud enough for a smirk to tug at Varco's lips.

"You can wash in that barrel." Varco pointed at a wooden drum full of rainwater. Ilona reluctantly dipped in her hands and splashed water on her sleep-hot face. The icy liquid refreshed her, and she greedily drank a handful.

"Are we going to eat?" she asked. As a maid, she had helped prepare many tasty dishes for the countess's soldiers. Would she now be on the receiving end of such delicacies?

"Later." Varco motioned her to follow him toward his men's building. "We'll have time to eat after the raid."

Raid? Ilona shuddered. She had hoped to have a chance to explore the woods around the castle and find the rathstone before she was made to join the soldiers in their hideous quests for girls. But now she wasn't even sure anymore that the rathstone was hidden in the forest. Her last dream had not been helpful at all.

How could she accompany the Wolves on a raid? She would have to pretend she was on the Unhallowed's side and at the same time protect the humans. It would not be easy.

Inside the low shed, Varco's men gathered around him.

"You will remember my right hand man, Zador." Varco clapped a hand on the young redhead's shoulder. "And Farkas." The man with the long scar dividing his face narrowed his eyes at Ilona.

Varco indicated the rest of his troop. "And these men here are called Gyala, Kardos and Dezso. All excellent archers and swordsmen, so stay on their good side." He said it with a twinkle in his eyes, but he wasn't joking.

Memorizing their names, Ilona gave each soldier a long look. Gyala was the oldest of the group, with a gray beard and equally gray eyes. He must have been the old lieutenant that Varco had replaced. Dezso was the shortest and youngest-looking, with scraggly brown hair and a pimply chin. Kardos's face was nearly covered by his black beard, and his small eyes glowered at Ilona. Ilona wondered where these men had come from, and why they would willingly kidnap girls that could have been their sisters or daughters or nieces.

All soldiers were clad in the same silver armor, with swords strapped to their sides and bows on their backs. Each was at least six feet tall—except for Deszo, who was a couple of inches shorter than Ilona—and broad in the chest and shoulders. They eyed her with distrust and open antagonism.

Ilona hitched up her shoulders and tried hard not to show her discomfort. Would these men watch her back if she needed them to? *Not likely.* And she wasn't sure she wanted to watch theirs, knowing what their mission was.

Farkas stepped forward, his dark eyes flaring. "Why is she here?" he challenged. "I refuse to work with this girl. Her place is in the kitchen."

Kardos bowed his head briefly toward Varco before he spoke. "Farkas is right, Lieutenant. How can a girl be a soldier?"

Farkas shook his long, scruffy hair. "Exactly. I don't want the Wolves to become a laughingstock. Who agrees with me?"

All hands flew up. Varco warded them off. "The decision wasn't mine," he said. "Ilona is here by Countess Bathory's explicit command."

The soldiers' hands sank back down, dismay spreading over their rough faces.

Farkas alone still grumbled out loud. "I don't believe you, Varco. Why would the countess want us to drag a girl along on our raids?"

If the challenge to his authority angered Varco, he hid it well. "Because Ilona is as skilled at sword fighting as any of us," he said calmly. "We've been a man short ever since we lost Bajnok."

The soldiers sighed at the mention of Bajnok. Varco added, with a pointed look at Farkas, "Anyone unhappy with the situation may feel free to speak to Countess Bathory about it."

Ilona guessed that none of them had the courage to irritate the countess by complaining about her presence. She was glad when the talk shifted to the next subject. Varco laid out the plan for the raid.

"We will travel some ways tonight to raid homesteads in the area around Nyirtelek. I heard the farmers there have very pretty daughters."

The men in the circle snickered and fingered their swords, as though itching to use them. Dezso wiped a long string of saliva from his hairless chin.

Bile rose in Ilona's throat at the thought of more girls stolen from their homes for the countess, just like Anci, Dorika, and Katalin. *And Jeanette.*

Instead of freeing the girls imprisoned in Castle Cachtice, I'll be adding to their number tonight, Ilona thought. *And I haven't gotten any closer to finding the rathstone. What a mess I'm making of this mission.*

Out in the yard, Varco pulled her aside. He handed her a silver sword and matching shield. "You drank the countess's wine," he said in a low voice. "So you'll be able to run with us."

"I'll try my best." Ilona chewed on her bottom lip, wondering what he meant. What had running to do with wine?

The soldiers crossed the courtyard and exited the grounds through the main gate. The moon hung low and heavy, its crescent shape half hidden by black night clouds. On the slope leading toward the village, the men broke into a loose jog. Moving through the mild night with fresh air filling her lungs would have been enjoyable for Ilona, if the soldiers' wicked intentions hadn't been foremost on her mind.

When the soldiers reached the edge of the forest, their speed accelerated. Ilona had imagined Varco leading his men, but he kept in the rear, near her. Did he worry about her dashing off? The thought had crossed her mind, but where would she run to?

The men moved swiftly out of sight between the dark shapes of the trees and Varco whistled. It was such a high-pitched sound that Ilona covered her ears.

"They'll wait," he said. His hand on her wrist made her stop. The cool air burned in her lungs, and she leaned against a tree trunk, trying to catch her breath. It irritated her that Varco didn't show any sign of exhaustion. His breath was even and steady and no sweat covered his brow.

Clouds floated away from the moon, and silver light flooded through the canopy of branches. Varco eyed Ilona carefully.

"Would you like to run faster, like me?"

"I'm running as fast as I can." Ilona didn't mean to sound angry, but she was frustrated with her own limitations. And *his* lack of them.

He smiled down at her. "Take my hand. I'll show you."

Curiosity won over trepidation, and Ilona laid her hand into his. Even on this cool autumn night his hand was almost hot to the touch. The warmth spread through Ilona's arm and from there throughout her body.

Varco pushed off the tree and began to run, clutching her hand.

The heat wove through her abdomen, then to her legs and into her feet, which moved as though on springs. Her breathing slowed, but the beat of her heart drumming in her head grew louder. With speed came exhilaration, the sensation of flying. Branches snapped around them; the trees rushed past and blurred into a gray-green fog. Varco kept her close to him, yanking her along. Ilona was certain she would have hit a tree if it weren't for his quick reflexes. They ran on and on, time blurring as much as the rural surroundings. Forest gave way to meadows, and village after village appeared and disappeared on the horizon. Armed men guarded each village, though the glances Ilona got showed defeated, weary acceptance in their faces. After a long time, they reached a small copse at the edge of a meadow, and their pace slowed.

"We're here." Varco stopped and let go of her hand.

Ilona skidded, tripped over a thick root pushing out of the earthy ground, and fell into a pile of damp leaves. "A little warning would have been nice," she grumbled as she pulled herself up on a branch. Her ears rang and her vision trembled. Her first steps felt shaky and uncertain as though she had spent weeks on board a ship again.

Brushing dirt and grass off her pants, Ilona noticed Varco's men ahead. They stood on the ridge of a hill, looking down into the valley. Her head still reeled with the unnatural speed she had achieved, and she wondered what Father Joseph would say about her sharing Varco's powers. Varco served the countess, which meant that even if he wasn't Unhallowed himself, he was in league with them. And so his powers must come from *them*.

Varco and Ilona joined the soldiers on the crest. The moon lit a peaceful pastoral view below. A field of glimmering wheat, another of what might be rutabaga. Behind, a cozy farmhouse with a porch running the length of it.

"No cattle," Farkas growled. "Some farm."

"We're not here for a feast." Varco's tone was sharp. "Look at the windows. The lamps are out—everybody is asleep. We'll be in and out." Ilona wasn't so sure about that. Given the armed guards she'd seen earlier, the humans in this rath seemed to be well aware of the dangers of the nighttime. She could only hope.

"No time for fun?" Farkas raised his thick eyebrows. When Varco shook his head, Farkas glared at Ilona as though this was her fault.

Is he restraining his men for my sake? That's all right with me, if it means no one will be hurt tonight.

"Let's go." At Varco's command, the men streamed down the hill, their movement as flexible as the bending wheat. Halfway to the farm, at the edge of the field, Varco slowed and motioned to Ilona and Zador.

"I want you to stand guard here."

The redhead nodded, and Ilona sighed in relief. She had been worried about being forced to take part in breaking into the farmhouse and pulling the girls out of their beds. From here she might be able to subvert their plans. She hoped her suspicions were right and that the inhabitants of this house were ready for them.

Standing next to Zador, she kept her eyes on Varco's receding back and watched his men slip down the path behind him.

The soldiers were already on the gravel path surrounding the house when the first window blazed with flickering light. The door burst open, and men clutching torches and pitchforks with iron tines poured into the yard, yelling.

Varco unsheathed his sword with an unearthly howl, and his men followed suit. Glowing swords crashed onto pitchforks and daggers.

Nerves shivered over Ilona and she gnawed on the edge of her thumbnail. She tried to control her outward reaction, because what she really wanted to do was cheer.

Zador laid a hand on her arm. "They're outnumbered. The farmers were waiting for us. We must help them. . Come on."

Ilona had been itching for battle for weeks now—but for a battle against the Unhallowed, not humans.

Reluctantly joining the soldiers, the Unhallowed sword's warm blue shine lit Ilona's way. Its hilt melted into her palm as though it had already accompanied her into a thousand battles. Ilona kept to the edge of the scuffle, wondering how she could make it appear as though she were fighting the humans without actually harming them.

A chunky man of middle age jumped in front of her, wielding an ancient-looking metal sword. *Iron.* This was the first time Ilona had seen actual iron in the rath. The countess had none in her castle. *Good,* Ilona thought. *They will be able to defend themselves.*

She smiled at the farmer and winked.

With an angry yell, he leaped forward and thrust his blade toward Ilona. Her fast reflexes made her stumble backward just in time, and his sword only sliced through her sleeve. While she wasn't here to fight, the farmers were, and if she didn't defend herself, they might kill her.

A few careful blows disarmed the farmer, who scrambled away in a panic. Ilona retreated, but another man blocked her path. He had a long beard and held a shovel. Pity surged through her, but was quickly suppressed when the blade of his shovel slammed against her shoulder.

A hard blow from the flat of her sword sent the shovel into a muddy puddle. The farmer sank to his knees. He cried out miserably, begging for his life.

Ilona bent down to him, smelling his rancid breath. "Run," she hissed. "Hide in the fields. I don't want to hurt you."

A booming crash made Ilona straighten. To her left, old Gyala sagged to the ground. Her head spun toward the farm house. A man stood on the porch, a musket leveled on his shoulder.

Varco cursed and dashed toward Gyala. Zador heaved the injured soldier onto Varco's back. The farmers, emboldened, attacked with renewed vigor, and Ilona had to defend herself against two men at once while glancing over her shoulder to see what was happening with Gyala.

A shrill whistle rang out over the din of the scuffle. "Retreat!" Varco yelled.

Thank heavens—finally. Ilona dashed after the soldiers, who were already halfway up the hill. Leaving the farmyard, Ilona's foot collided with something soft and night-dark. The creature yelped and hissed. Green eyes flared in the moonlight.

Another black cat, she thought. *Is this really a bad omen, like Anci said?* A rock hit her back and she glanced over her shoulder. The farmers waved their pitchforks at her. Several held big rocks in their hands, ready to throw. The musket man reloaded his gun and aimed it at Ilona.

She broke into a run, wishing she had Varco's powers of speed. The next instant, he was by her side. His hand entwined with hers, and her blood warmed with his magic. Her feet seemed to grow wings as they left the fields behind in a heartbeat.

Up on the crest of the hill they slowed. Varco released her hand. Gyala sat leaning against an oak tree, his lined face pale in the moonlight. The other men had gathered around him, and Zador crouched beside him.

Ilona glanced back into the valley, half expecting the horde of farmers to run after them. A few men still stood in the farmyard, but the man with his musket was now too distant to pose any danger.

"Are we safe?" Ilona said. "They can still see us."

Varco knelt next to Gyala and barely glanced up at her. "Of course we're safe. And we'll leave in a moment." He turned to Zador. "Get the bullet out."

Ilona stepped closer and peered down at Gyala. The shot had hit his side. A rusty circle spread on his green shirt. His gray eyes were glazed, and his breath came irregularly. Zador dug a finger into the center of the wound. Gyala roared and arched his back, but Varco restrained him.

Ilona's stomach turned, but her gaze remained on the scene with dark fascination.

"I've got it." Zador removed his bloody hand from Gyala's chest. It reminded Ilona of the Captain that Corrine always saw. The Captain with his bloody hand.

Zador dropped something into Varco's palm. Ilona

leaned against his shoulder to get a better look. It was a shiny bullet, the size of a pea.

"It's silver." Varco exhaled sharply. Then he chuckled. "Silver! Where do they get the idea that silver will harm us?"

Zador joined his laughter. "If they would have used iron . . . look what that pitchfork did to my arm." He pulled up his sleeve and showed Varco a wide welt of blistering flesh.

"Gyala'd be dead. He was lucky." Varco threw the bullet into the bushes and clapped a hand on Gyala's shoulder. "Let's get you home."

"We're leaving without the girls?" Farkas's voice was thick with contempt.

Varco helped Gyala to his feet. "Yes. We'll return another night."

One by one, the soldiers slipped back into the forest. Gyala walked slower than the others, but on his own.

Varco waited for the shadows to swallow the men before he took Ilona's hand once more.

"Is he going to be all right?" Ilona asked. The wound on the old soldier had looked serious, even if the bullet had missed his lung. Ilona wasn't sure why she cared, except that perhaps she didn't want *any* more people to get hurt—even these soldiers.

A wide grin spread over Varco's dark features. "He'll be fine by tomorrow. You'll find us a sturdy bunch, Ilona." His hand squeezed hers and sent a hot tingle surging through her spine. In her embarrassment she wanted to push him away, but she couldn't let go of him. She wanted to feel the unearthly sensation of running with him at least one more time.

TEN

THE NEXT EVENING, VARCO WOKE ILONA MUCH EARLIER THAN dusk. Ilona hazily blinked into the warm rays of the setting sun peeking over the treed horizon.

"It's not even dark yet," she mumbled, pulling her jacket tighter around her shivering frame. The reversal of night and day was confusing enough without being sleep-deprived. And for some reason she had thought that daylight would actually hurt Varco and his men. He didn't seem bothered by the sunshine, however. He stood in the middle of the yard, shaking his dark hair back over his shoulder, eyes sparkling in the light. *He's just an ordinary man,* she reasoned. *Not one of the Unhallowed.* But then, his running ability was distinctly beyond ordinary.

While Ilona washed her face in the barrel of cold water, she reflected on the night before. After returning from their botched raid, they had joined the other soldiers for a fancy dinner. Ilona ate only goat roast and fall vegetables, which she knew for certain had come from the local farms and wasn't tainted like the wine and waxy-looking fruit. One taste of Unhallowed wine had already changed Ilona enough for her liking. With Varco's help, she could run like the wind as his strange powers coursed through her, and she could wield an Unhallowed sword like any other soldier of the countess. But what would happen if she ate Fey food every night? Would her thoughts and feelings turn wicked, would she eventually become Unhallowed herself? The lovely taste wasn't worth the risk.

Now Ilona glanced around the courtyard, bathed in the late sunlight. No clashing swords, no swearing soldiers. Only the occasional shrieking of an early bat broke the eerie silence.

Ilona took a deep breath and leaned back against the barrel. "Why did you wake me so early?"

Varco gave her a long appraising look. "To have some extra practice time. Last night you held your own against the farmers. I think you earned my men's respect."

"That was nothing," she grumbled, hiding behind her long bangs. She knew Varco would be furious if he knew that she had stayed out of battle as much as possible. If he found out, she would no longer have even the possibility of freedom to look for the rathstone. "And I think you're wrong. Farkas doesn't respect me." *Farkas doesn't even respect you,* she added silently.

"I already knew your skills with the sword were impressive," Varco said, ignoring her remark about Farkas. "But how well do you shoot the longbow?"

The pride she'd felt a moment ago vanished into the cool evening air. Her lessons last year had been confined to fencing. She had used her older brother's hunting bow a few times, when no one was looking, but she never had any formal archery training. Her mother had tried to teach her sewing instead—a supremely useless skill, and one reinforced at Falston. She'd much preferred Father Joe's lessons on battles and strategy in history class.

Varco grinned, ducking his head to peer into her face. "You don't have to hide your talent here."

The part of her that wanted to be honest with him briefly struggled for control over the part that so badly wanted to impress him. *How hard can it be to shoot the longbow? If my clumsy brother can hit a rabbit, there can't be much to it.* She pushed off the barrel and tossed her head back.

"Sure I can. Any idiot can shoot the longbow."

Varco broke into a hearty laugh. "Any idiot? I hope you don't mean me." He motioned her to follow him to the shooting targets propped up against the stone wall and handed her a longbow fashioned out of gleaming yew. "Give me your hand."

Ilona hesitated, remembering the tingle of his powers flowing into her.

Varco wagged a shooting glove. "You should wear your protective gear."

"Oh. Of course." She pulled the soft leather over her right hand. Then she let him tie a leather guard around her fore-arm and hook a quiver filled with arrows onto her belt.

"You're all set." Varco's eyes rested on her with approval. "How far do you shoot for practice? Thirty yards? Fifty?"

"A hundred yards," Ilona claimed, then immediately chastised herself. Why did she have to brag like that? Shoot-ing from fifty yards would be impossible enough.

Varco raised his eyebrows and whistled. "One hundred yards? Unfortunately, the courtyard isn't that large. I usually practice-shoot from fifty yards away. Perhaps you'll show me what you can do from a thirty-yard distance."

Varco walked across the cobblestones, counting his paces. Ilona's heart sank. She hadn't realized how far even thirty yards were. Dragging her feet, she followed him. They stood near one of the castle's tall towers and Ilona, shielding her eyes with her hands, glanced upward, checking for the bats she'd seen flying in and out of the arched windows.

I'm stalling. Should I just tell him that I can't shoot the bow? But stubbornness and pride sealed her lips. She pulled an arrow from the quiver on her hip. Its tip gleamed golden in the sun. Ilona wondered if it was enchanted, too, like the sword blades. That might make things easier.

She placed the arrow on the narrow ledge of her bow and lifted it to aim. Instantly, the arrow slid off and tipped to the ground. Ilona suppressed an unladylike curse.

"Remember to tilt your bow," Varco said. "You haven't shot in a while?" His black eyebrows rose.

Ilona tried again. This time, she held the bow at an angle, making it impossible for the arrow to slip off its ledge. Taking a deep breath, she drew back the string. It took more effort than she had expected, and her arms trembled with the strain. She focused on the target on the far wall, but her fingers slipped too early and the arrow shot high into the cloudless sky. It arched through the air and disappeared on the other side of the castle walls.

"Good shot." Varco chuckled. "Were you aiming for a bat?" He pointed at a bat careening out of the tower window and streaking across the sky.

Ilona glowered at him, but he only winked and stepped closer.

"Your stance is a bit off. Allow me." His boot nudged her left foot forward so that Ilona stood sideways with her legs hip-width apart. "And hold the bow more like this." His hands lifted her elbow to point behind her. "When you pull back, your right hand should be near the edge of your mouth." His eyes met hers. "Right here." The tip of his finger lightly, deliberately stroked her cheek, gliding from her scar to the corner of her lips.

The touch sent an electric flare over her skin and Ilona jerked away, giving him a warning look. He had no right. Yet the sensation had been curiously pleasant.

Ignoring her racing heart and hoping her cheeks weren't as brightly colored as they felt, Ilona assumed the correct stance. Carefully, she pulled the string back until her hand was level with her mouth. Realizing she couldn't hold it like that for very long, she barely glanced at the target before she released. This time, luck was on her side. The arrow zipped straight across the yard and hit the outermost ring of her target.

"The sun must have been in my eyes the first time." Ilona was unable to suppress a triumphant grin.

"Oh, certainly," Varco said with a mocking smirk. He pulled another arrow out of her quiver. "Pass me the bow." He bent his knees slightly and without apparent effort shot his arrow into the very center of the target—bull's-eye.

"Show-off." Ilona took the bow back and tried again. Her next arrow missed the target by a few inches. She groaned.

Varco adjusted her stance once more and encouraged her to keep trying. Soon she hit the target every time, sometimes even near the center. Working up a sweat, Ilona shot arrow after arrow until her arms ached. Practicing with the longbow was more fun with a good instructor than it had ever been to shoot secretly, on her own. And Varco's intermittent praise gave Ilona a special, unfamiliar thrill.

The sun was dipping low behind the trees and the light

shifted to the hazy glow of dusk, when a long, tortured scream broke the yard's silence. Ilona released her bowstring without aiming, and her arrow shot into the side of the nearest shed.

"What's that?" Her voice was only a whisper while she strained to hear. Another cry rang out. This time Ilona was able to locate the source. The screams came from a window high above. They sounded like a girl fighting a terrifying and final battle against an unknown horror.

Ilona glanced at Varco, who stood listening, his body tense and unmoving.

"We have to help her," she said. The sound of pain and desperation chilled her heart and jumbled every thought in her brain. "Come on."

She turned to run to the castle doors, but Varco's hand gripped her arm and spun her around to face him. His kind eyes grew cold, glowing amber in the twilight. "You cannot interfere with the countess's pleasures," he growled. His voice was hardly recognizable, low and dangerous. "You don't possess the power to oppose her."

Another prolonged scream broke the evening's calm. Ilona tried to pull free. "But listen! Someone's in pain!" Her own helplessness made Ilona nearly frantic. *I have to stop the countess. I'd cut her head off, if I had my sword. I'd shoot an arrow through her heart of stone.*

Ilona's struggle against Varco's grip was futile, but she couldn't stop, like a rabbit caught in a trap. He put a finger to his lips.

"Calm down. Wait. It's almost over."

And after another tortured cry, a death-like silence descended over the courtyard, almost more difficult for Ilona to bear than the screams before.

She opened her mouth, but no sound came out. She cleared her throat, fighting back the horror.

"The countess killed her." She raised her eyes to Varco, challenging him to contradict her. He slowly released her from his grasp. "Why? Why does she have to kill them?" Ilona's voice rose with mounting frustration, and her fist pounded the stone wall beside her. "Why?"

Varco scratched behind his ears, shrugged. With a quick, fluid movement, he bent down and wiped a rogue tear from her cheek. He gave her a long look before he spoke.

"You know. Every so often, the countess needs mortal blood to sustain her."

Ilona swallowed her tears. She didn't want to cry in front of Varco. It wasn't news that the vampiric Fey fed on humans. She had known this even before she admitted to it, long before she and her friends had left their own world. When Kenneth was murdered at Fearnan, Ilona had faced the truth head on, vowing to defeat these monsters. She had promised to never let that happen to anyone ever again. How could she keep that promise when she was so powerless and lacked any allies?

"I've also heard that the countess likes to bathe in it to keep her youthful looks. I don't know if that's true, but . . ." Varco trailed off.

"She bathes in their *blood?*" An icy shiver trembled over Ilona's skin. She flashed Varco a questioning look. *Tell me it's not true.*

Varco shrugged and pointed a long finger up the ivy-covered tower. "It's probably only a rumor. But . . . her bath chamber is up there."

Ilona glanced at the arched windows. The room beyond

lay in innocent silence now. She couldn't help conjuring up an image of the countess, relaxing in a tub of rust-red liquid, its color an affront to the polished silver of the tub. Nausea twisted her guts, and Ilona thought she might be ill. *There's no point in dwelling on the worst. I'll find a way to help these girls. Maybe not today or tomorrow, but soon. Soon.*

She rubbed the bridge of her nose and forced a few deep breaths of soothing air into her lungs. "Only a rumor, I'm sure. Let's practice, shall we?" She took up the bow she had dropped and turned her back to the tower. "Show me how to shoot a bull's-eye."

When the sun disappeared behind the stone wall and the clouds turned from pink and orange to a threatening purple, the soldiers, stretching and yawning, left their sheds and began their nightly exercises. Farkas, Zador, Gyala, Kardos, and Dezso crowded around Varco and listened as he outlined their practice schedule. It was the perfect opportunity for Ilona to sneak away unnoticed.

She had put on a brave face for the rest of the evening and managed somehow to concentrate on her shooting. But at the back of her mind, a tortured girl kept screaming in terror. The unknown girl alternately became Christina, Katalin, and Jeanette. There was no way she could simply accept the death of another girl as calmly as Varco did. She had to find out what had happened to that girl in the bathroom.

At the entrance to the castle, she grabbed the silver knocker and banged it against the wood. *What if Madame Joo opens? What shall I say then?* But before Ilona could think up a reasonable excuse, the door opened and Anci's pale face peered out at her. Her eyes widened.

"You?" She leaned against the doorjamb and chewed on

a scabby knuckle. "We thought we saw the last of you."

Taken aback by the unexpected hostility in Anci's voice, Ilona narrowed her eyes. "What do you mean? I was worried about you. About all the girls."

Anci nodded slowly. "Sure. But you moved up in the world. You're a soldier now. We're your servants."

Ilona's stomach contracted. *Did Anci think that Ilona had left the girls behind on purpose?* "That's not how I planned it," she said. "And I'm still working on getting you all out. It might be easier with me on the outside."

Anci shrugged, looking unconvinced. She still blocked the entrance, leaving Ilona shivering on the doorstep. "What's your plan, then?" Her fingers dug deep into the pockets of her dirt-streaked apron. The glance she gave Ilona was cautiously hopeful.

"Just be ready. When I give you the signal, gather the other maids." Ilona's voice trailed off, and she avoided Anci's eyes. Embarrassment drove the heat into her face.

Anci laughed softly. "That's what I thought. There is no plan."

"There will be." Ilona's voice rose in pitch. "I made a promise, and I'm not going to break it." She took a few calming breaths and remembered why she had come. "Listen, Anci. Earlier tonight I heard screams from the western tower. From Countess Bathory's bathroom. Do you know—do you know anything about this?"

A shadow drew like a curtain over Anci's features and for a moment, she looked lost and unbearably sad. "Ilona," she whispered. "Don't think about it. It'll break your heart if you do." She squared her thin shoulders and straightened up. "I'm sure you'll make a great soldier. Just don't let Varco turn your head." She smiled at the last.

Ilona forced a grin. "Deal." She hesitated. Anci so obviously didn't want to talk about it. But she had to know. "I was wondering if you could do me one favor. Could you find out about Katalin?" Ilona would have liked to ask about Jeanette as well, but she hadn't mentioned her existence to anyone. It would only raise the questions of where she had come from and why. She gave Anci a pleading look from under her long bangs. *Find out if Katalin is still alive . . . or if the countess bathed in her blood this evening.*

Anci squirmed, then nodded. "I'll check on her. I'll sneak her a treat." Anci lunged forward and hung from Ilona's neck, squeezing tightly. "Be careful out there."

Ilona hugged back, feeling awkward. Anci smelled of kitchen soap and burned wood. She quickly let go. "So how are the other girls? Evike? Dorika? And Gizi?"

"They're fine." Anci shrugged again. "Hanging on somehow." She smiled, unsure and lopsided. "I'll tell them to look out for your signal, then. That'll cheer them."

A whistle behind Ilona made her spin around. Varco stood at the foot of the steps, cocking his head at her.

"I *knew* I was a man short. Who told you to take a break?" But the grin spreading over his face and the twinkle in his eyes belied his gruff tone. He clucked his tongue at Anci. "Are you bothering my soldiers again? Off to the kitchen with you!"

When he touched Ilona's elbow, she gave Anci a farewell smile and then followed him into the torch-lit yard.

ELEVEN

Two nights later, Varco gathered his men at dusk. There was an excited gleam in his eyes, and Ilona knew that he had something more planned than practice swordplay.

"The time is right," he announced. "The night of the autumn equinox has finally arrived, and the veil between worlds is thin." The men shuffled their boots, hands sliding to the swords at their sides. They grinned and elbowed each other.

Varco continued, "We'll be able to leave this rath and forage in the plentiful mortal world."

The Wolves' fists shot up with a battle yell, and cheers rang out all over the yard, as the other group leaders made similar announcements.

Ilona rubbed her cold hands together and blew on them. She was worried about being forced to participate in another fight with humans, and she didn't want any more girls harmed. She had hoped that they'd stay near the castle tonight so that she could try to find that hollow tree of her dreams. The little man had offered his help and had told her to find him. But how could she find the right tree if she was constantly supervised?

After each soldier had strapped on their weapons and silver armor, they filed through the front gate. Ilona watched out for any black cats to trip over, but none was in sight. She reached for Varco's wrist as he passed her.

"I have a question," she said quickly, before he could begin to run at his unholy speed again.

"So ask."

Ilona drew a deep breath. "You can leave the rath? I thought . . ." Something Corrine or Father Joe had said had given her the impression that it was difficult even for the Fey to pass the barriers between mortal world and their raths. Had they been wrong?

Varco glanced at his men running ahead of them toward Cachtice village. "We can't always. Only at certain days of the year that are holy to the Fey. Samhain, Beltane, the equinox, those kinds of days."

"And we'll visit the mortal world tonight?" Ilona felt stupid for asking the obvious, but part of her was afraid to use another portal. She'd much rather stay in this rath than take any chances.

Varco eyed her carefully. "Are you homesick? I guess I'd better keep an eye on you."

"I'm not going to run away." Ilona glared at him before dashing down the hill after the other soldiers. She was angry at his lack of trust, and shocked at herself for wanting his trust, from an ally of the Unhallowed. After all, if he knew her true mission, he wouldn't trust her.

Varco caught her halfway down and took her hand. With a dizzying flash, his power spread through her. The world around them grew silent, except for the rhythmic whoosh of air passing Ilona's ears as her feet pounded the ground. The dark world suddenly glowed as though a giant had lit an invisible torch. New smells rose up, of decaying leaves, of woodland animals and moist grass.

When they entered the village, human odors replaced these smells, the nasty ones of excrement and sweat, and then something much sweeter and inviting. A sudden thirst burned in Ilona's throat. A heady, delicious scent—reminiscent of the spicy Unhallowed wine—called to her. Tugging at Varco's hand, she slowed down, looking around the village for the source of the teasing, tempting smell. A boy, perhaps ten years old, stood on the threshold to a dilapidated shed holding a rusty spear. Ilona's eyes burned as her vision focused. His skin appeared to become translucent, and the dark vein on his throat pulsed out a rhythmic invitation.

I can smell the villagers' mortal blood. And I want it.

The boy hastily entered the shed, and Ilona broke free from Varco's grasp, heart pounding in her ears. *What happened?* Hands on her knees, she sucked in air, and almost immediately revulsion replaced the strange longing.

Varco had sprinted on ahead, but returned to her in a few long strides. The whirling world slowed down to a quiet village street. She hid her hands behind her back and glowered up at him.

"I don't want to run with you anymore."

Varco cocked his head, gave her an uncertain grin. "Who do you want to run with, then? Want me to get Farkas?"

Ilona shook her head defiantly. Varco motioned her to walk beside him. Side by side, they followed the path out of the village. Ilona didn't need to be told that they'd never catch up to the other soldiers at this snail's pace.

"The smells," she began, when they had left the last crooked house behind. "It was disgusting." She took deep gulps of the sweet fall air, as though it could erase the memory of the scent of human blood, of smelling it not with aversion, but with something else. Temptation. *Desire.*

Varco gave her a surprised look and furrowed his brows in thought. Then he brightened. "Humans do smell disgusting sometimes. Not *you*, of course, but those foul old farmers. Here in the forest, you won't smell them." Once more he took her hand, sharing his power with her, and they raced through the woods.

Varco pulled Ilona to a stop on top of a hill, where the other Wolves were waiting by two tall oaks. The wind blew gently through the vast canopy of the branches, rustling the remnants of yellow leaves. Ilona found she wasn't even out of breath. Exhilarated from the run, she scraped some cow dung off her boot.

"Are we the last group to go?" Varco asked Zador, who nodded in reply.

"What took you so long?" Farkas grimaced. "We've been waiting forever."

"Go ahead, then," Varco said, motioning toward the oaks.

Ilona wondered where the portal was supposed to be. She couldn't see anything auspicious. Then Farkas stepped through the narrow space between the two old oaks and disappeared.

Ilona's heart pumped faster. *A Fey portal.* What would happen to her if she used it? Would she feel the same disturbing sensations as when she ran with Varco? And could all this contact with Unhallowed power turn her eventually Unhallowed herself?

One by one, Zador, Gyala, Kardos, and Dezso entered

the portal between the trees. Varco waited beside Ilona. "You're next," he whispered.

"Why don't you go first?" Ilona suggested, wondering if she could possibly make a run for it and head back to the castle alone.

Varco grinned. "I don't think so." He nudged her forward. "What's the matter? Scared of fighting the mighty villagers?"

"I'm not scared!" Immediately Ilona regretted taking his bait. Now she had no excuse to hang back. She took a few calming breaths. How bad could the portal be? At least she'd be in her own world again in a moment. Away from murderous, inhuman Countess Bathory.

With firm, resolute steps, she walked between the mottled trunks, steeling herself for a rough entry. Grass crunched underfoot, and an owl hooted in the distance. The same valley spread brown and wilted below. Ilona turned. Varco stood behind her, frowning through the trees.

"Did I go through?" She hadn't felt the strange falling, spinning sensation, the momentary darkness or the nausea she had experienced with her last portal.

"No." Varco waited until she had returned to his side. He gave her a thoughtful look. "It seems my pretty mortal soldier can't use our doorway. I guess you didn't drink enough of the countess's wine for *that*."

She smiled. Or maybe only Unhallowed Fey and Half-Born humans like Corrine could use this portal. Then a horrible thought struck her. What if all portals only worked one way for humans without magical abilities? Maybe she couldn't leave this rath at all. *I'll be stuck here forever!*

"We'll go together," Varco suggested. "I'm sure I can pull you through."

Ilona wondered how he could be so sure, but the next moment, his warm arm encircled her waist. Before she could protest, he lugged her forward.

On the other side, Ilona dropped to her knees. The world spun like some unruly merry-go-round. She gagged and spat. Gradually the darkness around her flickered into focus and the voices clarified from an indistinct buzz into individual sounds.

"She's slowing us down." That was unmistakably Farkas.

"She'll be all right in a moment." Varco patted her shoulder.

Ilona fought through the fog and trembled to her feet. Her vision cleared. Six disheveled men in various states of impatience stared back at her.

"I'm fine," she mumbled, squaring her shoulders. "Where is our target?"

Varco pointed to a scattering of huts in the distance. A few windows were still lit, giving an impression of peacefulness. Walking at a normal pace, the group closed in on the village.

Once her nausea subsided, Ilona noted how very much the human countryside resembled the rath. Except they had left the rath in fall, and here, the spring she had left behind in the mortal world bloomed in vivid colors. The village past the crossroads ahead was decked in what appeared to be spring festival preparations, but the brightly colored flowers were curiously intertwined with ash boughs and wolfsbane. A crop of what Ilona assumed to be rye was just peeking up in the newly planted fields. The air was fresher here than it had been in the rath she'd just left, and the moonlight clearer and brighter, but otherwise it was rural Hungary on both sides of the portal. When Ilona mentioned her observations to Varco, he laughed.

"That's because those human villages in our rath were once on this side of the portal. When Countess Bathory's power grew, she expanded her rath. She swallowed up a few human townships, you might say. Or rather, parts of them. Some of the villages were split and left twins in the mortal world."

Now I understand how they knew my hometown, Ilona thought. *It must have a twin in this rath. How peculiar.*

"Her plan was to breed more humans," Varco continued, "so we'd have a steady supply—" He broke off after a glance at her face.

Ilona swallowed her distaste and aimed for a stony, untroubled look. "Ah. That's very . . . creative. And did it work?"

Varco guffawed. "For a while. But it seems that humans don't breed well, confined to a Fey rath. And it sure didn't help that the young girls disappeared much quicker than they could be raised."

Ugh. Ilona's hands curled into fists. Then she noticed Zador, waving wildly at them from the crossroads up ahead near the village entrance.

"Varco, look!" she said. Armed villagers, six or seven men, wearing floppy hats and irate expressions, strode up the path toward the soldiers. The village guard, Ilona assumed.

"Come on." Varco sprinted ahead, and Ilona followed at a trot.

When Ilona reached the crossroads, the brawl was already in full swing. She pulled her sword, heart clenching at the thought of fighting the mortal people of her own world. People she wanted to protect.

I can do this, she thought. *I can pretend to fight them, without actually hurting them.* Perhaps her new fighting skills would even allow her to help the mortals escape unscathed from her troop. But it was a careful balancing act, if Varco was not to notice any enthusiasm lacking in her performance tonight.

Ilona's scheming was interrupted by a man attacking her with a long iron sword. Without thinking, she crashed her blue blade onto his, and glowing sparks flew. His eyes widened under the brim of his hat, but he fought on. Ilona danced around him, lightly clanking her sword against his. His ability with the sword was laughable, and Ilona did not feel in danger.

Finally she jumped forward, bluffed-charged, then smacked the sword out of his hands. He cried out as his weapon hit the ground with a thud. Ilona kicked it away. The villager, tougher than she had expected, raised his fists.

"To the death," he snarled, revealing crooked brown teeth. He emitted a strong smell of pigsty and drink. No doubt his bravery could be traced back to a long night at the tavern.

"I don't think so." Ilona flipped her sword in her hand. She didn't want to hurt anybody but the Unhallowed, but she couldn't let herself get killed, either. She thwacked him on the head with the hilt of her sword. With a groan, he fell unconscious to the ground.

Ilona glanced toward the other soldiers. Wild-eyed, they wiped their red-stained swords on their pants. All the villagers lay in unmoving, whimpering heaps on the path. Ilona bit her lip, hoping they were not all dead. She suppressed her tears of anger. Once again, she had failed to defend humans against the evil Fey.

Varco sniffed the mild air. "We're taking the first house, the one over there." The dwelling he pointed at sat about a hundred yards away from the path. It seemed one of the more affluent houses of the village, with a neatly thatched roof and geraniums drooping from planters under the windows. An apple tree bloomed white on the front lawn and a painted gate marked the entrance. Wolfsbane and ash boughs marked this house, too, at which the soldiers laughed the way they'd laughed at the silver bullet that first night. There was something Ilona was missing here, but she couldn't quite place her finger on it.

Varco turned to Ilona. "I want you to stay on this path and whistle if there's trouble. Understood?"

Ilona nodded, still too upset to speak. She watched the soldiers leaping over the gate and surrounding the house. How could she protect this village and still accomplish her mission? She didn't think the Council had anticipated this kind of dilemma, and many innocent lives could be lost from that miscalculation.

Farkas and Kardos rammed their massive shoulders into the front door twice before it gave way. The other four followed them inside.

Ilona waited, shuffling from one foot to the other. The house behind the apple tree lay in serene darkness. *What's happening inside?* The men sure took their time. She glanced up and down the village streets. There was not a soul in sight. What if she warned the next house? Would the Wolves know it was her? She glanced at the next building, its lights low. No one appeared to be keeping watch—the villagers they'd met before must have been the sole source of protection. Calculating the distance, Ilona knew she wouldn't have the time to go knocking on any doors before her troop would return.

She had already failed the villagers at the crossroads; she could not let this happen a second time in one night. With a deep breath of the warm spring air, she opened the gate and approached the house.

When she reached the threshold, an unearthly howl shattered the quiet night. The eerie sound sent waves of shivers over her skin. Ilona stopped and peered around the shadowy garden, but couldn't see any wolves. Besides, it had sounded like it came from inside. Hesitantly she stepped over the doorstep and snuck into the house.

A short hallway led into a little sitting room. There was a sofa and a low table with a cup of cold tea. A basket filled with mending sat on a nearby stool. A vase of daffodils had tipped over, and the water dripped onto the wooden floor, next to a strange brown stain. Ilona bent down to examine it. It looked like a large, dirty paw print. *A wolf print. There's a wild animal in the house.* Ilona wiped her sweaty palms on her pants as she rose.

She tiptoed around it over the frayed rug and headed toward the next door. A crash and a bang came from deeper within the house, and Ilona stiffened. The idea of running back into the yard flashed through her mind. *Don't be such a coward!* Her hand glided to the hilt of her sword. A few more lithe steps brought her to a corridor. Strange noises came from ahead. With a pounding heart, Ilona crept toward them.

She peeked into a spacious country kitchen. And froze.

Four grizzled creatures prowled the room, hunched over, with mottled brown or gray fur hanging over tight green clothes. Huge ears stuck up from their heads, snouts protruded where lips should be. Exploring the room, they grumbled and growled, sniffing here and there. Gnarled claws ripped the doors off the cupboards and swiped down jars of sugar and spices, spilling the contents over the counters. One of the creatures tore at the upholstery of the kitchen bench with his yellow fangs. One pulled a ham out of the pantry and swung it over his head with a whoop. His huge jaws enveloped the entire ham and tore it apart.

Wolfmen. Ilona wanted to back away before they saw her, but her feet wouldn't obey her. Her hands clutched the doorframe, and she was unable to tear her eyes away from the scene of destruction. No wonder the villagers had posted wolfsbane and ash at the entrance, though apparently like silver, the folk remedies held no power over these creatures. At the far end of the room, a door swung open, and two more wolf creatures entered. They had slung two girls wearing nightgowns across their shoulders. One appeared asleep, or more likely unconscious, the other whimpered softly and stared around with glazed eyes.

"The parents?" a chocolate brown wolf snarled.

The one with the sleeping girl over his shoulder threw his black head back and made a strange sound. It took Ilona a moment to realize it was laughter.

"They'll fight no more." The wolf's long tongue slipped out and licked his lips. Then his eyes fell on Ilona, tawny eyes, glowing and mesmerizing. Ilona wanted to shrink from his gaze, but his look held her in place as her heart drummed in her ears. Then he growled deep in his throat. "Your maiden is here." His glance flickered back to the brown werewolf. "Take care of her before I do."

The shaggy brown head swung around and his amber eyes stared at her. In one leap, he was by her side. Ilona gasped.

"Ilona. You shouldn't be here!" Varco's voice rasped in her ear and his claws gripped her elbow.

Ilona shook her head. He was so right. She didn't belong here, with these Unhallowed creatures. She pulled her arm out of Varco's grasp and fled. Her feet finally back under her own command, she sprinted down the hallways and out the open door.

Ilona couldn't get her fencing partner Kenneth's horrible murder out of her head. She gagged at the memory of his body, ripped to nearly unrecognizable pieces by the Fey. Perhaps that had been the handiwork of these werewolves.

Ilona ran on, down the path, through the gate, and along the deserted village street, without stopping for breath, even when her lungs began to burn. Suddenly she heard thundering paw steps behind her.

Don't slow down now. Stupid, stupid Ilona. Playing soldier with the Unhallowed.

Running up a lush green hill, she convinced herself that the pack of Wolves was after her, that if she turned to glance back, they'd be upon her, tearing her to pieces. Her thighs screamed in pain and it hurt to draw air, but Ilona pushed herself farther, farther, even though she knew she had nowhere to hide.

"Stop!"

Ilona felt his hot breath on her neck, caressing her cheek. *I'm not going down without a fight.* Still running, she pulled her sword out of its sheath. She spun around.

"No!" The dark of night and the shadow of the looming forests made her blind, and she swung her sword around aimlessly.

"Put the sword down. I don't want to hurt you."

The moon peeked through the clouds and illuminated Varco. He was alone. The fangs, the claws, and the fur had disappeared—he looked like he had earlier that night. Human.

"You can't fool me," Ilona spat out. Her voice sounded small and childish in the vast night. "I know what you really look like." She lifted her weapon, but her hands trembled. She dimly remembered his warning about not raising the sword against one of her own. But then, she wasn't really one of *them*.

"I said, don't." Varco pulled his sword and, with a single strong strike, knocked Ilona's weapon out of her hand. He gripped her by the shoulders, as though he meant to shake her. But his hands were as gentle as the eyes peering into hers.

"It's not so bad," he whispered. "Once you're used to it."

~ TWELVE ~

*O*NCE YOU'RE USED TO IT. VARCO'S WORDS ECHOED IN Ilona's mind as the two of them slowly walked through the forest. How could one become used to being a monster? A creature of the night? A servant of the Unhallowed? Ilona vowed she'd never fall into that trap, never lose sight of her goals in the rath, no matter how many strangely pleasant shivers Varco's hand on her arm sent down her spine.

Because I can never really be one of them. The thought saddened Ilona a little. For the first time in her life, she hadn't felt like a complete misfit. Varco had accepted her and even seemed to like her, just as she was, and the rest of the group might follow suit eventually as well, if they had time enough to observe her skills as a fighter.

But she knew in even entertaining the thought that she was forgetting what master these Wolves served. Their goals weren't her own. She couldn't let herself get close to Varco.

Varco held up a wayward branch for Ilona.

"Thanks," she murmured. The dense forest was so dark that she'd bump into the trees every two seconds without his casually touch at her elbow every now and then.

139

"I didn't want you to see us tonight."

Ilona nodded, realizing he could see her as clear as in daylight, even though he was only a dark shape to her. She still couldn't speak to him. She'd thought he was a normal man, perhaps enslaved to the countess as she had been, but she had to admit she'd been blinded by his gentle attitude toward her. Even now, he was speaking gently, when Ilona had anticipated a fight.

"I expected you to obey my command and stay where I posted you."

Ilona's desperate laugh rasped over her throat before she could stop it. So he blamed her? "I would have found out sooner or later."

"True." He remained silent for a while. They walked on, until he swiped a long branch aside and revealed a moonlit clearing. The long oak branches threw weaving shadows over the mossy ground, and unseen animals rustled through the underbrush beyond. Varco sat on a fallen tree and motioned her to join him.

Ilona stood, tapping her foot. Heat rushed into her head. She wouldn't sit beside him—he had a way of tweaking her emotions. She mutely shook her head.

"Suit yourself." He sighed. "I thought . . . I want you to understand why."

"Why what?" She stepped closer and leaned against the trunk of a tall pine.

"Why I joined the Fey."

Ilona averted her eyes. Part of her didn't really want to know, didn't want him to talk about it. Wanted to pretend it had never happened. But she had to know. Deep down, her fascination with him had always been because she needed to know.

"Did they force you? Or bribe you?" She crossed the few feet to where he sat and sank down beside him.

Varco scratched his neck. "They didn't force me. I went willingly. But let me tell you from the beginning." He paused, as though waiting for her to interrupt, but Ilona chewed on her knuckle, determined to hear him out.

"I was born human, like you, in a small village in this rath, not far from here. The name I received from my parents was Laszlo Bencze. They were dairy farmers, but we didn't have many cattle and our land wasn't big. I was the oldest of eight children, and there often wasn't enough food for all of us. Many nights, I went to bed cold and hungry."

"Do you still see them sometimes?" Ilona interrupted. "Your family?" She tried to imagine such a meeting. The image of Varco in his werewolf shape sipping politely from a teacup drove rough laughter over her lips.

Varco raked his hands through his untidy hair. "No, Ilona. This all happened a long time ago, in another century."

Ilona shivered and drew her arms around herself. "How can that be?" she asked, but the answer already unfurled in her mind. Fey time was different from mortal time.

"I'll come to that in a moment." Varco sounded tired now, as though he found it trying to tell his tale. "As I said, we were poor. But that didn't mean we lived in misery. Most of our neighbors were just as poor. In our big family, we always had each other, and I took pride in helping raise my siblings."

As Varco paused again, Ilona listened to the sounds of the forest, creaking branches and hooting owls. Part of her expected howling wolves, but it never came.

"And then?" she prodded, when the silence grew uncomfortable. "Did the Unhallowed come and steal your little

141

sisters?" She knew she was being blunt, but she couldn't help herself. Any excuse he produced for joining the Unhallowed wasn't going to be good enough, would never justify what the Wolves did for the countess.

"No." Varco stretched his long arms. "No, it was the bubonic plague. The Black Death. One day it hit our village like a blizzard, touching all of us."

Ilona knew about the bubonic plague, about the devastation it had caused in Europe in the fourteenth century. There had been other outbreaks later on, but the disease was now gone from Europe. *The fourteenth century . . .* Varco looked about twenty years old, but he had been alive much, much longer. Goosebumps rose on her skin. *It's unnatural that he's alive at all, sitting here next to me.*

"What happened then? Did you get sick?"

"Not right away. My mother was the first one in my family to fall ill. Then the baby girl she still nursed. Then Janos, my brother closest in age to me. Then my other three sisters. Then my other two brothers," Varco recounted in a toneless voice. "And still I didn't get ill." "That's strange," Ilona said, trying to keep an emotional distance, and failing. His tale was too horrid, and she couldn't help feeling sorry for the boy he had been. The boy who had lost everybody close to him.

Varco's sigh was nearly soundless, little more than a quiet breath. "My father thought that perhaps God had spared us so we could take care of our family and nurse them through to their deaths. It made sense then."

"You believe in God?" It seemed inconceivable that someone in league with the Unhallowed could belong to a church.

"I haven't for a long time," Varco replied. "But back then, yes, I did. I prayed every night for their misery to end."

"I'm sorry." Ilona reluctantly put her hand on his arm. She hadn't gotten along well with her parents and brothers when she still lived at home, and sending her away to Falston hadn't improved things. Yet she understood how heartbreaking it would be, to lose them and her brothers forever.

"They all died?"

Varco looked at her, his brown eyes sad. "Yes. My father came down with the illness during the last days of my youngest brother—my last sibling to die of the disease. I thought my father would be next, but he had never been sick a day in his life, and he beat this one, too. He survived the plague. After a few delirious weeks, he was scarred but healthy."

"Oh." Ilona gave Varco a thoughtful glance. "That was good, then, wasn't it?" When he returned her look, it was so mournful that she knew she was wrong.

"It might have been. But my father lost everything . . . everything but me. He raged against God, and . . . I don't know. I think he might have gone insane with grief." Varco took up a stick and drew circles in the soft, moist ground. From deep within the forest, an animal made a shrill sound, cutting through the quiet night. "He hanged himself that spring. In the barn. And I buried the last of my family."

Ilona sighed. If there were words to help heal such pain, they eluded her. "I can't imagine," she said finally, in a low voice. "It must have been awful."

"Oh, but it gets better!" Varco said, with a forced laugh. "The night I buried my father, the first swelling appeared in my armpit. Within a few days, I was too ill to move from my bed." Varco drew a deep breath and gave Ilona a sidelong glance. "I don't know why, but I didn't feel ready to die yet. I clung to life. At first, I still prayed to God, but prayers had been useless to my family. So I turned to the dark powers."

"How did you even know about the Fey?" Ilona interrupted, trying to follow his twisted logic. "They don't teach about them in church."

"No, you're right. But if there's light, there's darkness, and I had heard all the old wives' tales, about witches and the Fey Prince in his court."

"Old wives' tales!" Ilona burst out. Her hands gestured around wildly. "This—this is not an old wives' tale!"

Varco smiled a true smile. He took her hand and squeezed it. "There's some truth in every tale. And so on the night I prepared to die, the Fey Prince sent an emissary to me, who healed me of my illness and brought me to this rath. Then he made me one of the countess's soldiers. In return, I swore the Prince eternal loyalty."

Ilona pulled her hand out of his. "I'm glad he saved your life. But . . ." She shook her head. What was the better choice? Death or serving the countess's bloodlust? Had Varco been wrong in his desire to live?

Ilona rubbed her aching head as her mind replayed the werewolves tearing through the kitchen. Claws, fangs, and the stale odor of blood. "And now you turn into this . . . this creature?" She couldn't keep the revulsion out of her voice, and for a moment, Varco looked hurt.

"We are shape shifters. The Prince bestowed this generous gift on all the countess's soldiers. Our group— the Wolves—can change into wolves. The group called the Bats change into bats, the Bears into bears . . ."

Ilona nodded at Varco's expectantly raised eyebrows. "I understand. The Rats turn into real rats. I don't see how that would help in catching girls, though."

Varco laughed. "Well, we keep our human size when we transform."

Ilona shuddered at the thought of huge rats prowling the village streets at night. It wasn't a very comforting image. "And you're not upset by what you are?"

Varco shrugged. "I am what I am. I've lived like this for a long time and will for much longer than most humans will live their boring little lives."

His voice was rough and sure, yet something in his eyes told Ilona that Varco wasn't completely at peace with his twilight existence. She saw the remainder of the human soul he once possessed at war with the evil in this rath. But even though she felt sorry for his lost life and for what he had become, she couldn't imagine making that same choice for herself. Nothing justified serving the Prince and the countess in their killing and destruction.

"We can't change the past," she said after a long pause, "but I don't like seeing you in wolf form. It's unnatural."

Varco got to his feet and pulled her up from the log. "Then I'll do my best to keep to my human shape when you're present."

Ilona smiled at his sincere expression. "You'll do that for me?"

He slowly returned her smile. "I promise."

Varco led Ilona out of the forest into a meadow. Stars had come out and the sky glowed lavender on the eastern horizon, the first sign of the coming spring dawn. A mild wind caressed Ilona's face and swept across the meadow, bending the long grass.

"What are we doing here?" Ilona said. "Shouldn't we

get back to the others?"

"They'll meet us here. You'll see." Varco shrugged off his jacket and spread it on the lumpy ground. He motioned for her to sit.

Ilona sat down on the ground, inches from his jacket. He didn't have to treat her like a delicate maiden. Especially not after tonight.

With a chuckle, he sat beside her. He pointed down the slope, at a dense hawthorn grove.

"Keep your eyes on those bushes."

Ilona yawned. The excitement of the night was wearing off. She still wasn't completely used to being up all night long and sleeping during the day. And watching bushes came awfully close to counting sheep.

They sat quietly together, Varco's watchful eyes scanning the horizon. Ilona's eyelids grew heavier and heavier, and she thought she might curl up for a little nap, when Varco clucked his tongue.

"Look."

Ilona blinked and rubbed her eyes. She sat up straighter and squinted through the hazy dawn. Dark shapes hurried across the meadow, forming an undulating line. As the shapes drew closer, Ilona could make out their forms more clearly. They were bears, huge rust-red grizzlies with humped backs and tiny black eyes. But unlike any bear Ilona had ever seen, these bears walked on their hind legs. They wore the same green uniform she wore, and several of them carried a small, unmoving bundle on their shoulders.

"It's the Bears," she whispered. "Where are they going?"

"Just watch."

The bearmen walked straight toward the hawthorn grove. The first one stepped between the bushes and disappeared. The rest of them followed.

"It's a portal?" Ilona gave Varco a quizzical look, and he nodded. "Why aren't we using the oak tree portal we came through?"

"Many of the portals work only one way. We cannot go back through it."

Ilona scanned the hawthorn grove. It looked so ordinary. She would never have guessed that it contained a portal to a Fey rath.

Moments later, a swarm of bats appeared over the northern horizon. Bats were common around the castle, but these creatures were twenty times the size of regular bats. Several of them gripped motionless girls in their black claws.

"The Bats," Ilona commented quietly. The oversized bats landed on the lush grass. Now Ilona could make out their peculiar shapes. Their chests, clad in soldiers' garb, resembled human torsos, as did their muscled arms, which seamlessly turned into large, leathery wings. Their faces were grotesque, more human than bat, but with the high, pricked ears and jutting incisors of the animal. The men-bats walked the last few paces toward the hawthorns. One turned around and looked straight at Ilona, its eyes glowing red as though lit from within. With a hiss, the creature stepped into the bushes and was gone.

Next came the Copperheads, slithering through the grass, then the Hawks and last the Rats. To Ilona's mind, those were the worst. They walked at a crouch, sniffing along the way, with their whiskers trembling and their black eyes gleaming in the dim light. There was nothing human left in their features except their size. Even from the distance, Ilona could see sharp teeth protruding from their snouts. Their tails swished back and forth, thick and white, like African earthworms.

"Shouldn't we go through, too?" Ilona suggested after the last rat had disappeared among the hawthorns. The chill of night seeped through the ground into her bones and she wanted to get moving again.

"Not yet." Varco whistled shrilly. Ilona thought her ears would fall off if he did that again. "We'll wait for our men and go as a group. I wanted you to see the other soldiers pass through first."

"Why?" Ilona rubbed her upper arms and glanced at him sideways. He was chewing on a long blade of grass, looking unbothered by the chill. *He's probably never cold*, Ilona thought, remembering the warmth of his hands. Of his hands on her arms. *No. I cannot let myself forget what he is. And whom he serves.*

"Why did you want me to see the others?" she repeated.

Varco jumped to his feet and stretched languidly. "So that you can watch out for them." He ran down the slope, whistling softly to his men, who were arriving from the eastern path. Ilona followed without haste, reflecting on his last statement. Did he mean she should offer protection to *all* the countess's soldiers? But the idea of her being of assistance to a gigantic Rat was ridiculous. Or had he meant, rather, that she should be wary of them?

Approaching the hawthorn grove, Ilona decided it didn't matter. She'd battle the lot of them if she had to. *Just let them come.*

THIRTEEN

THE NEXT FEW NIGHTS WERE ALMOST PEACEFUL. THE WOLVES rested, gorged themselves and did some half-hearted target practice. A few times Ilona tried to sneak off into the forest to find the hollow tree of her dreams, hoping to meet the little woodsman who had promised her help, but to her great frustration Varco kept his promise to the countess and made sure Ilona stayed in the yard.

She became accustomed to sleeping the day away and being awake and alert at night. Her muscles weren't sore any longer, and her sword fighting and archery skills improved.

One night, when the moon hung bloated and yellow above the naked branches of the treetops, Varco called his group together and explained to them that the Captain would bring them several girls for the countess. They were to meet him in one of the meadows around the village.

The Captain with his bloody hand? Ilona's heart raced with worry. He had fought her in London and might very well recognize her. She pulled her cap down low into her face and decided to stay in the rear during the meeting.

Despite her anxiety over the Captain, it was pleasant to be out in the mild night, with the Fey sword at her side light as a toy, and her longbow slung over her shoulder. *Don't fool yourself,* she thought. *Playing soldier with Varco helps nobody. It's the rathstone that's important.* She accelerated her pace in a poor attempt at driving away the rising guilt. Too bad the Wolves weren't running tonight. She missed the exhilaration of speed.

Varco walked a few hundred yards ahead of the men, leading them along an invisible path. Ilona hoped fervently that they wouldn't turn into their wolfish shapes again tonight. It was a sight she wanted to avoid if she could. *Varco promised he wouldn't turn into a wolf in front of me, but none of the other Wolves have made such a vow.*

In a cleared rye field that rolled in all directions, Varco stopped and gathered his troops around him with a high-pitched whistle. Strands of a thin, damp mist rose and swirled around them like dancing ghosts. The village farmers had stacked the hay, creating squat figures supervising the fields. Ilona tugged at her pants and wiped her long bangs back under her beret. The other men shuffled restlessly, scratching their ears and spitting on the ground.

"He's late," Varco said with a glance at the low, fat moon. "Let's try for those deer while we're waiting." He pointed at the far end of the field. With quiet grunts of joy, the men bolted across the hay-stubble, tugging at their swords and bows.

Ilona squinted after them. Through the weaving fog and the enveloping darkness, she saw only shadows and the dark tree trunks seaming the edge of the meadow. Varco stepped closer and wrapped his hand around her wrist. She glared at him and tried to jerk out of his grasp. He held firm and his warmth spread up her arm into her shoulders and neck.

"Look *now*." His chin motioned toward the shadows.

Her vision focused as though through a powerful mono-cle. The mist parted and the edge of the field rushed toward her. A stag glanced up with pearly dark eyes, uncertain and ready to bounce away. It seemed close enough to touch.

Varco released his grip on her arm. Immediately, her vision darkened, but Ilona kept her focus on the black spot within the gray shadows. Her hands slid up and wrestled the bow off her shoulder. She pulled an arrow from her hip quiver and raised the bow to aim. Breathing slow and steady, she let the arrow fly. It raced across the field, disappearing from her view.

She turned to Varco. "Did I miss?"

The yellow moonlight illuminated his wide grin. "You did not."

She grinned back, pride warming her cheeks. It had been an impossibly far shot—and she had done it!

Once more, his hand tightened around her wrist. "Come on. I'll show you."

Ilona ran alongside Varco toward the fallen buck. Her feet nearly flew above the ruddy terrain, and her vision cut sharply through the shroud of darkness. Only yards away from her kill, Varco yanked her to a sudden stop. Farkas and Kardos had beaten them to it.

Farkas gave Ilona a lecherous grin, a long tongue spilling out over his furry chest. Then he threw back his head and howled. His jaws elongated and his teeth grew. Frozen by inexplicable fascination, Ilona couldn't avert her eyes, but watched as his ears became pointy and a tail burst out of his pants. Farkas turned to the deer and leaped at its carcass, pushing away the wild creature which only a second ago had been Kardos.

With deep, snarling grunts, the wolfmen ripped the deer apart. Blood dripped on Farkas's heavy fur and splattered his shirt. Kardos pulled a long string resembling a sausage link out of the carcass. Farkas pushed him over, digging his claws into his fellow soldier's chest and tried to rip the intestines out of Kardos's mouth.

Intestines. Ilona bent over and vomited onto the chill ground.

"Are you all right?" There was concern under the amusement in Varco's voice as he finally released her wrist. Merciful darkness hid the disgusting view of the fighting Wolves, but it couldn't stop the wet crunching, breaking, ripping sounds.

Ilona covered her ears and ran blindly, hearing the violent, mindless feeding, and tasting the bile in her mouth. Instead of fading, the noise seemed to become louder and louder, and then she collided with another tall, furry body. Amber eyes glared at her. It was Zador, turned into a wolfman.

"Leave us, mortal," he snarled.

In the glow of the moon, Ilona made out two more soldiers, Gyala and Deszo, kneeling over another animal corpse. Their muzzles dripped with blood and gore, and when they looked up, they growled deep within their throats, their snarling lips revealing long canines. Zador shielded them, his hunched shoulders thrusting his distorted face into Ilona's.

"Leave us," he repeated. He sniffed and she knew what he smelled, remembered the scent. *Human blood.*

"Go, before we kill you, too."

Ilona swallowed something vile-tasting. His frank words cut through her trance and, heart pounding, she ran on. She stumbled and tripped over rocks, invisible in the darkness. Her driving thought was to get away from these tainted creatures, as fast and as far away as she could.

A heavy hand fell on her shoulder and shoved her to the ground. She cried out, her thoughts spinning. Why hadn't she pulled her sword earlier? How could she have left her back unguarded? But then, how could she hope to defend herself against a pack of primeval monsters?

"Calm down, Ilona." It was Varco's voice.

She ignored the hand he offered and rolled into a crouch, panting. "Aren't you going to join the feast?" She straightened and wiped dried leaves and soil from her pants. Out of the corners of her eyes, she noticed that he was still in his human shape. Not that it mattered. He probably smelled her blood and waited to pounce.

I hate him. She blinked back angry tears. *I hate this whole rath.*

"I . . ." Varco looked almost embarrassed, and Ilona's anger dissolved. He scratched behind his ear and gave her a lopsided grin. "I'm not hungry."

The obvious lie made Ilona smile. "Of course not." Then she remembered why she had run, and became serious again. "Zador threatened to kill me."

"Oh?" Varco quickly glanced behind him, in the direction of his feeding pack. "He threatened you? Or was it more of a warning?" Varco stepped closer, hooked his finger under her chin and lifted her face. He gazed intently into her eyes. "Never come between a wolf and his kill. That's vital."

Ilona jerked away. "I *wasn't!*"

Varco raised his hands. "All right." Then he stood still, as though listening for something. "He's here."

Varco dashed off, whistling to gather his men.

Ilona stood alone, straining to hear what Varco had. But only the wind gently brushed the branches and, underfoot, mice rustled through the wheat stalks and fallen leaves.

The moon shone down yellow and sickly as Ilona squinted around her. The mist had thickened once more, making the dark shapes around her impossible to identify. Hay stacks? Wolves? A draft rubbed Ilona's neck like a cold hand from a grave. *He's here. The Captain.* Did she have enough courage for this encounter?

A soft moan, carried on the wind, was followed by a prolonged sigh that wormed into Ilona's heart. Her head jerked around. A weaving white circle, about thirty yards in diameter, appeared around the field. Green lights danced and throbbed, throwing a cool emerald glow. The wide ring sucked in the wispy swirls of fog and tightened around the Wolves. Shapes within the gray circle darkened and solidified as they came closer.

Hooves flogged the soft damp earth, sending grass and dirt spinning. Then the band of mist slowed, and the green lights grew brighter and brighter, until Ilona could make out the horses and their riders. The mounts were blacker than night, absorbing the darkness, with a velvet gleam on their sweaty flanks. Cloaked men slouched on top, their hoods drawn too low for Ilona to see their faces.

Where was the Captain?

A whistle cut through the sounds of the horses and their mysterious riders. Varco waved at her from the middle of the field. The other soldiers had reverted to their human shapes, although their faces and clothes still showed dark stains from their grisly feast. Ilona dashed toward them, suddenly glad for their presence. She didn't want to face the Captain alone. What if he recognized her as Corrine's friend, the one he had held at knifepoint in the slums of London—the one he'd dueled, who had nearly defeated him when someone noticed she was a girl?

Varco motioned her to stand behind him, next to Zador. Ilona's hand gripped the hilt of her sword, although she knew she couldn't attack the Captain, if he was to believe that she was fighting for the countess. Though she would have liked to.

The horses halted in front of the Wolves. A man, wrapped in a hooded black cloak, slid from his mount. Ilona peeked around Varco. A middle-aged man with sad, tired eyes and long, curly brown hair stood before them wearing a blue uniform. He held up a bright red hand in greeting—a hand dripping fresh blood. Ilona recoiled.

"My honor, Captain." Varco bowed. Ilona and the other soldiers followed suit.

"Lieutenant Varco." The Captain's voice came thick and warbled. Ilona couldn't be sure what defect prevented him from speaking clearly. He looked fine, though exhausted. She almost felt sorry for him. "The honor is mine." He glanced behind Varco and his gaze met Ilona's. "I heard you have a new member amongst your group."

Varco pulled her to the front. "Yes, sir. Ilona has proved a worthy addition. She's a strong fighter and skilled bowman. Uh, woman." Varco winked at her, but his words drove heat into her face. Varco wasn't usually so forthcoming with his praise.

"Yes, so I've heard." The Captain smiled. He took Ilona's hand in his bloody one and pressed it, cold and sticky. Ilona fought hard against the urge to fling it from her. She held her face averted and didn't meet his eyes in order to keep him from recognizing her. "Enchanted." He lifted her hand to his lips. An icy kiss sent a chill up Ilona's arm, and her stomach rolled in revulsion. No matter how nice he looked, the knowledge of who he was and the coldness in his eyes told her to be on her guard more than ever.

"You brought us more girls?" Varco pointed at the riders. For the first time, Ilona noticed the bundles tied to several horses. Solid shapes of flesh and printed cotton. Girls.

The Captain nodded. "Yes. The Prince sends a gift to the countess. More girls to *protect.*" The Captain laughed.

"Wonderful." Varco ordered his men to lift the girls from the horses.

Ilona hung back. She didn't want anything to do with capturing more girls. The Captain appeared at her side. He took her elbow and steered her away from the horses.

Curious, Ilona gazed at him from under her long bangs. Up close, his human outline wavered and shimmered as though it was only a reflection in a well. And underneath the kind, regular features of his face, Ilona glimpsed something else. Pale skin, charred in places, his hair patchy and thinning, the sad eyes covered by an oily yellow film. *He must be wearing a glamour,* Ilona realized. *But it's as weak as the trolls'.* The Captain wouldn't know that she had tasted the Unhallowed wine, which had changed her somehow, made her see more—even more than she wanted at times.

Ilona averted her eyes, not wanting to be caught staring. She had to pretend that she only saw him as a man—even if he smelled as though he had just crawled out of his grave.

"And how do you like working for Countess Bathory?"

the Captain asked. Through the glamour, Ilona saw a black tongue protruding from his mouth as he tried to form intelligible words.

"I like working with the soldiers," Ilona said. It wasn't even a complete lie. Maybe this conversation wouldn't be so hard after all.

The Captain nodded, then gripped Ilona's elbow again. He peered into her face. "And Corrine? I trust you left her we-e-e-e-ll?" The last word came out as a long sigh, his misshapen tongue getting in the way. His touch, his *words* chilled Ilona to the bone. So he did know who she was. This couldn't be good.

But she wasn't ready to surrender. "Corrine?" she said airily. "I don't know anyone of that name, sir. Perhaps you confuse me with someone else?"

The Captain made a wheezy chuckle. "You can try to deceive me. But the Fey Prince knows you and yours." He coughed and pulled his bloody hand across his dry lips. "That's why I'm here tonight. The Fey Prince gave me a message for you."

"Oh?" Ilona's heart pounded faster. Euan—the Prince—knew she was in this rath. It was a near direct failure of her mission.

The Captain pulled his black cloak tighter around himself. His sad eyes regarded Ilona for a long moment. "He wants you to join his army. He said he has a special position for you, should you assent."

"What?" Ilona knew this was a rude response, not at all within the proper conversational lines. But how dare the Prince assume she would want a place in his army? *He taught me much of my fighting skills,* she thought. *And he values them.* It would have been a compliment from anyone else.

But pretending to be one of the countess's soldiers was bad enough. How could she willingly serve the Fey Prince—the one responsible for abducting and killing several of her friends? It was a preposterous notion—but an outright refusal might cause him to become suspicious.

Still hesitating on her answer, Ilona turned to the Captain. His gaze on her was eager. His features twisted and contorted, and it took Ilona a moment to realize that he was trying to smile.

"The offer extends to Lieutenant Varco as well," he said, the corners of his mouth drooping. "And you don't have to answer right away. There is no hurry. After proper consideration, I am sure you'll find yourself *unable* to decline."

His tone was grave, and surges of power emanated from him in reaching tendrils. They wavered and blurred, as though he struggled to hold on to such power, as though it was fading from him like daylight, like life itself.

Then he turned and walked to his black horses. Ilona stared at his back. Had he meant to threaten her? His very being was vile, his words confounding. But Ilona held powers of her own. Her strength. The enchanted sword in its sheath. And Varco. He wouldn't let the Fey Prince steal her away.

~ Fourteen ~

"ILONA!" VARCO YELLED. "GIVE ME A HAND HERE." He stood over two girls who had curled up next to his feet, with another threatening to slip off his shoulders. Suppressing her trepidation, Ilona hurried to his side.

"Are they hurt?" She bent over one of the girls, rolling her over onto her back. Long copper curls fell away from a pretty young face. Pale blue eyes stared unseeing at the stars.

"They're fine." Varco nudged the other girl with his boot. "They have been enchanted for easier transport. But there are too many for us to carry. We need to wake them up and make them walk."

"Oh." Ilona heaved her girl to a sitting position. The girl drooped like a doll, her arms limp. A string of drool ran down her chin. "I'm so sorry," she whispered into the girl's ear. Her instinct was to protect this helpless bundle, not to haul her to a horrid fate. She glanced up at Varco. Anger seeped into her voice. "It might take a while to wake them. They're completely dazed."

"Why are you glaring at me? I didn't enchant them." He grinned. "Maybe I could scare them out of it."

Ilona gently shook the girl. When there was no response,

she slapped the pale cheeks. The girl blinked once, twice. Ilona slapped her again. "Wake up!" she yelled. She hated to be rough, but if she couldn't wake the girl, one of the other soldiers would. And his treatment was bound to be even less gentle.

The Wolves had formed a half-circle around Ilona and the girl. They watched her efforts with smirks. Each of them carried two girls.

"What? You can't carry two girls, Ilona?" Zador teased.

Farkas mumbled something harsh-sounding.

Ilona pressed her lips together and ostensibly ignored both of them. She didn't need another reminder that she wasn't as strong as a man. Especially these unnatural men.

She shook her girl again. "Wake up!"

Varco slid the girl from his back, then stretched his arms wide and yawned. "Wolves, run on home and present the Prince's offer to Madame Joo. Ilona and I will follow on foot."

Still grumbling, the Wolves began to trot across the trampled field. Accelerating to their Unhallowed speed, they disappeared.

Varco crouched next to Ilona and helped revive the girls. He lifted one by her ankle and dangled her upside down. "Moves the blood to the brain," he explained at Ilona's raised eyebrows. When the girl coughed and moaned, he turned her around and stood her on her feet. One by one, the girls came out of their enchantment enough to walk. Their eyes were still dazed and they didn't speak, but Ilona was glad for it. She couldn't have dealt with crying, struggling girls. The guilt would have been too great.

Varco roped the three girls together and secured the other end of the cord to his waist.

"They still don't look very alert," Ilona pointed out. "They'll trip."

"Aye," Varco agreed with a sigh, glancing behind him at the bespelled girls. "It'll be a long walk home."

The moon illuminated their path as they set out for the castle. Ilona was quiet, upset that the other Wolves had mocked her physical weakness. It was so unfair that men developed stronger muscles and that she would never be as physically powerful as them, no matter how long or often she trained.

The Captain's words returned to her in a flash. *The Prince wants you to join his army. He has a special position for you.* But why would the Fey Prince want her? Perhaps it was a trap.

"Varco, how well do you know the Captain?"

"I've only met him a few times," Varco said, chewing on a long blade of grass. "Each time he dropped off girls for the countess, much like tonight. Why? Did he catch your fancy?"

Ilona scowled at the suggestion. "He said the Fey Prince wants me to join his army. What do you think of that?"

Varco pulled to a sudden stop. The girl directly behind him stumbled into his back and fell with a small yelp.

Varco stared at Ilona. "Really? He said that?"

Ilona wiped her long bangs aside and nodded. "You're surprised."

"No, no." Varco walked on, yanking on the rope. "You are a good fighter. I'm not at all surprised that the Fey Prince wants you."

Ilona couldn't help feeling flattered. "He also said you may join as well," she added. "The offer was for both of us."

Varco's eyes lit up, glowing amber in the moonlight.

"Oh? Now that's interesting!" He clucked his tongue. "I've heard that the Prince is assembling a splendid army, Ilona. I don't know what he plans to do with it, but I'm sure there will be exciting missions, thrilling battles, glorious victories!" A wide grin split Varco's face, revealing his long incisors. "No more fighting simpleton farmers who can barely button their overalls. No more lugging nitwit girls about." Varco spread his arms and gestured around. "We'd live at court and eat like lords. We'll receive new weapons and perhaps even new powers!"

He cuffed her ribs playfully. "Right?"

Ilona shrugged at his quizzical look. She hadn't expected Varco to be this enthusiastic about the Captain's proposal.

"Sounds great," she lied. She stared over the fields, her mind miles away. Under different circumstances, a soldier's life *would* suit her well. The freedom of wearing unrestricting clothes, of sword fighting and archery. And Varco. Fighting side by side with him in a well-equipped troop would be fabulous. *If* it were any other army than the Prince's. Because how could she abandon Jeanette to the countess's blood-thirsty schemes? And Christina, and all those other girls, including the three behind her. The Prince was the cause of all this suffering, so why would she join his army?

She sighed. No, she would do her best to complete her mission, to find the rathstone, free the girls in the castle and then return home to her friends. Even though at home she'd once again be considered strange and boyish, instead of strong and capable.

Ilona's foot hit a soft shape in the darkness. She swore and fought for balance.

"Mrrrrow!" The dark form stirred against her leg, before racing up the path toward the castle.

"Another black cat!" Ilona said. "There are so many of those around here. And always underfoot!"

Varco growled and kicked at a rock. "I hate cats. This one especially. He's the countess's special servant."

Ilona laughed. "Don't be dumb, Varco. How can a cat be a servant?"

Varco opened his mouth, but the girl behind him began to pull on the rope, whimpering.

"Where am I?" she cried. "Why am I roped? Don't you know that I'm the daughter of Lord and Lady Emmerly of Sundale Manor?" Her voice rose in pitch until it stung Ilona's ears. The girl dug in her heels and Varco had to drag her along, rolling his eyes at Ilona.

"You can tell your sorry tale to the countess," he muttered. "I sure don't care."

But the girl's pitiful sobs cut through Ilona's heart like a troll sword. They were on a death march, taking these kidnapped girls to the countess's castle where they'd be drugged and ultimately killed. How could she even for a second contemplate accepting the Fey Prince's offer?

In the castle's courtyard, Varco parted from Ilona, intent on taking the girls to the countess. Varco motioned toward the far end of the yard.

"Dawn is near. You might as well take your rest now." He pulled on the rope, and the quietly sobbing girls followed him to the entrance. Ilona watched Anci open the door. After he entered with the girls, Anci closed the door firmly, but not before giving Ilona a small smile.

Ilona turned to her shed with a sigh. Maybe Anci and the other kitchen maids had forgiven her after all. She might need their help again soon. Perhaps they'd cover for her if she'd find a way to sneak into the castle to search for the rathstone. For it was ridiculous to wait for the little woodsman of her dream to come to her aid. And the faster she found the rathstone, the faster she could return home—before she did something incredibly stupid like joining the enemy's army.

And if I stay here too long, the Captain might come back for me. He knows who I am. I should try to get into the castle right now. The idea sent a shiver of excitement down her spine. Why didn't she think of it earlier? The entrance by the kitchen garden!

Ilona hurried across the cobbled yard. Varco had forgotten to take her sword. She pulled it out of its sheath and admired the cool, blue gleam in the twilight. *I could sneak upstairs and kill the countess in her sleep,* she mused. *Slit her throat and drain her of her precious blood. Prevent her from ever harming an innocent maiden again. And then search her chambers at my leisure.*

But even as she thought this, Ilona knew that she wouldn't attempt it. It was too risky. If she were caught, it would be all over. And even if she weren't caught, Ilona doubted that she could kill a sleeping woman. Even one whose death would save a hundred or more innocents.

Ilona opened the door to the stable—her bedchamber—and, still swinging her sword about, entered the stuffy room. Something on the floor made her trip and she nearly impaled herself when she crashed to the ground. The cat hissed and jumped onto Ilona's bed of straw. It regarded her with cool green eyes and began licking its dainty paws.

Wincing, Ilona got up. She kicked her sword aside and lunged at the cat.

"I've had enough of you!" she yelled. "What's the matter

with you? Why do you keep bothering me?" She grabbed the screeching animal by the scruff of its neck and shook it violently, fury replacing rationality. "Answer me! What do you want from me?" With a moan, she dropped the cat and sank on her bed. Now she was talking to cats! Clearly, the situation was getting to her.

The cat had landed on its feet. Now it stretched and yawned. "Thank you for releasing my binding," it said in a pleasant male voice. "It is good to speak again."

Ilona stared at the cat. Quite possibly she was going mad. It was no wonder, considering. "Did you just say something?"

"I did." The cat looking up at Ilona.

Her thoughts revolved until she hit on the one that felt right. "You're enchanted."

The cat puffed up its glossy coat, making it look like a fluffy kitten. "How very astute of you. Yes, Countess Bathory put a spell on me. By bidding me to speak, you broke the enchantment."

Ilona reached down and lifted the cat onto her bed.

"Pour little guy," she said and ruffled the tuft of fur on his head. Any enemy of the countess could only be an ally to her.

"Do you mind?" The cat slunk back. "This is not the way to pay respects to an elder Fey." When Ilona simply stared at him, he added. "My name is Vencel Miklos Istvan Laszlofi the third. You may call me Vencel."

"I apologize. Let's start over." Ilona shook his delicate paw. "A pleasure to meet you, Vencel. I'm Ilona Takar."

"Miss Takar," Vencel said. "I've been watching you since you arrived in our rath. I attempted to alert you to the dangers of this rath by sending the serpent to the graveyard.

But you didn't heed my warning. I've tried to discern your purpose here, but I have failed. Enlighten me, please."

Ilona sighed. She couldn't blame the cat. She hadn't advanced her purpose one inch yet. But she couldn't tell him why she was here—how could she be sure that he was trustworthy? Varco had said he was Countess Bathory's particular servant.

"It would take more than a little snake to scare me off," she said. "And who exactly are *you*, Vencel?"

Vencel yawned, a great toothy cat yawn. "I see. You do not trust me. It is wise to be careful in this rath. Mortals are in grave peril here, even more so than we Hallowed."

"You are one of the Hallowed?" Ilona couldn't hide her puzzlement. He didn't look like she had imagined the Hallowed. Not in the least. "Isn't this an Unhallowed rath?" she asked. "What are you doing here?"

Vencel mewed and settled down on his hind legs.

"Once, a long time ago, all Fey in this rath were Hallowed. But as the dark Prince's influence grew, many Hallowed turned and joined him. For a while, Hallowed and Unhallowed held a balance of power. Then the Prince found a willing ally in Countess Bathory, bestowing upon her special gifts of power, which made the people believe her to be a shaman and trust her with their daughters, until they discovered that they hadn't sent their daughters to a better life but to die for the countess's love of beauty."

Ilona glowered at the countess's deceit. "And now she steals the girls from the villagers outright, a shaman in name only."

Vencel's furry head bopped up and down. "Her power has increased tenfold since she aligned herself with the Prince. One by one, she enchanted or turned the Hallowed

Fey in this rath, until you could count us on the fingers of one hand. I used to be a wood sprite, protecting my forest and moving through nature as I pleased. Countess Bathory entrapped me in this useless body and bound my voice. Her spells force me to obey her demands and to protect her and her soldiers."

Vencel's green eyes sparkled at Ilona, as though asking for her sympathy. "Our powers are weak now. But it wasn't always so. And it won't always remain thus."

Ilona chewed on her thumbnail. "Did you say *wood sprite?* I dreamed of a strange little man living in a hollow tree—was that you?"

The cat's grin widened. "Yes. I sent the spirit maidens to guide you to my home. At least in dreams I still hold my true shape."

"In my dream, you offered your help. Do you know where Countess Bathory keeps the rathstone? You know, that special stone of power, one of the keys to opening Hallowmere?"

Vencel sat unmoving, staring at the door. Only his tail swished slowly back and forth. "Moonshine's cold glare, her power is everywhere," he said mysteriously.

"I beg your pardon?" Ilona felt a renewed urge to shake the cat. Why was he talking in riddles now? "I asked you a simple question," she said, her voice rising. "Can't you give me a simple answer?"

At a loud knock, the cat jumped off her bed and slunk into the shadows.

"Ilona!" Varco called through the door. "You forgot to hand in your sword."

"Right," she yelled back. "Just a moment." She knelt on the dusty ground and peered through the dim light at

Vencel, who was only a bundle of darkness. "Quick, tell me," she whispered. "Where's that stone?"

"Mrrow." Vencel's green eyes were wide and luminous, and his head bobbed as he motioned toward the door with his chin.

"Are you scared of Varco?" Ilona tried to pick Vencel up. With a hiss and a swipe of his sharp claws, he escaped her reach and dashed away.

"Ilona." Varco banged on the door again. "What's taking you so long?"

"Coming." She slid the bolt aside and opened the door a crack. Varco stood in the first rays of morning sun. His eyes glowed hazel in the warm light. Vencel pushed through Ilona's legs and sprinted across the yard.

"Stupid cat." Varco sniffed after the receding black shape. "Why did you let it into your chamber?"

Ilona hid behind her bangs. "I didn't. It snuck in." She untied her belt and handed Varco her sword. "Here. Good night."

"Wait." Varco's hand shot out and gripped her wrist. When she glared up at him, he slowly released her. "I . . . I wanted to apologize."

Ilona folded her arms across her chest. The rising sun was now behind him, and she couldn't make out the look in his eyes. "What for?"

His boot scuffed the ground as he fumbled for words. "You know. Out in the fields."

"What, when you scared me silly? Or when you all turned into bloodthirsty, savage creatures?" *How can he have the audacity to ask my forgiveness?*

"Yes, that." Varco gave her a long, appraising look. Ilona met his eyes.

Varco sighed. "I know what you're thinking. You think I'm cursed. You think I'm wicked. You think I was wrong to accept the Prince's gift."

"I do." Ilona tapped her foot. The Fey Prince's special *gift* was something they'd never agree about. Unhallowed was Unhallowed, no matter what.

"I want to show you something," Varco said. He turned and motioned her to follow.

Ilona hesitated, still defiant.

Not checking to see if she came along, Varco strolled across the yard. Curiosity won out, and Ilona ran after him. They left the castle grounds through the wooden gate and walked down the slope toward the village. Birds zipped from tree to tree, trilling at the early sunshine. Dew drenched Ilona's boots, and she pulled her jacket tighter. The morning was bright but cold.

"You're always shivering," Varco observed. "And it's only autumn, not winter."

A smirk tugged on Ilona's lips. "I'm sure it's beautiful here in the summer." *Not that I'll stay long enough to find out,* she added in her thoughts. *I hope.*

Varco smiled. "It is. And I don't mind autumn. But then, I'm never cold." He tugged at her elbow. When she jerked away, he said, "If you give me your hand, I can show you what I mean."

Narrowing her eyes at him in warning, she held out her hand. He pressed it with his own. Immediately heat ran from his hand into hers and coursed through her veins up her arms and into her legs.

"Are you still cold?" he asked.

Ilona shook her head.

Varco regarded her with a dark intensity. "I want you

to see the world through my eyes." His hand gripped hers tighter.

A sudden surge of Unhallowed power made Ilona stumble against him. Her vision changed so abruptly that her stomach heaved and she couldn't stop blinking. Her sense of smell intensified and Varco's musky aroma added to her nausea. Searing heat ripped through her limbs and sent waves of fire into her face. She tried to pull away from Varco, but his hands were like silver shackles, clasped and burning around her wrists.

"I can't I can't I can't." Ilona's words slurred together as though her mouth had forgotten how to form proper sounds.

"Give in to it," Varco urged. "Then it'll get easier."

The pretty fall scenery spun, the birds screamed, and a scent like caramelized bones filled her nostrils. "No no no n-n-n-n—" Speech became harder, so she clenched her mouth shut and mentally fought the onslaught of powerful sensations. They penetrated anyway.

"Stop struggling. Open your mind and heart. You might not get another chance." Varco's voice was a murmur in her mind, ringing and echoing. "Deep breath," he whispered. "Let it come."

The moment Ilona stopped resisting the hot flow of power, a weight lifted from her chest, and air swooped into her lungs. Sweet morning air, carrying a heady mix of smells. Wildflowers, the brackish waters of a small pond downhill. Varco's old boots. And rabbit, tasty, delectable rabbit, zigzagging through the meadow.

Ilona stood still to listen to new, amplified sounds. The twittering sparrows, loud and annoying, the wind in the trees, a squirrel in the nearby forest, gnawing on an acorn.

Yes, she could hear the entire valley. Where was that rabbit? Her eyes scanned the horizon. Colors had faded to browns and grays, but she could magnify her vision to focus on a mouse ducking under a tuft of grass.

"Let's run, Ilona." Varco's deep voice was a mellow growl by her ear.

Hand in hand, they dashed down the slope and back up on the other side of the valley. The sun gleamed off the meadows. Poppies stood stark against the pools of glistening light. Ilona leaped over them, the warm air tousling her hair. Then they entered the forest, full of delicious smells and enticing movements. Branches flew by on both sides and Ilona delighted in her speed, her strength.

She wanted to pause to listen to the woodpecker or follow the trail of a badger into the underbrush. But Varco ran on, pulling her through the trees and back out onto the crest, where he stopped.

Below them lay the valley, golden and sweet. Varco let go of her wrist and spread his arms. "Look!" He spun around, his whoop turning into a pleased howl.

Ilona took a deep breath of the fragrant air, whooshing over the peaceful valley. A hawk circled overhead, eyeing a timid mouse. She could roam here forever. All the rabbits of the soft gleaming fields were hers for the taking.

Varco stepped close behind her. "How do you like my world now?"

Ilona smiled, intoxicated. "It's beautiful."

~ Fifteen ~

In her dream, Ilona was fighting a grizzly bear deep in the darkness of the forest. He was old but tough, with mean little eyes. She stabbed him repeatedly with a dagger. Thick, crimson blood oozed from his wounds. His ragged, putrid breath blew hot against her face. The bear swiped his paw at her again and again with a fierce growl.

"Ow." Ilona rubbed her arm. "Die already!" Her eyes blinked open, then squinted at the radiant day. She rolled onto her stomach and covered her face with a groan. Dry grass and rocks poked through her shirt, and something scraped her arm.

"Wake up, Ilona." The voice purred softly into her ear. Ilona pushed a small paw away and sat up, sleep slipping off her like a blanket.

"It's you." She scowled at the black cat sitting daintily before her. "You scratched me."

"I wanted to wake you." Vencel licked his paw, his features calm and unconcerned. "What are you doing out here? I had a hard time finding you."

Ilona shielded her face. The sunshine's glare was too bright. It hurt her eyes and numbed her senses. What *was* she doing, sleeping in the meadow? Where was Varco? She hugged her knees to her chest and tried to remember.

Heat flushed her face when the memories came. He had transferred his Unhallowed powers—his *gift*—to her. Together they had roamed the hills and forests, hunted rabbits and rolled in the long grasses. Ilona groaned and buried her face in her knees, hiding from the cat's stern expression.

What have I done? How could I lose control so completely?

Vencel nudged her with his furry head. "I came to take you to meet my friends."

"What?" Ilona pushed him away. She had no patience for his nonsense now. She had to figure out how to deal with Varco. He needed to understand that she would not join the Fey Prince's army, under no circumstances, never. Ever.

No matter how much fun it had been, racing over the hillside, taking hedges at a leap, the strength of her muscles as she dug out that rabbit . . . She shook her head to clear the image away. Guilt and embarrassment drove heat into her face. *Was that really me?*

"Ilona." Vencel pawed her again. "You are not listening to me at all, are you?"

"Did you say something?" Ilona sighed.

The cat looked at her out of deep green eyes. "Yes. You asked me about the rathstone. I think my friends will be able to help you with that. They are expecting you now. Follow me." He got to his four feet and parted the high grass with his purposeful stride.

"Wait. Who are your friends?" Ilona jumped up and ran after him. The movement caused dizziness and a sudden tightness in her throat. The colors of the trees and blossoms stung her eyes and blurred her vision. Her head pounded out a frantic beat.

"Slow down," she mumbled. "I don't feel so great."

Vencel turned his emerald eyes on her. "What's the matter with you? Did they put a spell on you, too?" He sniffed her trousers with trembling whiskers. "You don't smell enchanted."

"I'm not." But Ilona wasn't sure if that was completely true. Ever since she had taken that one sip of wine, she had felt a little different, more susceptible to Unhallowed powers. "Where are we going?"

"Down to the pond. Can you make it?" Vencel swaggered on, his tail a dancing black snake between the bushes.

"Of course." The nausea faded with every deep breath of fragrant fall air. Still, Ilona felt sluggish and slow, as though rocks had been tied to her wrists and ankles. Her nose was plugged as with a cold, and the day seemed much too bright. Part of her just wanted to crawl into a dark cave and sleep it off.

The path Vencel chose was rocky and overgrown. Tiny white blossoms grew on spindly stems. Ilona pushed them aside, impatient to get this meeting over with. She seriously hoped that Vencel's friends wouldn't all be cats.

They walked in silence. Vencel would dash ahead and chase a butterfly, then return to the winding path with a satisfied smirk on his furry face, regardless that the insect usually got away.

The afternoon was so warm that Ilona unbuttoned her jacket and slung it over her shoulder. She yawned. "How much farther?"

Vencel answered without turning. "Just behind that grove of poplars. Not far."

Tall trees surrounded the pond, casting shadows with their long, waving branches. Reeds and lily pads floated on the green water, which sparkled in the sun. Two white swans glided majestically along.

Ilona glanced around the overgrown banks. There was no one in sight. She sat on the pebbled beach and stretched out her legs. She had become used to sleeping during the day and now exhaustion sent shivers over her skin.

Vencel sat facing the gently lapping waves. He lifted a paw and meowed.

"Looks like your friends are late," Ilona said. She peeled off her right boot and examined a broken blister on her heel.

Vencel made a hiccupping sound she guessed was his way of chuckling. "They live here."

Ilona looked up from her foot, craning her neck. "Don't tell me you mean those swans." Vencel gave her an unfathomable look. "Just wait and see."

The swans swam through the reeds and up to the beach. As soon as their feet touched the ground, they began to transform. Their necks shortened and their legs elongated, becoming human calves and ankles under long, white robes. Snowy wings flapped until arms appeared, and the swans' heads changed into human heads with female faces. Water droplets sparkled in the sun, casting tiny rainbows, which shimmered around their silvery white hair and tall frames.

Ilona jumped up with a quick inhale. She stepped forward, sharp little rocks imbedding themselves in her calloused naked foot.

Two older women smiled at her. Their faces were wrinkled and haggard, their long hair thin and wispy. Their gleaming white robes fluttered gently in the breeze. Vencel sat between them with a raised paw.

"Ilona, meet Edina and Prioska. They are the last of the

Hallowed in this rath and protectors of the region."

Edina leaned forward and took Ilona's hand. "You have come from afar. Vencel told us that Countess Bathory has forced you into her service." Her voice was deep and gentle.

Prioska ran a wrinkled hand through her silver hair. "He also said that you are looking for the rathstone. Why?"

Ilona was speechless. Finally she had help, allies she could trust! The relief not to be alone any longer with the burden of her dangerous mission was immeasurable. "Well, it's a long story."

Where to begin? Collecting her thoughts, she sank back down on a patch of grass between the rocks. Deciding to give them a full account, she started with the time Corrine came to Falston, and the strange events that had happened before the school went up in flames. Then she explained about the mysterious old letters from the monk, Angus O'Neil. Long after her throat had turned parched, she ended with how the Council had fixed on finding the rathstones to save Hallowmere from being destroyed by the Fey Prince and his allies of vampiric Fey.

The Hallowed spirits had listened in silence. Their gazes attentive, they held their hands folded in a saintly way over their flat stomachs.

"Do you believe me?" Ilona asked when she ended her tale. "I didn't make all that up, you know."

Prioska sighed. "We believe you, Ilona. We have seen much evidence in this very rath to sustain your story. The Prince's supporters have grown in number, and the remaining Hallowed have become weak. We cannot defend ourselves alone."

Edina laid a hand as light as parchment on Ilona's arm.

"This is why we have been sending the spirit maidens to lead you to us. We are grateful that you came to help us."

Ilona let her long bangs fall into her face to hide her embarrassment. "No trouble," she muttered in a rough voice. Then she took a deep breath and swallowed her pride. "But I don't really know how to help you, to be truthful. I don't even know what exactly the rathstone looks like." Edina and Prioska exchanged a glance.

"We can help you with that," Edina said in her deep, ringing voice. "The rathstone you're searching for is the large sapphire in the countess's wedding necklace. She has not taken it off since her husband died."

"In her necklace?" Ilona smacked her forehead. "Then I've seen it! But why would she parade it around like that, for all to see?"

"Don't question the Hallowed's answers." Vencel jumped on her lap and glared into her face. "These are powerful ancient spirits. Their benevolence is infinite, and their wisdom beyond human understanding. You are lucky to have their advice."

"It's all right, Vencel," Edina cut in. "The answer is simple. Countess Bathory doesn't know that she is holding the rathstone in her possession. She believes her powers come from drinking mortal blood, and from the gifts of her master, the Fey Prince. The Unhallowed cannot detect the rathstones. This is a great advantage to us."

"Countess Bathory feels secure in her power," Prioska added. "She fears no challenge. It will take all your courage to take the pendant from her."

"Oh, I'm not afraid of her!" Ilona grimaced. "I only have to figure out how to get close to her—I'm not allowed into the castle at the moment." With a few words, she told the Hallowed how she had led the kitchen maids in their revolt.

A grin widened Vencel's cat face. "Well done."

Ilona smiled and scratched the little tuft on his head. "That's why I came, to battle the Unhallowed. And I'm not done yet."

Prioska's face became very serious. "It's not going to be easy. Attempting to take the rathstone will put you in mortal danger. If the countess ever suspects your deceit, she will kill you."

Ilona remembered the gruesome screams of the countess's victims. She didn't need the Hallowed's warning to be aware of the risk. She wiped a strand of hair from her face and shrugged.

"I've been in mortal danger ever since I came to this rath. I hunt with vicious wolfmen at night and sleep next door to the local *táltos*. Do you really think I'm scared?" Jutting her chin forward, Ilona dared the Hallowed to call her a coward.

Edina laughed. Her lined hand reached out and touched the unruly lock on Ilona's forehead. "You are a valiant girl-knight. If anyone can take on the countess, it's you."

Ilona smiled, trying hard not to let the flattery go to her head.

Vencel stood. His tail swished from side to side as he grinned at the two maidens. "I told you! Ilona is our girl. She will defeat the countess and restore our power!" He pulled himself up onto his hind feet and danced, his paws waving in the air. "And I shall be a cat no more!"

Ilona got to her feet with a sigh. "We are all looking forward to that, believe me!" She smiled at the Hallowed.

"But first I'll have to find a way to be allowed back into the castle."

"Yes," Prioska said. "Unfortunately, we cannot help you with that. Keep your eyes and ears open—perhaps an opportunity will present itself. And," she added, her face grave, "do not trust anyone besides Vencel. Our intentions must be kept secret. Beware of too much beauty."

"Of course. I shall not speak of it to anybody," Ilona promised. She thought she knew what they meant—how beautiful the castle had looked to her at first, but inside it held insidious evil.

Edina and Prioska waded into the murky water of the pond and turned back into swans. Vencel and Ilona waved good-bye and then made their way toward the looming dark towers of the countess's castle.

When they returned to the castle, the sun dipped low on the horizon and a cool wind nipped at their necks. Ilona thought she had never been this tired in her life. The last few hundred yards she had been ready to fall asleep standing up. Vencel kept nudging her on as her eyelids drooped.

The front gate was locked, and Ilona didn't want to attract attention to the fact that she had been away from the castle grounds all day. Vencel led her around the wall to a spot low and chipped with the wear of weather. Ilona easily climbed up and sat atop the wall, surveying the yard. Usually at this time of day, the Wolves still snored on their beds of straw. But Ilona spotted Farkas, Kardos, and Dezso huddled together behind the shed housing the Wolves.

Vencel leaped onto the wall and sat next to her. "What are you waiting for?" he hissed. "Jump down!"

Ilona slipped to the ground and motioned Vencel to be quiet. Farkas didn't turn around—he must not have heard her. *But what are they doing up so early?*

Ilona couldn't suppress her curiosity. She snuck closer, using water barrels and outhouses as cover. Vencel tried to deter her with a low meow and a stern cat frown. When he didn't succeed, he slunk toward the kitchen.

Ilona leaned back against the wall of the shed. Farkas and the other Wolves were standing just around the corner. They spoke in quiet, urgent whispers. Ilona held her breath and closed her eyes, trying to catch at least some of the words.

"Can't stand it . . . night after night . . . getting worse." That was Kardos's voice. Ilona didn't like Kardos. His long, dark beard made him look sinister, and he had never once addressed her directly. Dezso was friendlier, but he was so much smaller than the rest of them, he always seemed to beg for everyone's approval.

"I don't know. She *is* a good fighter," Dezso's shrill voice squeaked. The other two immediately shushed him. A silence followed. Ilona guessed they were waiting to hear if Dezso had woken anyone. The yard remained quiet, bird trilling the only sound.

"Never mind that now. When I'm in charge . . ." The rest of the sentence was lost in a low growl. Farkas always sounded like an irate bear. Ilona could just imagine him, his dark red scar glowing on his angry face. So he wanted to be in charge? The idea occupied Ilona's mind, and she missed the next part in the grumbled conversation.

On the opposite side of the shed, something clanked and then a door banged open. The group around the corner fell silent, and Ilona pressed her back even more against the splintering wood. If Farkas found her eavesdropping, she'd be dead.

Footsteps came closer. Ilona held her breath. Another conspirator? He'd have to pass her to get to the three behind the shed. Her muscles tensed and she wished Varco hadn't taken away her sword that morning.

Abruptly, the footsteps shuffled toward a new direction. A figure appeared in her line of vision: Varco crossed the yard, walking toward one of the large barrels holding rainwater. He ripped off his shirt and threw it on the cobbles. His hands gripped the sides of the barrel as he dipped his entire head into the water.

Run. Now. Ilona dashed along the path toward the vegetable garden, navigating tightly around the corners of the squat buildings. Her heart hammered in her chest. Varco hadn't seen her—not with his head under water—but she couldn't be certain he hadn't heard and identified her footsteps. His senses were more acute than hers. As for Farkas, no, she didn't even want to contemplate the possibility.

In the garden, she crouched among the winter squash, regaining her breath. The soil radiated a chill underneath Ilona's limbs. The sun was only half visible now, casting purple shadows over the vegetable patch.

What should she do about Farkas and his plans? Tell Varco? Indecision and exhaustion made her dizzy. He had forced his powers on her, then left her sleeping in the meadow, defenseless. She didn't have any reason to show loyalty to him. But Farkas would never accept a girl among his Wolves. If he replaced Varco as their leader, he would certainly find a way to rid himself of her.

Physical and mental fatigue swirled Ilona's thoughts

around and around. *I need sleep. And time to think.* But neither would be available tonight.

A shimmering green light danced out of the kitchen door and flew in tightening loops toward her. Instinctively, Ilona reached out for the tiny fairy.

"Vanillina."

The pixie spread out her wings and sailed down into her palm. She smoothed her hands over her skirt of leaves.

Ilona held the little creature close and peered into the delicate face. "Do you have a message for me?"

Vanillina sat, dangling her legs off the side of Ilona's hand. "No."

Ilona waited and watched the fairy twist her pewter hair into a ponytail.

Finally, Vanillina spoke again. "Anci is in the kitchen crying. I thought you might want to know." She leaped to her feet and flapped her wings. "I have to go now."

"Wait." Ilona grasped the fairy's skirts between the tips of two fingers. "Why is she crying?"

Vanillina pulled free with an indignant *humph* and zipped into the air above Ilona's head. "Why don't you go ask her?" And with a fading buzz, the fairy disappeared.

~ Sixteen ~

$\mathcal{I}$LONA SOUNDLESSLY PUSHED THE KITCHEN DOOR OPEN AND slid inside. A single torch cast gloomy, flickering shadows on the walls. The smell of old cabbage hung heavy in the air. Anci sat alone at the rickety table with her back to Ilona. Her shoulders shook and she emitted strangled sobs like a mewling kitten.

Ilona's heart contracted painfully. Anci had been the closest friend she had made in this rath. It hurt to see her so upset. But maybe this was Ilona's chance to show the maids that they could still trust her—that she was one of them, no matter what.

She crossed the kitchen and laid a hand on Anci's arm.

Anci flinched. When she saw Ilona, she crumpled into a heap, tears streaming down her pale face.

"It's you. I thought . . ." She lifted her apron and blew her nose into the graying fabric.

Ilona slid into the only other chair, across the table from Anci. The fire in the hearth had gone out, and a cold draft blew in under the door. She gave Anci a tender smile.

"It's all right. Cry all you like. God knows you have reason to."

Anci shook her head, then wiped her eyes with the back

of her knuckles. "I'm not crying for myself, if that's what you're thinking."

Ilona wasn't sure what to think. She didn't cry much—there didn't seem a point to it, and it conveyed weakness. Her father's nose had twitched in disgust whenever she cried as a small girl, and Ilona had learned fast to keep upsetting emotions under a tight rein.

"What is it, then?"

Again, Anci shook her head, but her tears started to flow anew. "There is no end to their cruelty, Ilona," she whispered. "And now they're planning a new scheme, to trap even more girls."

The door banged open and Gizi and Evike entered, followed by Dorika. They glanced from Anci to Ilona with knitted brows. Evike hurried to Anci's side and protectively slung an arm around her shoulder. She glared at Ilona.

"Do you have to come here and make poor Anci cry? What has she ever done to you?"

Ilona jumped out of her chair. "I didn't make her cry! Tell them, Anci."

"It's true, Evike," Anci said. "I'm worried what will happen when the countess opens her school."

Dorika chewed on the end of her thick braid. Gizi nervously pulled on her harelip. Evike sighed. "Nothing will change for us."

Anci wiggled aside on her chair, making room for Evike to sit next to her. Ilona still reeled from the sting of the girls' hostility. They had each other; they didn't need nor want her help. For a heartbeat, Ilona was tempted to run back out into the yard, leaving the maids to their own problems. But Anci had vital information that Ilona had a feeling would be the turning point for her in reaching the rathstone, now that she knew where it was.

"What school? What are you talking about?"

The girls shuffled on their feet, glancing at each other.

I may never regain their trust, Ilona thought. The realization stabbed at her heart.

Finally, Anci spoke. "Countess Bathory's soldiers are returning with fewer girls from their raids than ever, and we hoped that her powers would weaken when she had no maidens left in the east wing."

It's not the blood that gives her power—it's the rathstone. But Ilona kept her thoughts to herself, as she had promised the Hallowed.

"But now she has found a new source," Anci continued with a deep sigh. "She is opening a finishing school for young ladies. It will bring so much more heartache and sorrow for us all."

Ilona tapped her chin. "I cannot imagine. Who would send their daughter to this horrible place?" *And who would send their daughter into a Fey rath?* "It's not going to work."

"Don't be so sure," Dorika said. "She already has a list of applicants and invited the parents to bring their daughters to start the term at Michaelmas. She'll host a fancy evening dinner for them."

"Michaelmas is only two days away," Anci added, throwing her braid back over her shoulder.

Ilona shrugged. Some plan. Surely the parents would see what sinister women ruled this place the moment they clapped eyes on Madame Joo and the countess, despite the castle's fine furnishings. *Only it will be too late.* A vivid image flashed through her mind; of doors slamming shut, torches dimming, and troll guards charging. No, there would be no school. As soon as the countess had lured her victims to her lair, there'd be no further need to pretend.

Heavy footsteps outside in the corridor made the girls scatter. Gizi hastily crouched by the fireplace, sweeping out cold ashes with shaking hands. Dorika grabbed the rusty buckets, while Evike pushed dirty dishes into the sink.

Anci gave Ilona a quick hug. "Perhaps I'll see you at the Michaelmas dinner? The countess ordered a special security troop to be placed inside the castle. She'll appoint one of the lieutenants as their commander."

Ilona squared her shoulders, an idea forming in her mind. What if she could be part of the security troop? This might be a good chance to get close to the countess, to take the rathstone from her.

"Can you do me a favor, Anci?" she asked. "Could you leave the door to the kitchen garden open for me tonight? And don't tell the cook. I have to speak to Madame Joo."

Anci shuddered. "You do? But why don't you go to see her now?"

"Because I have to get something first."

Ilona hurried up the winding staircase of the tower. Narrow vertical openings in the stone walls showed glimpses of the yard below. She didn't have much time before Varco would miss her at sword practice. In front of the heavy wooden door, she arranged her thoughts, while trying to control her rising excitement. She had the perfect plan. If Madame Joo made her commander of the security guards at Michaelmas, she would be able to get close enough to the countess to steal the pendant with the rathstone. And at the same time, she could find a way to release *all* the girls in the castle—prisoners, maids, and new arrivals. All she had to do was to win Madame Joo's trust.

When Ilona raised her hand to knock, a scream burst out from behind the door, followed by sobs and a familiar cackling laughter.

"Be quiet," Madame Joo said. "Or I'll give you something to cry about."

Ilona quickly banged on the door, before the screams could start up again.

"Yes?" Madame Joo stuck her head out. She glared at Ilona, making her face appear even more wrinkled than before. "It's *you*. I thought you weren't allowed into the castle. What do you want?"

"I—I have something for you. A present."

Madame Joo raised her eyebrows, speechless for a moment. She tapped her foot and eyed Ilona up and down.

"Do you, now? Well, well. Step into my . . . *parlor*, then." She laughed, the hairy mole on her pit bull's neck dancing up and down.

The torture chamber lay in moody darkness. The only light came from the skull candles and the fire in the grate. Next to the hearth stood a small, hairy troll.

A girl in a nightgown crouched on the wooden floor. Bruises marred her white arms and cheeks. Ilona winced and fought the impulse to attack Madame Joo. She didn't have her sword, and besides, she needed Countess Bathory's right hand to believe that Ilona was on *their* side.

"As you see, I'm very busy," Madame Joo said with a sneer at the crying girl. "What have you brought me?"

Glancing from the troll to the girl, Ilona hesitated. "Would it be possible to show you in private, Madame?"

Madame Joo narrowed her eyes and gave Ilona a penetrating look. "All right. But your present better be worth my while or I shall try out my devices on *you*." She prodded the maiden with the tip of her boot. "Take her away," she instructed the troll, who immediately slung the girl over his shoulder and tromped out of the torture chamber.

When the door swung shut behind them, Ilona pulled a small parcel out of her jacket pocket and handed it to Madame Joo. The old woman pulled off the rough paper and examined the device Ilona had hastily constructed, consisting of six wooden sticks connected by strings.

Madame Joo gave Ilona a puzzled look. "What is it supposed to be?"

"It's called a *tean zu*," Ilona said. "It comes from a strange land in the far east. The police there use this to make prisoners testify." When Madame Joo still looked dubious, she quickly continued, "See, you put a girl's fingers between the sticks." Ilona demonstrated on her own hand. "Then slowly pull these strings until the finger bones are crushed." Ilona pulled the device off her hand and gave it to Madame Joo, who turned it around with sparkling eyes.

"Fascinating. I've never seen one of these before."

"They are . . . um, new." Ilona shrugged, heat rushing to her face. She had learned about the Chinese *tean zu* in one of the penny dreadfuls she'd read in London. "They are easy to build—I made this one myself."

New appreciation flickered in Madame Joo's eyes. "Are you a fellow scholar of pain, then? I had no idea!"

Ilona grinned and winked. The idea of being anything like Madame Joo was repulsive, but she had to play this role well to gain the woman's confidence.

"I am very interested in all forms of torture," Ilona said. "Your chambers are exceptionally intriguing to me."

"They are?" Madame Joo's bulldog face lit up. "Then let me show you around!" She strode to the workbench pushed against the far wall and picked up a small device. She held it high for Ilona to see.

"These are my thumbscrews. They elicit nice wails." She dropped the tool of torture and took up another. "I heat these pincers in the fire . . . guess what part of the body is the most sensitive to burns?"

Ilona aimed for a nonchalant look. "The . . . elbow?"

Madame Joo snorted. "Don't be silly. Try again." When Ilona didn't respond, Madame Joo pointed at her chest, her lips turned up in a maniacal grin. "That's right. Young girls' fleshy pink parts."

Ilona turned away, ostensibly to examine another tool on the bench. Madame Joo was cruder than her troop of unwashed soldiers. Her gaze fell on a rod bearing several long rawhide straps with braided ends.

"What's this?" she asked.

Madame Joo lifted it from the workbench and caressed its long pole. "It's the cat o' nine tails. A special kind of whip. One lash is usually enough to bring the most defiant girl to her knees. It's one of my favorite tools."

A loud cawing came from the corner of the room. Ilona spun toward the sound. In a golden cage sat a huge, black crow. It cawed insistently, until Madame Joo approached the cage and fed it a wriggling worm from pinched fingers.

"You're a little greedy guts today." She opened the cage and stuck her hand inside. The bird hopped onto her finger. Madame Joo pulled it out and stroked its black feathers.

"Good boy," she cooed. Her high-pitched tone sounded fake, like a witch trying to lure children into her gingerbread house.

"He's tame." Ilona was surprised. She had never seen a domesticated crow before.

"He's my pet." Madame Joo smiled. "He's also one of my discipline tools. I trained him to peck out eyes on command. He likes to eat them for a snack."

The idea was sickening, and Ilona tried hard not to picture the scene.

Madame Joo put the bird back into its cage, then a devious look passed across her features. "So, soldier Ilona. Has any device in particular caught your eye?"

Ilona wildly glanced around the room. Picking the item Madame Joo would consider superior to all others would further her chances to win the old torturer's esteem. Her gaze fell onto the studded wooden chair in the next room, which she had briefly examined on her last visit—the one the ghost girl had died on.

"That chair," she blurted. "Without doubt, one of your finest instruments."

Madame Joo chuckled and motioned her to follow through the arched doorway.

"My Chair of Pain. It is one of Countess Bathory's favoritesas well." Madame Joo pointed at the iron studs poking out of the wood. "We push a girl into the iron points until she dies of blood loss, sooner or later. Of course, we rather prefer later . . . more fun for us to watch."

Ilona leaned forward. There was a hole in the seat of the chair. "What is that for?" she asked, pointing.

"It's to drain the blood, of course. I usually collect it in a bucket for the countess."

Madame Joo stooped low and pulled a stained pail from underneath the torture chair. Dark red liquid sloshed around inside. The old woman took a golden flask from a nearby table and measured some of the blood into it.

"Now it's ready to be served." She grinned at Ilona. "Surely you didn't expect a countess to drink from a bucket like a dairy maid?" Madame Joo shook the pail with the remaining blood under Ilona's nose. "Would you like a taste?"

Repulsion shivered through Ilona and she fought for composure. "No, thank you," she said with a forced smile. "Another time, perhaps."

Madame Joo laughed. "If you believe the alchemists at the Prince's court, it holds the promise of eternal youth."

Maybe you should have a bucketful then, Ilona thought. But she didn't dare say it out loud. She desperately needed to stay on the old woman's good side.

"It keeps the countess alive and vibrant." Madame Joo swished the blood around in the pail, staring at it with something like awe. "And if the blood of common little farm girls can do that, just imagine what the blood of young noblewomen will do!"

"Oh." Ilona scratched her arm where a droplet of the repugnant liquid had hit her. "So that's why the countess is planning to open a finishing school."

"You're quick to catch on, aren't you? Yes, we'll have twenty beautiful, aristocratic girls at our disposal, every one of them ripe with superior blood."

Ilona decided that now was as good a time as ever to go forward with her plan.

"I heard you need someone capable to command the security guards at the Michaelmas dinner," she began.

Madame Joo stuffed the golden flask into a fold of her dress. She leaned back against the table and crossed her arms. The dark eyebrows arched above her cold eyes.

"And?" she wheezed. "You want to nominate Lieutenant Varco for the job?"

"Uh . . . no." Ilona chewed her lip. "I was thinking that I'd be the right person for the position. I know how important it is for the countess that none of the girls escape from Castle Cachtice."

Madame Joo opened her mouth, and Ilona thought that she would chuckle. But then her lips shut as tightly as a clam, and she shook her head.

"It is indeed of utmost importance. And that is exactly why I cannot give such a vital position to a young girl like you," Madame Joo said. "The great honor of this task will fall only to the very best soldier at the countess's command."

"I've been noticed by the Prince himself, ma'am. He even offered me a position in his army! I'm sure you won't be disappointed if you give me the opportunity."

Madame Joo spat on the ground. "Is that the truth? Even so, I would think that your lieutenant would be better qualified for the position."

Ilona saw herself losing ground. What if she failed again? Where was her backup plan? No, this was her best chance. Possibly her last chance.

Cornered, she spoke in haste. "I'm a better fighter than my lieutenant," she said, chin raised. "I could beat him anytime."

Ilona and Madame Joo glared at each other for one long moment. Then Madame Joo pushed herself off the table. "Fine. You can command the guards at Michaelmas. Under one condition."

Ilona's heart accelerated. She'd done it! The rathstone was as good as hers!

"What condition?"

"Prove your haughty claim. Challenge Lieutenant Varco to a sword fight. If you win the duel, the position is yours."

Ilona sucked in a long breath and nodded. What else could she do?

Madame Joo walked toward the door, motioning Ilona to follow. With a dismissive glance over her shoulder, Madame Joo said, "The duel will take place tomorrow night, after sunset. I'll meet you in the courtyard."

~ Seventeen ~

$\mathcal{I}$LONA WENT INTO THE COURTYARD TO LOOK FOR VARCO. Torches lit the cobblestones and the soldiers' raucous shouts and laughter rang through the night. The lieutenants had most of their men engaged in combat or archery practice, while other soldiers sharpened weapons.

Varco was supervising a sword fight between Zador and old, grizzled Gyala. Their blue blades clanked together again and again, moving at lightning speed. Their talents seemed to be equal, but Ilona suspected Zador would eventually let Gyala win.

She scanned the yard for Farkas and his two confidantes. They sat around a fire lit within a ring of stones, talking quietly among themselves. Were they plotting against Varco again? And should she tell him about it?

Uncertain, she moved closer to Varco's group. As she approached, his head turned toward her, as though he had caught her scent on the breeze. Relief, followed by anger flashed over his face. Then a grin brightened his features.

"Ilona!" He turned from the duel and sprinted to her side. "Where were you? I thought you had gotten lost!"

His skin glowed orange in the firelight, and the memory of their morning running through the fields and forests returned with blinding force. *I would never have abandoned control like that on my own. He let me make a complete fool of myself.*

Anger heated her face, and she punched his arm. "You left me sleeping in a field like some dumb animal!"

His expression turned sheepish. "I didn't want to wake you. We were close enough to the castle for you to find your way home."

Ilona only glared, not giving him the honor of a response.

"Well, I'm glad you're back." He smiled. "If I had lost you, Madame Joo would have had my head." With a casual shrug, Varco turned back to Zador and Gyala.

The mention of the countess's head torturer reminded Ilona of the ridiculous claim she had made. She reached out and grasped his shirt. "There's something I need to tell you." Varco raised his eyebrows. "What?"

What would he say? Would he laugh? Or get angry? "I applied for the position of commander of the security guards at Michaelmas." She took a deep breath. "And Madame Joo said I could have it, if I beat you in a duel tomorrow night."

Varco's laughter was a snickered growl. His hand shot forward and pulled her sword from its sheath, while his foot knocked her leg from under her, making her stumble. He caught her with his left hand and raised her sword with his other hand. The gleaming blade lightly touched her throat.

His expression became grave. "Do you really think you could beat me in a duel?" A feral shadow flashed over his face, and his eyes shimmered amber. A growl purred from deep inside his chest.

Who was she fooling? He was a much better sword fighter than she was. *And in his werewolf shape he could tear me to pieces.* Heart pounding, she shook her head.

Varco pulled her up and slid the sword back into the scabbard at her hip. His hand wiped a strand of messy hair out of her face. He leaned close and whispered, "But I've never liked Madame Joo. I'll help you deceive her."

Stunned by his unexpected words, Ilona let Varco pull her along toward Zador and Gyala.

"Good effort, Zador," he said.

They lowered their swords and wiped the sweat from their foreheads.

Varco picked up several pieces of armor and two shields from a pile on the ground.

"Take a break, boys, and then practice your bows. I'll be busy tonight giving Ilona some one-on-one combat lessons."

Zador winked. "Is that what you call it now?"

Ilona sucked in her cheeks. She was ready to attack him for his idiotic, rude comment, but Varco yanked on her sleeve, and so she only gave Zador the most evil look she could muster.

Varco shook his head at Ilona. "Let it go. We have work to do, if we want to be ready for the duel by tomorrow night."

He led the way on a narrow path along the outer wall of the castle grounds, behind the sheds and stables. He stopped when they were well out of sight of the other soldiers, and set down their equipment. Scratching behind his ear, he asked, "So you want to command the security guards at Michaelmas. Any particular reason why?"

It was too dark to see his expression, but his eyesight

was certainly keen enough to see her blushing. Ilona tensed. He wouldn't help her if he knew.

"Are you planning something?" His voice was a low rumble, barely audible. His hand gripped her arm, hard. "If you are, you'd better tell me."

Ilona pulled free. Her pulse drummed in her ears. "I *can't.*" She had promised the Hallowed.

He stared at her through the darkness. "Fine, then. Stubborn wench!" He turned to light a torch. "It's best if nobody watches us practice. You never know whom you can trust around here—they might tell Madame Joo."

Trust. The image of Farkas and his gang whispering secrets flashed through Ilona's mind. She couldn't tell Varco what she meant to do at the night of the Michaelmas dinner, but she could tell him the truth about Farkas. Ilona spoke quickly, before she could change her mind.

"I overheard Farkas plotting against you. With Kardos and Dezso."

Varco briefly glanced up, then finished fastening the torch to the low wall. Wiping his hands on his trousers, he turned to her.

"Yes, I know."

"You already know?"

"It's no secret that Farkas wants to be leader of the Wolves. When Gyala decided to retire from his position of lieutenant last month, the rest of us fought for the post. I won by defeating every Wolf in battle, but Farkas never accepted me as his leader." Varco kicked at a rock, deep in thought. "If he defeated me directly, he wouldn't have to challenge every wolf in the pack or wait for me to retire."

"But Kardos—and Dezso! I thought they were your friends!"

Varco gave a mix between a growl and a laugh. "Friends! There is no room for friendship in a place like this." He shook his long hair out of his face and smiled. "Don't worry about it, Ilona. I can take care of myself."

He tied on his chest plate and threw her a silver shield. "How shall we start? We need to make the fight look natural."

Ilona fumbled with the leather strings of her armor, chewing on her lower lip. "I guess we'll have to put on a bit of a show."

Varco grinned. "Yes. We should create a set of movements and memorize them. That way, I won't accidentally hurt you." His booted toe drew a line in the sand. "Sword fighting is similar to dancing—you need to be able to move in rhythm."

Ilona grimaced. She had heard this comparison before, from her fencing teacher Euan, who had turned out to be the Fey Prince. But recalling every humiliation of Mrs. Alexander's dancing class at Falston made it difficult for her to link sword fighting to dancing.

Varco lifted his sword and, in a slow, controlled movement, thrust it toward Ilona's shoulder. She parried easily and smirked.

"Why so slow?" She lunged ahead, making him jump out of her way. With two large steps, he slipped behind her, his blade hovering inches from her throat.

"Because if I move any faster, you cannot win."

The amusement in his voice angered Ilona. Her elbow jerked backward into his ribs and she broke free. "You don't have to keep pointing that out."

Varco resumed his position across from her, a contrite look on his face.

"All right. Let's get serious. Why don't we start with some simple exchanges with a bit of fancy footwork thrown in?"

Varco demonstrated what he had in mind, and they worked on refining their routine all night until the stars faded into a brightening sky.

They sat on the low wall to rest and stretch their legs. Ilona's muscles burned from the vigorous exercise.

"How are we going to end?" she asked. "How will I defeat you?"

Varco tossed up his sword. It rotated a couple of times before he skillfully caught it again by its hilt.

What a show-off. But Ilona smiled anyway.

"Easy. A nice, heavy thrust in the shoulder. On my sword arm side." He pointed to his armor. It covered his chest, but his shoulder was unprotected.

Ilona winced.

"First, you trip me," Varco continued. He got up and motioned her to stand across from him. "Like this." His boot shot forward and hooked her foot. "A quick pull and I stumble. Try it."

With a doubtful smile, she copied the movement. There was no way she had the speed or strength to trip Varco in a fight if he didn't want to be tripped. Would this look believable to Madame Joo?

Varco teetered on his heels, arms waving for balance. His mouth formed an overly dramatic *O*, before he fell backward, sprawling over the stony ground. "Now put a foot on my belly and stab me in the shoulder."

"Gladly." Ilona's foot stepped down hard, close to his unprotected groin. Her sword dangled above his shoulder. She mimed the thrust, grinning down at him. "You don't think she'll know that you let me win?"

With a quick, fluid motion, Varco pushed her foot off and jumped to his feet. "I'm a great actor. She won't suspect a thing."

"And the shoulder wound? That's going to hurt."

Varco shrugged. "It won't kill me. And you know we heal very fast. Remember when Gyala got shot with that silver bullet? He was better within days." Varco lifted his shirt and pointed at his ribs. "Do you see this scar? Zador accidentally stabbed me during practice two nights ago. It's already healed."

Curious, Ilona traced a finger over the silver line of the scar. On a mortal, this wound would still be raw and oozing.

Before she knew what he was doing, Varco's arm encircled her waist, while his other hand lifted her chin. His movements were much too fast for her to react. His lips touched hers before she could even think of pulling away.

How dare you? Ilona meant to kick him for his audacity and foolishness. But the heat of his lips melted the fight inside her, softened her objections, liquefied her anger. She leaned closer and opened her mouth to his kiss.

When he finally let go of her, she dashed away to the sanctuary of the horse stables, heart pounding and thoughts scrambled into pulp.

But she couldn't stop smiling.

The shape beside her was as familiar as her own four paws. They ran as one unit. When he sped up, she followed at his heels, and when she broke away and raced up the wooded slope, he always stayed by her side. Together, they sniffed out the rabbit tracks and dug into the soft hillside.

Afterward, they shared the rodent's warm flesh. Its blood ran down her throat hot and sweet.

The moon was their torch, and its silver glow dressed their world in silk armor. The male wolf playfully jumped into her side, and she bared her teeth and snapped at his neck, joining the game. Life was joy. There were no secrets between them, and their desires were the same. They shared the past, and an eternity together lay before them like a wide ribbon unrolling. Time fed their power, and death meant nothing.

A new scent on the gentle wind caught her attention. Her ears pricked and she saw her alarm mirrored in her mate's features. His fur stood on end and his lean muscles tensed. The sharp smell of burning wood irritated her sensitive nostrils. She sneezed and shook her head. Age-old instinct told her to run. But the wolf beside her remained still.

The dark blue night sky lightened with the expansion of the slashing red line on the horizon, which grew until she could make out individual greedy flames devouring the forest. Their forest. The male wolf threw his head back and howled. And still he didn't run.

The air around them became hot; desert winds brought singed leaves and ashes down on them. Ilona began to shake. Her fangs, her muscles, could not fight this enemy. Her powers were small and meek in comparison. Run, run, run, she soundlessly begged the other wolf. His amber eyes were somber. Then he gently nudged her side.

She turned and ran alone, down the hill toward the valley and the cooling river. But the fire had beaten her to it. She spun and dashed through underbrush, past thorny bushes and brambles and came out in a field. A red and bubbling field. The heat surrounded her now on all sides, singeing her fur and burning her eyes. It inched nearer, tightening its suffocating grasp. Her breath became shallow as the smoke-filled air closed in.

There was no way out. She howled in desperation.

Ilona pushed up onto her elbows. Her clothes were drenched in sweat and her heart galloped against her ribs.

She rubbed her damp face. Already the dream was slipping from her. All she could remember was an anxious, claustrophobic feeling, as though she had been locked into a coffin.

It's only nerves about the duel tonight, she told herself. Slowly she rose and peeked out the door. Twilight tinged the sky purple—time to get ready. She quickly washed, using the cold rainwater in one of the barrels, then found Varco in the main building of the soldiers' housing, along with the other Wolves. He already wore his armor.

The sight of him brought back the memory of their kiss, but Ilona pushed her confused emotions into the far corner of her mind. *Concentrate on the fight. Pretend it never happened.*

"Are you ready?" she called to him from the door. The stench of unwashed male bodies made the place as uninviting as an outhouse.

Varco grinned and playfully whacked Zador on the head. "I told the boys to come and watch. Maybe they'll learn something."

Ilona's stomach flopped. There'd be an audience? She wiped her sweaty palms on her legs and took a few long breaths. *It'll be all right. I can do this.*

Varco handed Ilona her sword, shield, and chest protection. While she pulled the armor on, the Wolves passed her. Zador winked at her and Gyala nodded, but Farkas blew a cloud of putrid breath into her face with a menacing grimace.

In the main courtyard, the soldiers from the other divisions had formed a wide circle. Varco pushed his way through, and Ilona followed.

Ilona glanced around the crowd of excited faces, looking for Madame Joo. She wasn't there yet. A cheer went through the audience when Varco appeared, followed by rumbled encouragements.

I'm the underdog—they don't want me to win. Suddenly Ilona wondered what losing the duel would do to Varco's reputation among the soldiers. Would they still respect him after he lost to a girl? Or would it give Farkas additional reason to challenge his authority?

The door to the castle banged open, and Madame Joo stepped out, her wrinkled bulldog face blotchy and puckered like a badly stitched wound. She pulled a thin girl behind her, who wore a nightgown and had a dazed look in her yes.

One of the countess's maidens, Ilona thought. *Poor thing.*

Madame Joo parted the crowd with a single wave of her hand. She glared at Varco, then focused on Ilona.

"As you know, the winner of the duel shall become the commander of the security guard for the Michaelmas dinner. I also brought this maiden as an added prize. If Lieutenant Varco wins, the Wolves shall dine on tasty human flesh tonight."

The Wolves growled appreciatively, and although Ilona couldn't imagine that this slender girl would make a good feast for six burly men, her stomach rolled.

She cleared her throat and raised her voice above the din. "And if I win? Will you release the girl?"

Madame Joo's eyes widened. Perhaps she hadn't expected her to speak up. "I don't imagine that you will, soldier-girl. But if you do, I'll promise you that this girl will safely return to the maidens' chambers." She chuckled, and the men joined in.

"That's hardly fair," Ilona muttered, kicking up dirt with her boot. But it didn't really matter, as she meant to free all the girls in the castle anyway. Soon.

Madame Joo glared at her. "Before we start this *interesting* duel, hand me your shields and armor—both of you," she added with a nod at Varco. "You'll fight *au natural.*"

Ilona sent a look of panic in Varco's direction. Fight without their shields and armor? That's not how they had practiced it.

Varco smiled at her, but there was worry in his eyes.

Ilona dropped her shield and armor at Madame Joo's feet. How she wished she could fight the old woman instead of Varco. She'd gladly deliver a deadly blow to *her.*

"Assume your positions," Madame Joo shouted. "Let the duel begin!"

Ilona took a few deep belly breaths and flexed her arms and legs. Then she pulled her sword. *Focus. You only get one chance.*

The battle began well. Already, the steps they had practiced the night before were old routine to her feet and arms. She ducked, parried and thrust on cue. Varco's elaborate arrangement of movements made it look like they were evenly matched. But Ilona still had to pay close attention—they had to improvise the parts that had called for their shields in practice.

A few minutes into the duel, the crowd began to cheer for Varco.

Concentrating on Varco, she couldn't chance a look in Madame Joo's direction, but she was certain that the old woman was smirking now. A *no one's cheering for you* kind of smirk.

There was only one person here who wanted her to win. Varco.

Her hand on the hilt tightened, and her next blow

against Varco's blade came down much harder than intended. Frowning, he blocked her attack.

A few drops of sweat rolled down Ilona's temple, but there was no time to wipe them away. She was dimly aware of her shirt sticking to her damp body and the dull aching in her sword arm from over-exercise.

"Don't be such a weakling, Varco!" Madame Joo shrieked. "I want to see some blood. Cut her head off!"

Varco gave no sign that he had heard the old woman. They were approaching the end of their choreography. Ilona's foot shot forward, hooked around Varco's ankle and pulled. He fell back, leaving out the theatrics this time. His body hit the cobbles with a thump that was echoed by the gasping crowd.

Ilona stepped closer and set her foot on his stomach. She lifted her sword for the final thrust, held it suspended over his chest. But without his armor to guide her, she wasn't sure exactly where to aim. *What if I hit a major artery? Or his lung? What if he bleeds to death? He's the only one here who's rooting for me.*

Varco's dark eyes beckoned her. *Do it now,* they said.

The blade in her hand began to tremble; the Unhallowed blue glow dimmed in the darkening night. *I can't hurt him.*

His eyes turned amber, glowing like coals in his face. His jaw began to elongate. Bones and joints cracked as they grew and twisted. Hair sprouted on his cheeks, fangs protruded and gleamed. Claws developed on the ends of his fingers, black and long like talons. The man-wolf growled at her.

"No!" Angry tears blurred her vision. *He promised not to turn into a wolf in front of me.* She brought her sword down with all her strength. Ilona felt her blade rip through his muscles and tissue, rasping past bones. Dark blood pooled where sword met flesh.

With a roar, Varco arched his back and grabbed at the blade in his shoulder. His change reverted, and he turned back into his human form.

What have I done? The sight of her sword in his body sickened Ilona. *I could have killed him.*

The soldiers tightened their circle around them. Their faces showed incredulity. They eyed her with suspicion and hatred, hissing and growling.

Varco's eyes sought Ilona's, and for a brief second, they connected. He gave her an apologetic look, and Ilona understood. If he hadn't shape-shifted, she would have lost the fight. She gave him a brief nod. *It's all right.*

Madame Joo took her by the arm and pulled her away from the crowd. Her face scrunched up and her grasp tightened painfully.

"That was disgusting," she said, but her tone was approving. "No girl I ever met could fight like that. It's like I found a daughter!"

~ Eighteen ~

*M*ADAME JOO STOOD ON THE STEPS LEADING TO THE CASTLE doors, holding Ilona's arm up in a gesture of victory. "Meet Countess Bathory's new Commander of the Guard."

The soldiers in the yard glared at Ilona in hateful silence. A circle had formed around Varco, and Zador knelt by his side. With a knot in her heart, Ilona watched Zador pull her sword out of Varco's shoulder. It made an awful wet sucking sound, and Varco's quiet groan sliced through her soul.

Madame Joo spun Ilona around and smiled at her. "Don't mind them. Report to me tomorrow at dusk." She let go of Ilona's arm and entered the castle. The door slammed shut behind her.

Ilona leaned against the polished wood, trying to gain control over her twisting and rippling emotions. She had gained Madame Joo's trust and found a way to get close to the countess. Tomorrow night, the pendant would be hers for the taking, and she could finally free Jeanette. So why did she feel so miserable?

Zador approached her, holding her sword by its hilt. Brown liquid dripped down the blade and onto the cobble stones.

"Your sword, Commander." He gave her a puzzled look.

He opened his mouth as if to speak, then closed it again. Shaking his head, he turned and made his way through the crowd.

He must know Varco let me win. What if he tells Madame Joo?

Her stomach cramped when Zador and Gyala grabbed Varco at each end and carried him off to the sheds. Each lieutenant barked out orders for his group's training exercises, and the crowd slowly dispersed.

I hate this place. I hate what it's made me. She rubbed her knuckles across her forehead and tried to pull air into her lungs. Still, the castle walls seemed to suffocate her. She pushed off the door and dashed down the steps, taking two at a time. The soldiers took no notice as Ilona wrestled the heavy bolt of the gates aside and slipped out.

Ilona ran down the sloped path, skidding on loose gravel and damp rocks. The moon, a pale and distant shard, cast an eerie light across the landscape. She dashed through the scraggly grasses of the valley's meadow and up the hill on the other side. There she sank onto a flat boulder, face cradled in her calloused hands, glaring at the flickering torchlight of the castle yard.

What have I done? How could she have stabbed Varco as though he were her worst enemy? Her hands still trembled, recalling the sick feeling of slicing through the tissue of his body. No wonder the countess and Madame Joo thought that she wasn't really a girl at all.

Not that this was news. It had been a familiar chorus growing up at her father's house. She vividly remembered her mother scolding her for climbing trees with her brothers, or getting her pinafore dirty playing in the muddy fields behind their home. And Mrs. Kertész, pulling her out of a scuffle in the school yard, telling her in no uncertain terms that *girls don't fight*. How her parents suffocated her interest in archery and swords, and sent her to Falston after she punched a girl at her last school. Falston was a last resort, a faint hope that a fine school could make a lady out of her. And her mother's last words to her, handing her the packed trunk. *Please try to put those boyish ideas out of your head. Or you'll never find a husband.*

Ilona snorted. Falston hadn't managed to change her one bit. She would never be like the other girls there, who took pleasure in such tedious and pointless activities as dancing, cooking, and fine needlework. And so what if she never married? You didn't need a husband if you were strong enough to chop wood and knew how to use a sword to protect yourself.

But . . . Varco. He liked her anyway. He didn't care that she hated embroidery and never wore her hair in a fancy chignon. Instead of finding her strange and disgusting, he had enjoyed their friendly competition, their shared interests. And she had enjoyed his company. His archery lessons, their wild run over the hills, his kiss . . .

Ilona kicked at a lanky poppy until its petals drooped. It was useless. Varco had willingly put himself into the service to the Fey Prince. He was part of the evil she came to fight. And if he was evil, and she lost her heart to him, what would that make her?

I'm not evil. Her knuckles dug painfully into her eye sockets, willing them to stay dry. She wasn't evil and neither was Varco. *But he steals girl—like Jeanette—to fill the countess's castle. He turns into a beast with fangs.*

Ilona groaned. It was all too confusing. Maybe she *was* evil. Maybe her place was here, next to Varco. Maybe she should join the Fey Prince's army and command his troops of Unhallowed soldiers.

"Meow." A pink nose pushed against her knee, and cool green eyes stared up at her. "Good job tonight. You fooled Madame Joo."

Ilona shoved Vencel's furry frame away. "What are you talking about?"

He jumped onto the boulder and sat next to her. "Come on. Varco let you win. Didn't he?"

Ilona crossed her arms over her chest. She could trust Vencel with the truth, but she wanted to keep Varco out of this. Their friendship was none of his business.

"Anyway," the cat continued when Ilona remained mute, "tomorrow night is Michaelmas. The countess will have a fancy dinner for her new students and their chaperones. That's your chance to steal the pendant from the countess."

"I know." Irritation crept into Ilona's tone. "That's what I was going to do."

"We should tell the other Hallowed about your plans. Maybe they can help you." Vencel leaped off the boulder and pranced ahead. "Let's go."

Ilona followed reluctantly, wondering if she would be missed at the castle. But Vencel dashed ahead, not waiting to see whether she came along. He faded into the darkness.

"Not so fast! I can't see as well in the dark as you can." Ilona hurried after the black cat, who slowed to a trot.

The pond shimmered silver in the moonlight, like a polished mirror. The bare branches of the poplars reached toward the water, raking across the gray waves. Ilona shivered. The rush of the duel had worn off and now exhaustion sank in. They stood on the pebbled beach and looked out over the gentle waves.

"Where are they?" she whispered.

"Why, here we are."

Ilona whipped around at the bell-like sound of a voice. The two elder Fey ladies stepped out from between the trees, their white robes glowing in the night. They stepped toward her, hands outstretched.

"You have returned. Already you have completed your mission and brought us the rathstone," Edina said. Prioska crouched and stroked Vencel's fur, damp with dew.

"Um." Ilona glanced at Vencel for help, but he purred and twisted under Prioska's touch. "I don't have the rathstone yet. I'm hoping to get it tomorrow night."

Vencel finally pulled away from Prioska. "Ilona has a plan. But she'll need help. What can you give her?"

In a few words, Ilona told the Hallowed about her opportunity to steal the rathstone at Michaelmas. They nodded, their plain faces somber.

Prioska and Edina held hands and exchanged an unfathomable look. Then Edina turned to Ilona. "We will give you a glamour. It will change your appearance for a short time. Use it wisely, and you will deceive the countess long enough to take the stone."

Prioska opened her wrinkled hand and held it out to Ilona. A sphere the size of a large pebble lay on her palm. Ilona plucked it from Prioska's hand and lifted it high to examine in the moonlight. It was heavier than it looked, and the ochre surface turned soft under her touch.

"It looks like a sweet." Ilona sniffed it. It smelled faintly of almonds.

"It has a sugar coating," Edina explained. "To entrap the spell and sweeten its bitter taste." She smiled, which made her look younger and prettier. "Put it in your pocket to keep it safe. And don't let it get wet—it'll melt."

Ilona obediently stuffed the glamour into her trouser pocket. "I have a question for you." She eyed the ladies reluctantly, trying to line up her bewildered thoughts. "What will happen to the countess's servants after I defeat her? To her soldiers?"

Edina and Prioska's eyes widened and they grasped hands.

"She means what will happen to her shape-shifting friend Varco," Vencel added, parading around with his tail high in the air. "Her beau."

"He is not." Ilona lunged at the cat, who swiftly escaped her grasp and darted into the long grass.

Edina stepped forward and laid her hands on Ilona's shoulders. "Your soldier friend made the decision to hitch his fate to that of the Fey Prince a long time ago. It was a very bad decision indeed. And he needs to suffer the consequences for his actions."

Ilona pulled away from Edina, her hands tightening into fists. "He made a mistake. That doesn't mean he's all bad. He could change."

Again the Hallowed hesitated. Prioska leaned forward. "If he repented his association with the Prince, we could release his soul from this half-life form. As a favor to you."

Ilona frowned. "But then he'd be dead? Is that the best you could do?"

The ladies nodded gravely.

Ilona wasn't sure what she had hoped for. That the

Hallowed turned Varco back into a mortal so she could take him home with her? As a little prize for a mission accomplished?

"I don't think he wants to be dead."

"Then we're sorry. There's nothing else we can do."

Vencel broke through the grass and returned to Ilona. He rubbed his damp fur on her shins, purring gently. Ilona stroked his head. She wanted to weep for Varco's soul, but numbing sorrow left her eyes dry.

"And what about the countess's maidens and the kitchen servants?" Ilona's chest tightened. "I'm not leaving this rath without my friend Jeanette. And all those other girls—I have to free them before I leave. But the countess drugged her maidens with Unhallowed fruit and wine. I'm not sure they would follow me out of the castle."

"There is an antidote to the Unhallowed poison in this rath," Prioska said. She pointed up a hill to a cluster of tall shrubs, silver in the moonlight. "The fruit of the elderberry will dissolve the magic in the maidens' blood. One tiny berry for each girl should suffice. Pick them on your way home. Hopefully, you will still find enough of them. They are almost out of season now."

Ilona nodded gratefully. "I will."

The Hallowed began to look drawn and weary. Ilona wondered if it tired them to be in human form. "We must leave you now," they said. "Good luck. Return to us when you have the rathstone. Then we will help you return home."

Ilona climbed the hill, staring at Vencel's undulating tail in front of her. The Hallowed's uncompromising view of the countess's soldiers had dampened her excitement about her imminent victory. One thing she could be certain about was that Varco wouldn't pick death over joining the Fey Prince's army. That wasn't much of a choice.

When they reached the cluster of elderberry bushes, Ilona picked as many of the small, bluish-black berries as she could find and tied them up in her jacket. Then they quietly walked through the night back to the castle.

They had reached the crest of the last hill when shouts drifted up from the valley, along with muffled clanks of swords. Ilona squinted through the darkness. Black shapes moved in the fields below, but she couldn't see how many, or what they were doing.

When Vencel stopped, she nearly tripped over him. "Let's circle around," he said. "You don't want to be involved."

The castle was directly ahead of them, and the shortest way by far led through this valley. Ilona picked up Vencel and stared into his eyes.

"Here's what we'll do. You run down there and see what's going on. Come right back and report to me."

"Me?" Vencel swiped a paw at her ear. "Why me?"

"Because you're small and hard to see in the dark. Now go."

Grumbling, Vencel set off at a trot. Ilona rubbed her arms and hitched up her shoulders against the chilling breeze. A howl rose from below, making the hair on her arms stand on end. One of the Wolves . . . *Varco!* She couldn't have said how she knew.

Without thinking, she ran down the slope. Halfway down, she met Vencel. He climbed her legs like a tree trunk and jumped into the crook of her elbow.

"Let's go. Hurry," he hissed. "We must take a different path."

She grabbed him by the neck and pulled him off her. "Not so fast. Varco's down there." *And he's hurt. He can't defend himself well with a shoulder injury.*

"You can't fight tonight," Vencel insisted. "What if you get harmed? I won't let you endanger our plan for tomorrow."

"You won't let me?" Ilona's voice rose in pitch. "Try and stop me." She threw the yowling cat into the meadow and rushed on, toward the clashing blue swords and the dark shapes.

There were four of them, all in their wolf skins. Ilona tried to find ways to identify them. There was Farkas, tall and muscular, his long scar dividing his furry face like a river of blood. He held his brightly glowing sword in both hands. Next to him was Kardos, with sleek black fur, and the smaller Dezso, both shuffling on their feet, sharp claws and fangs ready to strike.

Ilona skidded to a stop. She was upwind, so they hadn't smelled her yet. Her gaze shot to Varco. He stood hunched over, as though in pain, russet fur falling into his eyes. His shoulder wound was bandaged, but a brown circle spread on the white cloth. A fresh wound gaped on his left leg. His sword dragged on the ground, yet the glow in his amber wolf eyes was fierce and full of fire.

Ilona's breath caught in her throat. *They're killing him.*

Farkas's sword came down hard, and Varco lifted his arm just in time to block the attack. Wincing, Ilona noticed he used his left hand. What a handicap. Farkas jumped to Varco's right and aimed a blow at his injured shoulder. With a roar, Varco swiveled around and parried. Then he backed away a few steps and rested on his knee.

He's exhausted. How long has this been going on?

Varco struggled to his feet. Then he turned his head and sniffed. His gleaming eyes scanned the dark night and his gaze stopped on Ilona. Behind him, Farkas raised his sword.

Watch out! But before the words could leave her mouth, Farkas's blade sliced through Varco's jacket. With a howl, he spun around and blocked the next blow.

Vencel frantically scratched Ilona's pant legs.

"Let's go, let's go," he hissed. "It's not too late."

Ilona crouched, her eyes still on the fighting pair. "Run to the castle, Vencel. Find Zador and Gyala and bring them here. Run as quickly as you can." Without waiting for a reply, she shoved the small creature forward, then sprinted into the valley.

When she approached, Deszo bared his teeth and Farkas growled out of the corner of his mouth.

"Leave. This is not your fight." His voice was rich and nasty.

Varco leaned on his sword as though it were a cane. His breath rattled in his chest and sweat matted his long fur. His amber eyes connected with her, and he began to change. His frame shrank, fur turned to skin, claws became defenseless fingers.

"No!" Ilona dashed to his side. In his human shape, he stood no chance against the Wolves. He was weak, and weaker still for being hurt. His face was pale and drawn. He pulled his mouth into a lopsided grin.

She threw the jacket holding the elderberries under a bush and pulled her sword from its sheath. Flakes of Varco's dried blood rained from the blade as it began to glow.

Farkas didn't waste any time. His sword clanked against hers. His teeth gnashed as he snarled.

Ilona ignored his attempt at intimidation and focused on her attack. To make up for her lack of strength, Ilona had to be swift and surprise him with unexpected moves.

Farkas's jaws tightened under her string of quick blows, and he yelled at his comrades, "What are you waiting for? Get him!"

Kardos and Dezso pulled their swords and advanced on Varco.

Out of the corner of her eye, Ilona saw him parry with his left, staggering forward to meet their attack.

Cowards, she thought. *Two against one wounded.*

Her arm muscles screamed as she thrust her sword forward, pushing Farkas away. She tried to aim for the unprotected curve of his throat, but he didn't give her an opportunity. It was all she could do to hold her ground and keep Farkas's blade from piercing her flesh.

After a few minutes, sweat streamed down her temple and coated her face. She wouldn't be able to last much longer. Farkas was ten times stronger, and fueled by Unhallowed powers as well as intense hatred.

A few yards away, Kardos struck Varco on the side of the head. Varco silently sank to his knees. Dezso made a sound somewhere between a snicker and a roar.

A shrill whistle echoed through the valley. Farkas's ears pricked up.

Ilona used his momentary inattention to thrust her blade into his arm. With a howl, he jerked backward, eyes narrowed. A thin line of blood ran down his hairy wrist. He licked it, then attacked again, driving Ilona into the field behind her.

Then Gyala was by her side, in the shape of a light gray wolf, and with two blades in synchronicity, they knocked Farkas's sword out of his hand. When it hit the ground, he tilted back his head and howled at the moon. Gyala dived to pick up the sword before Farkas could reach for it.

Zador disarmed Dezso and Kardos. They threw themselves onto their backs and exposed their scruffy bellies, making high-pitched whining sounds. Zador roared at them, then lunged at Farkas. He grabbed Farkas's arm and pushed the tip of his sword into the soft spot of Farkas's neck.

"Traitors must die," he growled.

Farkas's eyes rolled, showing yellow. His tongue lolled out of his mouth, and his jaws stretched into a grotesque grin.

"You fool," he panted. "There's a traitor among us, but it's not me."

Varco rose behind Zador in human form and hobbled toward the group. His numerous wounds leaked through his tattered clothes, and the sight of him tore through Ilona's heart.

He put a hand on Zador's sword arm. "Let him go."

Zador pushed his blade deeper into the flesh until he drew blood. "Swear loyalty to your Lieutenant, traitor."

Farkas roared and tried to pull away, but Zador dug his claws into Farkas's arm. He kicked Farkas's knee and pushed down on his back.

"Kneel and swear loyalty. Now."

Farkas fell to his knees. His eyes dark slits, he whispered, "I swear loyalty to Lieutenant Varco."

Zador gave Farkas another shove. He scrambled away into the darkness, Kardos and Dezso at his heels.

With a creaking of bones and a snapping of joints, Zador and Gyala turned back into their human shapes.

Varco sat on the ground. Zador crouched next to him, examining Varco's wounds.

"You had quite a night, my friend. Let's get you home."

Ilona touched Zador's elbow. "Thanks for coming to our rescue. I don't think we could have defeated them on our own."

Varco groaned in agreement.

"You're welcome," said Zador. "Your little cat friend was very insistent, else I wouldn't have bothered to come. I hardly believed my ears when I heard him speak to me."

"What cat friend?" Varco gave Ilona a quizzical sideways glance.

"Never mind," she mumbled, hiding behind her long bangs. But the mention of Vencel reminded her of the elderberries. She dashed to the bush where she had thrown her jacket and retrieved them.

"What were you doing out here, anyway, Varco?" she asked when she returned to his side. "Shouldn't you have been resting?"

He laughed softly, a warm rumble in his chest that made Ilona long to reach out to him. "I was worried about you. I saw you leave the castle, and Farkas followed me with his gang, that old weasel."

Ilona was racked by guilt as he described the Wolves' ambush. It was her fault. He shouldn't have been out here, alone and injured. Perfect prey for Farkas.

Zador hoisted Varco onto his shoulders. "Gyala, escort Ilona back to the castle. I'll attend to the Lieutenant." He turned and disappeared into the darkness at Unhallowed speed.

Gyala sighed. "Let's walk, then, Commander of the

Guards." His eyes twinkled when he said it, and Ilona smiled back at the old man.

She remembered what Varco had told her about him and said, "Why did you retire from the position of the Wolves' lieutenant, Gyala? I'm sure you made a fine leader."

Gyala's face was hard to read in the dark.

"I suppose I was," he grumbled after a pause, "in my day. But now my nights of running with the Wolves are numbered."

"You're not that old, are you?" Gyala looked about her father's age, only in much better shape from his nightly exercises.

"I'm older than you can fathom, young lady," he answered lightly. "Older than I care to be. I'll be glad when it's all over and done." He cracked the knuckles of his fingers—a sound like dry branches breaking.

How bleak. But somehow fitting for someone in the service of the countess. And then she thought that this was how Varco someday would end up. Old and alone and longing for the release of death.

Ilona bit her lip. *And if I could change that somehow, I would. I swear I would.*

~ NINETEEN ~

*A*FTER THE EXCITEMENT OF THE NIGHT, ILONA SLEPT deeply and dreamlessly. When she woke, the sun's rays fell through the small window at a slant. *Tonight is Michaelmas. The countess's guests will arrive soon.*

Ilona jumped out of bed, thinking about her plan. First she would use the glamour to deceive the countess, then use the elderberries to revive the maidens. She peeled the small, black berries out of her jacket. Many had been squished to a pulp, but she still had enough for all the countess's maidens.

Hurrying, she strapped on her armor and belted her sheath. She pulled out her sword and stroked a finger along its cool blade. It was a nice piece of equipment. Too bad it was tainted with Unhallowed magic.

With a sigh, she heaved the door open and stepped into the yard. She wanted to see if Varco was all right before getting ready for the dinner.

I'll tell him everything, she thought, her chest aching. *All I know about the Fey Prince and his intentions. And the promise the Hallowed made. Maybe then Varco will decide to break free of this wickedness.*

The sun just peeked over the horizon, and most soldiers were still sleeping in their barracks. She glanced around.

Where was Vencel? It would be nice to have some support at the dinner. But then, it might look conspicuous if he stayed too close.

Ilona approached Varco's shed, steeling herself against the familiar stench of unwashed bodies and rotting food. She entered quietly and snuck through the building on the tip of her toes, scanning the snoring shapes on the straw for the one that mattered.

She found him sleeping in a corner, on his side, his still blood-matted hair obscuring his face. He had taken off his ruined shirt, and his bare torso sported a few new bandages, including one on his shoulder. A strange desire to run a finger over his back, to feel the muscles under his smooth skin, drew Ilona closer. But then she only crouched in front of him, staring at him in silence.

His hand shot out from under the threadbare blanket and gripped her arm. His eyes opened to slits, and he growled.

"It's you." He released his grip and rolled onto his back. He stretched his arms and yawned.

On the next pile of straw, Kardos groaned and kicked his foot.

How can Varco sleep next to such a backstabber? Ilona put a finger to her mouth. "Shh. Can we talk outside?" When he nodded, she rose and crept toward the door.

Varco stepped outside right behind her, blinking in the fading sunlight. "Are you ready for tonight?"

She nodded, swallowing all doubts. She had to be ready. She had to do this right. So many lives depended on it.

Varco dipped his head into one of the rain barrels, then shook his wet hair out like a dog. He looked much better than he had the night before and no longer moved like an invalid.

"Come on. Let's find a place where we can talk," he said. They slipped out of the castle grounds and walked across the meadow. The evening was mild, and birds chirped in the poplars. The late sun tinged the landscape golden.

Almost impossible to believe that this is a rath ruled by the Unhallowed. Even the countess's close presence wasn't enough to destroy all beauty.

Varco stopped by a grove of oaks and leaned against a broad trunk. A single bead of sweat glistening on his forehead gave away his exhaustion.

Ilona frowned. So he didn't heal as fast as he had made out.

"What did you want to talk about?" He reached for her hand, and she let him pull her close.

"Our future." Ilona bit her tongue. She hadn't meant to sounds so sentimental. "I mean, your future. And mine." She groaned in frustration over her foolish stuttering.

Varco grinned and wrapped his arms around her. She hid her face in his good shoulder, breathing in his distinct smell. *Home,* she thought. *Why do I feel so at home right here?*

When she lifted her face, his lips were on hers. Their kiss seemed to last forever, and Ilona never wanted it to end.

Then Varco spoke again. "I'm so glad you are considering our future together. I was hoping you would."

Ilona, still leaning against him, wiped a strand of short hair behind her ear. She opened her mouth to speak, but he was faster.

"If we both join the Prince's army, we'll be together for all eternity. We'll look out for each other. We'll always fight side by side. It'll be wonderful."

His fingers interlaced with hers, and the warm glow in his eyes was nearly unbearable. Ilona stared at her boots.

"That's not what I meant," she whispered. But it was *almost exactly* what she wanted. To use her fighting skills to become a great army leader. To be with Varco for all eternity. To be a girl *and* a soldier. But a soldier for a *good* cause.

"I can't." She pushed away from him and crossed her arms over her chest.

He hooked a finger under her chin and forced her to look at him. "Can't or won't?" His eyes narrowed as he searched her face.

She pressed her lips together and yanked free.

"You don't have to decide right now." His voice turned flat. "But the Captain will certainly want an answer tonight."

"He's coming?" Ilona's heart beat faster at the memory of the Captain's bloody hand.

"Who else could escort the young ladies to their new school?" Varco grimaced. "It's not like they'd be able to find their own way here."

Ilona understood. Someone had to guide them through a portal. Someone like the Captain. "It doesn't matter. My decision is already made." She hesitated, then added, "The Fey Prince is scheming against the mortals. He's using men like you for his purposes. He's drawing you in with his *gifts*, and then . . ."

Varco's fingers gripped her wrist like shackles. His dark eyes flared.

"You don't have to become a wolf, if that's what you're worried about." He yanked her into his arms, wincing when her chin hit his injured shoulder. "We could take care of each other. At least think it over. Promise you will."

Tears filling her eyes, Ilona pulled free.

"You don't understand. I've made other promises already. And I have to get home." She stepped backward, chewing a knuckle. "As long as you serve the Prince, there's nothing I can do for your soul."

"My soul?" His gaze hardened, and his hands clenched into fists. "What about my soul?"

"If you repent . . . if you want to break free of your ties to the Prince . . . there's a way." Ilona struggled with feelings of dread. Part of her couldn't bear the thought of him cold and dead. But it was the only way to save him from the evil that had drawn him in and held him captive.

"There's a way for me to become a mortal human again?" Varco gave her a dubious look.

Ilona shook her head. "As a mortal, you would have died such a long time ago. But there are forces in this rath who could end this horrible life for you and return your soul to the light. They promised me."

She bit her lip and choked on the lump in her throat. *This is too hard.*

"You already arranged this for me?" Varco sounded equal parts hurt and astounded. "You want me to surrender and die?"

"And save your soul." Ilona gave him a pleading look.

"How sweet of you." Varco's tone became low and sarcastic, and the corners of his mouth lifted into a fierce snarl. "But if you thought a few kisses would make me roll over and submit to your outrageous request, you're wrong." A vein pulsed on his forehead and his hands curled into fists.

He's going to become a wolf and tear me to pieces. Ilona stared at him as though mesmerized, unable to break away. But he didn't change. Instead he spun around and sprinted through the forest.

Away from her.

"Varco." The word was only a whisper, drifting on the breeze. He was gone.

Ilona kicked at a boulder. *I'm so stupid—asking him to die for me. Now he thinks I'm his enemy.* Desperation settled over Ilona like a heavy cloak. Her friendship with Varco had no future. She had promises to keep, girls to save, a rathstone to return. And she'd have to go back to school, have to try to fit in with the genteel young ladies who raised their eyebrows and giggled when they saw the mess Ilona made of her needlework.

She pulled her sword from its sheath and swung it at the bare-branched bushes.

"It's all so stupid, stupid, stupid," she yelled as she chopped off the heads of long-dead flowers.

Then she stopped. Perhaps there was another way. She could pretend to accept the Captain's proposal. Once the Prince bestowed Unhallowed powers upon her, she would be free to travel back and forth between this rath and the human world at will. She would be able to finish her mission, then return to Varco. But they wouldn't join the Prince's army—never that. They'd run away together, to a place far from all this.

Ilona sighed and strode down the path toward the castle with quickening steps. Before she spoke to the Captain, she had to find out if Varco would be willing to leave the countess and the Prince *for her.*

As she ran across the castle yard toward the Wolves' sleeping quarters, Zador stepped into her path. "The countess's messenger is here for you."

"I beg your pardon?" Ilona stopped and gulped down the lump in her throat.

He motioned toward the ground, where a black, spider-like creature crouched. "The daoi."

"Oh." Ilona eyed the Unhallowed being with disgust. "What does it want?"

The daoi made a series of beeps and grunts, shuffling on its many legs. The sight sent a shiver down Ilona's back.

"He says the countess wants you in the banquet hall right now," Zador translated.

"All right." Reluctantly Ilona followed the creature into the castle, her hopes of speaking to Varco before the festivities crumbling.

In the great banquet hall, the servants had pushed several long tables together in a horseshoe shape. China and ancient silver gleamed on the snow-white linen. Vanillina flitted around the chandeliers, lighting the candles with little sparks.

Countess Bathory and Madame Joo supervised the maids who darted around bearing napkins and flower arrangements. The daoi scurried to the countess. She leaned down to scratch his hairy body.

Ilona approached with a grim smile on her face. "You asked for me?"

The countess shooed her creepy messenger away. The silver necklace with the blue rathstone sparkled around her neck.

Ilona's fingers itched. She might never get this close to the rathstone again. *Control yourself. Madame Joo is staring at you.*

"It is time for you to assemble your guard, Commander," Madame Joo said. "Our guests will be here within the hour."

The countess flicked an invisible piece of dirt from

her heavy brocade dress with two red fingernails.

"Your assignment tonight is simple." Her eyes pinned Ilona. "Once my guests arrive, make sure they don't leave the hall. Have one group of soldiers accompany the young ladies to their quarters in the east wing, and instruct the rest of your men to liberate us from their chaperones."

The close presence of the countess nauseated Ilona. She straightened her spine and nodded.

"If you have any trouble, Madame Joo will assist you. I will refresh myself in my chambers and then dress for dinner." She glanced at Madame Joo. "I want to look as beautiful as possible for my guests tonight. Have you followed my instructions?"

Madame Joo nodded eagerly. "Everything is ready for you."

Gracefully, the countess glided out of the room. Ilona stared after her in confusion.

"What did she mean about the chaperones?" she finally asked. "I have to liberate them?"

Madame Joo scowled. "Stupid girl. You're supposed to kill them." She chuckled. "What else?"

Two trolls Ilona didn't recognize sauntered through the arched doorway. Where did the countess get this seemingly endless supply of trolls? Did they breed in a dungeon underneath the castle? The idea was as disgusting as absurd, yet in the realm of possibility.

The trolls saluted first Madame Joo, then Ilona. "At your service."

"Is this it?" Ilona gave Madame Joo a panicked look. "I only command two trolls?"

"Don't be ridiculous. Each division contributes two of their finest men. They should arrive any moment."

On cue, a draft swept through the hall and the pounding of feet on the stone floor rang from the corridors. A dozen young men in full battle armor stomped into the banquet hall and lined up before Ilona and Madame Joo.

They bowed, armor clanking. Madame Joo stretched her thin lips into a grin.

"Here they are. Your men." The old woman set off in the direction of the kitchen, probably to torment the poor maids.

Her men. Fairies seemed to flutter through Ilona's insides. These men would follow her orders and fight on her behalf. An amazing feeling of power surged through her. She scanned the line for familiar faces. There was Zador, shaking his red mane back over his shoulder. Further down, Farkas shuffled from one foot to the other, his face an angry grimace. Her stomach contracted. *Not him.*

Zador stepped forward and saluted. "Allow me, Commander." He handed her a silver shield and matching armor.

She pulled the chest plate over her head and tied it with barely shaking hands. *Varco must have realized that I left them behind. So he's not angry at me anymore.*

"The Lieutenant?" she asked Zador in a low voice.

He lifted a bushy eyebrow in response. "I haven't seen him since last night, Commander."

Ilona swallowed hard. "My mistake."

Zador gave her a quizzical look, then leaned forward and whispered, "Will you station some of us at the castle gates?"

She squared her shoulders and hissed under her breath, "I was about to." She cleared her throat and raised her voice.

"You there." Ilona pointed at a broad-shouldered, six-foot soldier with a scraggly brown beard. "You'll greet our guests at the gate and bolt it behind them." *Who else?* "Farkas. You'll help him." She couldn't work properly with him glowering at her back anyway.

The bearded one exchanged a look with Farkas. Neither one of them moved.

I see. Ilona bit her bottom lip. "That's an order. Now!"

An amused smile played around Farkas's lips. "Make us."

Ilona narrowed her eyes and gave the men an evil stare, hand on her hilt. But the power she had felt earlier was draining through her fingers like sand. *I can't make them do anything.* Yet Ilona wasn't ready to admit defeat.

"If you don't want to follow my orders, I'll have to report to Madame Joo and request a replacement from your house."

Farkas and the bearded one stood their ground, although at a decidedly less confident stance.

"Zador." He was the only one who might be trusted. "Report to Madame Joo on these soldiers' inability to follow simple orders."

Zador saluted and turned to go.

"Wait." Farkas sneered. His yellow eyes regarded her and Zador with open hatred. "Call off your poodle. I'm on my way to the gate." He motioned to the bearded soldier, and together they trotted out of the hall.

Ilona wiped her sweaty palms on her pants. So Madame Joo didn't terrify only young maidens. For once she was glad of it.

~ Twenty ~

JLONA SQUARED HER SHOULDERS AND WALKED ALONG HER line of soldiers. "One, two, one, two," she counted them off. "Group One will be in charge of taking the girls to the maidens' chambers." It took all of her efforts to keep her voice steady. "Group Two will then kill their parents on my command." A shiver ran over her skin. *This is how it would be if I worked for the Prince.* In his army, ordering mortals killed was routine.

A tall soldier stepped forward. Scars criss-crossed his face and his heavy-lidded eyes shone with a menacing light. "Where shall we dump the bodies, Commander?"

Ilona swallowed hard. *Dead bodies?* It was too ghastly a scenario to consider. "You can unload the bodies in the same place you use for any dead maidens," she snapped. *Wherever that is.*

Ilona drew a deep breath. She was walking a fine line. First, she had to make sure her men would obey her commands—and she wasn't yet convinced they would. These surly glances they gave her . . . Then she had to make sure they would *not* carry out these orders. And above all, she needed to appear calm and collected.

Ilona placed her men at intervals around the hall, as

though their only concern was overseeing a safe and joyous meal. She hid the trolls behind the floor-length velvet curtains parting the arched doorway. In plain sight, their grotesque hideousness, even behind a glamour, would send the wrong signal to the guests. Ilona's heart pounded like a drum as she gave the trolls her commands, but the two ugly creatures obeyed without a fuss. Perhaps she had already earned a reputation as a troll slayer.

She leaned her shield against a stone pillar as Countess Bathory entered the hall with fluid strides, Madame Joo at her heels like a mean old lapdog. The countess's black hair was pinned up and laced with silver and emeralds. She wore a richly embroidered blood-red dress with a high neckline and slashed, puffed sleeves. A wide cartwheel of linen ruffs hid her pale neck. To Ilona's relief, her wedding necklace with the blue rathstone dangled underneath. She looked magnificent, yet her clothes were so hopelessly old-fashioned, Ilona wondered what her nineteenth century guests would make of her.

Countess Bathory's glance swept over the hall and her lips curled into a satisfied smirk. Then her gaze pierced Ilona. "They're here. Come with me. We'll greet them in the yard."

Ilona glanced at her soldiers. They stood each at their designated posts, scratching their heads or picking their noses. Ilona had the niggling feeling that they couldn't be trusted the moment she turned her back.

Madame Joo gave her a curt nod and crossed her arms over her chest.

They won't desert their posts while she's here, Ilona decided and followed Countess Bathory's gently bobbing hoop skirt.

The air outside was moist with the promise of rain, and

heavy clouds obscured the moon and stars. Farkas and his comrade stood by the open gates. Through the wide doors, the path leading to the village curled like a gray ribbon in the night.

A row of black coaches thundered up the road, pulled by horses. Ilona hadn't seen many horses in this rath, and when Farkas smacked his lips beside her, she realized why. An image rushed through her mind, of the Wolves tearing the poor animals apart, devouring them before they had even died. She shook her head to get the horrid picture out.

More than half a dozen carriages entered the courtyard. The countess's menservants rushed to steady the horses, open the carriage doors and help the young ladies out.

Ilona scanned the yard. Had Varco returned to the castle? Or was he still roaming the woods, angry and disappointed in her? She had hoped to have a quick word with him before the dinner began, but now there was no chance of that. The guests were here.

Behind the last carriage, a night-black horse pushed through the open gates. Mounted atop was a cloaked, hooded figure. The Captain. He must have worn his glamour again to convince these fine ladies and gentlemen to bring their daughters here, because Ilona couldn't see how a grotesque, cloaked stranger would appeal to them.

The girls in their wide crinoline dresses, silken shawls, and upswept golden hair gathered in the yard, next to their mothers, fathers, aunts, or uncles in more somber but not any less fashionable evening attire. The men in their brown suits and vests eyed the castle and exclaimed loudly about the solid appearance and the height of the towers.

Countess Bathory stepped forward, her chin raised and her cool eyes appraising the crowd.

"Welcome to Castle Cachtice. I am Countess Bathory." Her melodic voice rang out deep and enchanting, and the narrow-eyed gentlemen relaxed their guard and twirled their mustaches with a mellow smile.

It will be easy for her to bespell these parents, Ilona thought. *They* want *to believe that this is a respectable school for their daughters.* Perhaps, as with Ilona herself, traditional methods of upbringing had failed these girls. *A bunch of little trouble-makers. They'll need their spirits tonight.*

The countess threw the castle doors wide and motioned her guests to step inside. Ilona hung back, making sure Farkas and the bearded soldier locked and barricaded the front gate. *That'll make a quick escape hard tonight,* she thought grimly. *But perhaps once I have the rathstone in my possession, locked doors won't be a problem.*

In the entrance hall, Ilona overheard the guests praise the artistic portraits, the soft Turkish rugs, the polished wooden floor and silver fixtures. Ilona wondered that they didn't feel the icy chill or smell the penetrating odor of mold. But perhaps the countess had thrown a strong glamour over her castle to dazzle her guests.

The girls whispered and giggled under the high chandelier, hands modestly covering their mouths. Ilona followed the countess's gaze to their bare pale throats, choking down disgust. These girls were so innocent and beautiful. Their long, ruffled gowns and frilly hairstyles made Ilona become painfully aware of the odd contrast she provided, sweating under her armor, the choppy hair stuffed carelessly under her beret.

Countess Bathory clapped her hands as though addressing small children.

"Before I will show you around the premises of the

school, let me invite you to take a seat in our banquet hall and join me for refreshments."

A cold, damp hand clasped her forearm. Ilona swiveled around to the Captain. His hood hung low and half hid his destroyed features, which shimmered through the human face of his glamour.

He whispered, "A word with you, Commander." He motioned her to follow him back out into the yard.

Ilona hesitated. Now he would ask if she accepted the Prince's offer. And she didn't know what to say. Somehow, she feared he wouldn't take no for an answer. *I guess I'll have to speak to him. What else can I do?* With a quiet groan, she stepped outside once more.

The Captain held a shuttered lantern, which threw a pale yellow light. When she approached, he pulled his hood down. His red burn marks seemed lit from within when he smiled. Ilona squinted. When she tried hard enough, she managed to only see him the way he wanted her to, as a tired, middle-aged man in a blue uniform.

"Ilona Takar." His bloody hand reached for hers. "I heard of your promotion, Commander. We-e-e-e-e-ll done." After his warbled speech, his blackened tongue lolled between his lips as though forgotten.

She briefly pressed his limp hand, then wiped hers on the back of her pants. *Her promotion.* It sounded strangely pleasing. She cleared her throat.

"I suppose the Fey Prince wants an answer tonight?"

The Captain dipped his head once.

"Please tell him that I'm greatly honored by the offer from my old sword master and his trust in me. But . . ." Ilona hadn't thought of an excuse that would sound reasonable to the Captain, and she couldn't tell him the truth.

"But?" The Captain inclined his head further toward her, and it took all of Ilona's efforts not to draw back in disgust.

"But my place is here," she continued. "Countess Bathory needs me, and I've sworn her loyalty."

The Captain made a strange choking sound. It took Ilona a moment to realize that he was laughing. "That shall not impede us. I'm certain the countess will release you to the Prince's army. I will speak to her before the night is over."

Ilona shook her head. "I don't . . ." She fumbled for words, thoughts spinning. "But if I can't—there's someone eager to join the Prince's army: my lieutenant, Varco. He'll make a fine general." She slowly backed away from the Captain toward the castle's door. She didn't have time to argue with him, and what did it matter what he thought, anyway? If her plans succeeded, she'd be home by morning.

"I have to go. My men are awaiting my command." She hurried up the steps to the door. "Give my regards to the Prince. Tell him I'll join him another time, perhaps." Without glancing back for the Captain's response, she entered the castle.

Running down the dimly lit corridors, she reached into her trouser pocket for the Hallowed's glamour. The thick sugar coating was hard and cool.

I'll swallow the glamour before dinner is over. Then I'll lure the countess away from her guests and take the pendant. I'll dismiss the guards and free all girls.

Ilona accelerated her steps and almost fell over Vencel, dashing down the corridor.

"There you are. Nervous?" His voice was a low hiss.

"I'm not nervous." Ilona bent down and rubbed his little head. "Just eager to begin."

"Have you fed the elderberries to the countess's maidens?" Vencel asked.

"Not yet. I'm going to take the rathstone first."

"That's not a good idea," Vencel countered. "It takes almost an hour before the elderberries revive the girls."

"An hour?" Ilona picked up the cat and glared at him. "That's too long! The soldiers will arrest me once they find out I defeated the countess. Madame Joo will lock me into her torture chamber in the tower! Why didn't you tell me earlier?"

"I thought you knew," he yelped, struggling out of her grasp. "But it's not too late. Go to the maidens' chamber right now. Then the berries will have time to work while the countess and her guests eat dinner."

"All right." Ilona dropped Vencel.

"I'll be around if you need help." He chafed once more past her leg and then slunk back into the shadows.

And what kind of help would that be? I'd like to see you hold a sword in your tiny paws. Groaning, Ilona turned on her heel and ran back into the yard. In her shed, she scooped the elderberries into her beret and raced to the east wing, hoping not to run into anyone.

At the locked door to the maidens' chambers, Ilona knocked three times. When the troll guard opened, Ilona motioned him to step out. He complied with a growl, looking her up and down.

"I'm commander of security tonight," Ilona said, hand on hilt. "Countess Bathory requests that all trolls help out in the banquet hall."

The troll scratched the chin under his bone visor with a claw. "And leave the maidens unguarded?"

"Of course not," Ilona snapped. "That's why I'm here."

The troll raised his eyebrows. "Really? But Madame Joo told me 'splicitly to stay 'ere all night. Can't go against Madame's orders, can I now?"

Ilona groaned. Then she pushed her beret under his nose. "I brought the maidens a snack."

"In your hat?" The troll narrowed his eyes. His hand slid down toward his sword. "I don't believe a word!"

They glared at each other for a moment, then they both reached for their weapons in unison. His sword came at Ilona fast, but she threw her beret with the berries in his face and stepped aside.

The berries scattered and the troll shook his head. During his moment of confusion, Ilona whacked her sword into his unprotected upper arm. The blade sliced neatly through the rough shirt and the dim-white flesh underneath. The troll fell to his knees, roaring with pain.

His groans echoed down the corridor behind the open door. A second later, the other two guarding trolls rushed out.

"What's happening?" When they saw their injured companion, they advanced, swords aimed at Ilona's throat.

She parried their blows with fast, decisive movements, using her slim body to dart around them as Varco had taught her. Even as she leaped sideways and blocked their blades, her mind formed a plan. The trolls wore bronze chest-plates, but their backs were covered only by plain brown and black cotton shirts. *I'll need to get behind them.*

Ilona's sword clanked from one troll blade to the next. Her arm muscles screeched with the effort and sweat dampened her forehead, gluing her bangs into one thick forelock.

The injured troll rose and tottered toward her. Black

goo seeped through his ruined shirt. His shiny eyes fastened on Ilona as he lifted his bronze sword. With a fierce yell, he ran at her. Ilona sprang to the side. His blade rasped along the stone wall. Sparks rained down, gleamed and glinted.

Ilona raised her sword and sank it into the flesh between his shoulder blades. She heard his tissue rip and something popped. Gaping and clawing at his chest, the troll went down. Ilona pressed her lips together as though she could swallow her disgust. With one foot on his side, she pulled her sword out of him.

The other two trolls stared at her, mouths open and eyes wide. Then they attacked Ilona once more. But their thrusts lacked conviction now, and Ilona used their hesitation to stick her blade just above the knee of the smaller of the two. He yowled, but kept on fighting. Ilona tried the same maneuver on the other one—bluff-step to the left, jump to the right, shove the blade into his leg with all her might.

This time, it worked better. The troll bent forward, cradling the injured leg. Ilona raised her sword as high as she could, then thrust it into the center of his neck. His face slammed into the ground and his battered helmet rolled off, clanking over the stones. It stopped in front of Ilona's toes. The troll's eyes stared blankly into the ceiling.

Following a sudden and compelling instinct, Ilona scooped up the troll helmet. It was well-worn: the metal skull cap dented and scraped; the bone visor brittle. As she pulled the helmet over her head, the aroma of stale troll breath nearly made her gag.

The last troll standing breathed heavily. He backed away until his rear met the wall. He shook his head, over and over. "You're a worse witch than the countess," he whispered in a toneless, broken voice. "Your powers can't be fought with our simple troll swords."

His face paled behind his visor. His heavy hand holding the sword trembled as his gaze swept over his dead comrades.

Ilona straightened her shoulders. "Then surrender! Drop your weapon."

The troll complied. Ilona took his sword, wondering what to do with him. "Give me your keys, too," she ordered. "I'll have to lock you up somewhere." *But I can't lock him into the maidens' chamber.*

The troll gave her a questioning look. "The latrine tower is nearby, Commander. That might be convenient."

"All right." Ilona pointed her sword at his back and herded him down the corridor. "But don't try any tricks on me."

After locking the troll into the smelly latrine, Ilona returned to the entrance of the maidens' chambers. She crawled over the dirty ground, collecting all the elderberries back into her beret. Many had been trampled, but Ilona took them anyway, hoping their powers would be undiminished.

She raced through the parlor and past the curtain on the right into the first maidens' chamber. Hastily, she pried each girl's lips open and stuck in one elderberry. Fortunately, their drugged state made them compliant, and every girl swallowed obediently.

In the second chamber, Ilona's gaze immediately swept toward Jeanette's bed. It was empty, the sheets neatly pulled taut, the pillows fluffed.

"No." Ilona ran to the bed, threw back the blankets, even

checked underneath the wooden frame in her desperation. Jeanette was gone.

"Where did you go?" But it came to her instantly. The countess. What had she said to Madame Joo about needing refreshment before dinner? "She has Jeanette!" Ilona groaned. How much time had she already wasted fighting the trolls and feeding the maidens?

Ilona wanted to run up to the countess's chambers *now*, but it probably would be too late for Jeanette already—the countess had gone to her chambers long ago. And Ilona had to finish feeding the elderberries to the maidens.

Her stained beret in hand, she hurried from bed to bed. When she came to Katalin, she noted that the girl still breathed, shallow and slowly, but unmistakably. Ilona forced a thick, juicy berry into Katalin's mouth and held her nose until the girl swallowed.

"I'll come back for you soon," she whispered. Then she left the countess's maidens and headed back toward the banquet hall. Racing around a corner, she collided with Gizi, carrying a silver tray with a glass decanter. The tray slipped from her grasp and crashed on the stone floor. Glass splintered all around.

"No!" The maid fell to her knees and hastily swept the shards together.

"I'm so sorry." Ilona crouched down to help. "I didn't see you."

Gizi's hands trembled, and one of the larger splinters slashed her finger. She stuck the digit into her mouth and sucked. "You know Madame Joo. I'm in trouble now."

"I'll speak with her," Ilona promised, piling the remaining glass onto the tray.

Gizi snorted through her long nose.

"Don't bother. We know whose side you're on." She took the tray and scrambled to her feet. "You've helped capture more girls for the countess. And now you're joining the Prince's army. So don't pretend you're our friend." With small, hurried steps, Gizi disappeared down the corridor.

"Well, you're wrong," Ilona mumbled after her. "You'll realize it before the night is over."

But maybe I should speak to Anci, she thought. It couldn't hurt to have the maids ready to fight or bolt when the time came. Rather than cross through the banquet hall, where Madame Joo might stop her, Ilona wound her way through a maze of corridors toward the kitchen.

Steam from multiple pots misted the maids' faces and made Ilona's eyes itch. Every single servant of the countess seemed to be working tonight, and the kitchen was over-crowded with tense, rushing maids. Even the cook worked, though it was still daylight, wielding a spoon on the slower maids. Ilona weaved around girls carrying silver platters with mouth-watering roasts and tureens of fragrant soup, girls decorating little cakes, girls chopping and arranging Fey fruit into crystal bowls.

She's serving them Fey food. Ilona grimaced. *I have to hurry.* She spied Anci by the stove, stirring a thick, creamy sauce.

"Anci."

The maid spun around. Thin strands of hair had escaped her *basma* and hung limply around her narrow face. The corners of her lips curled up when her eyes met Ilona's.

"Hello, Commander. What are you doing here?" She focused her attention on the sauce, sprinkling herbs onto the velvety surface.

"I . . ." *I'm here to rescue you tonight. This time, it's for real.* But how could she speak up with this gaggle of girls around? *I need to give her a sign. Something only she will understand.*

"Hoping for a treat, I suppose? Well, you'll have to wait." Anci's voice was light and casual. "We're extremely busy."

"Yes. I see that." Ilona scratched under her tight armor and moved aside to let a girl with a large tray pass.

"We need the second course, NOW!" Madame Joo's shrill voice rang above the din. Ilona ducked. Too late. Madame Joo rushed toward her with narrowed eyes. "Ilona! Where have you been? Get back to the banquet hall immediately. And where did you get that helmet?"

Ilona's hand shot to her head. She had forgotten that she was still wearing the dead troll's helmet. "I borrowed it," she said.

As a girl was trying to sneak past them, Madame Joo grabbed her by the collar of her dress. "And you! Where are the meat pies? Serve them immediately, or else!"

The girl nodded wildly as tears streamed down her cheeks. "Yes, ma'am. Right now, ma'am."

Madame Joo released her and gripped Ilona's wrist instead. "What are you waiting for, Commander? Your troops are getting restless."

While shuffling after the old woman, Ilona frantically searched her brain for something that would remind Anci of their attempted escape plan. Halfway through the kitchen, she turned her head and yelled, "Anci. I'm planning on getting my hands on your tasty casserole dish later!"

Anci's shoulder's stiffened in response, but then Madame Joo dragged Ilona out the door and down the corridor. Had Anci gotten Ilona's hint?

~ TWENTY-ONE ~

IN THE BANQUET HALL, DINNER WAS WELL UNDER WAY. MAIDS with shaking hands ladled fragrant bouillon into the guests' bowls and scooped away plates crusted with dried gravy. The young ladies sipped their mulled wine and chatted, cheeks flushed as red as the Unhallowed apples sitting in a wicker basket at the center of the table.

The parents also seemed to enjoy themselves. They shoveled meat pies and scalloped potatoes into their mouths as though they hadn't eaten in months, chattering to each other happily about how lovely the school was.

Ilona wandered about the room, her gaze flitting between her soldiers and the guests. Neither had moved an inch since she had left. She took up her shield, still leaning against the stone pillar where she had left it, and hooked its leather strap around her wrist. Then she noticed one of the trolls she had positioned behind the drapes wiggling his fingers at her, making hissing noises.

She approached the velvet curtains.

"What's the matter? Getting bored?" She stepped around the drapes and came face to face with the troll. His thick lips, half-covered by his bone visor, curled into a wide grin.

"Somebody's here for you, miss. I mean, Commander." He hitched a clawed thumb behind him.

Varco stepped out of the shadows. His face was calm and serious. "Do you have a moment?"

"Of course." With a last peek at the feasting dinner guests, Ilona slipped into the corridor. Her heart hung in her chest, twisted and aching. Was he still angry?

Varco motioned her to follow him down the passage and into a small antechamber. The sounds of chatter and clanking dishes faded. Instead, Ilona's heart beat so loud it rang in her ears.

Varco gave her a searching look. "So, Commander," he said finally. His hand reached up as though he meant to tuck a stray strand of hair back under her helmet, but then stalled and dropped to his side.

"I just spoke to the Captain." He carefully watched for her reaction.

Ilona sighed. "I spoke to him as well, when he arrived."

"I know. You refused the Prince's offer." Varco's voice was thick and heavy, like sludge. "I had hoped—" He broke off and inspected his boots. When he straightened, his face was absent of emotion. "The Captain offered me a position in the Prince's army. I accepted."

"I knew you would." Ilona nodded eagerly. "But Varco, I've thought about it all, and there's a way we could still be together."

Varco's eyes sparkled with new interest. "Really? How?"

Ilona took off the troll helmet and shook out her tangled hair. "What if I spoke to the Captain again tonight and pretended I changed my mind? Once the Prince gives me the power to travel through the portals, we could leave this rath together and roam the world, just you and me."

245

Ilona gave Varco a pleading look. "We'd finally be free."

Varco growled. His fist hit the paneling on the wall, making it crack. "Ilona. That's the dumbest thing you've ever said."

Sudden tears stung her eyes. "Why?"

"Because once you pledge your service to the Prince, you'll *never* be free again. I'm tethered to this rath. Yes, I can leave, but only for short periods of time. The Prince would not willingly let us go. And if we ran, he'd send his army to find us. If we openly defied him, he'd kill us. Do you understand now why your idea isn't going to work?"

Ilona nodded. She forced the next few words past the lump in her throat. "So I won't ever see you again?"

"I'm leaving with the Captain tonight." Varco's face became anguished. "I only came to say good-bye. And to give you this."

Varco reached into his jacket and pulled out a small parcel. He held it with the tips of his fingers, as though the contents were hot to the touch, then handed it to her.

Ilona pulled off layers of dirty cotton and found the little iron dagger she had brought into the rath with her. She gave Varco a questioning look.

"It's yours." Varco shrugged. "I thought you might need it tonight."

"Thanks." She slipped the dagger into her boot, lacking another place to put it. There was so much else she wanted to say. How sorry she was that they had to part ways. How much she'd miss him. But the lump in her throat was too great, and she couldn't speak.

Varco swept her into his arms. "Are you sure you cannot join me in the Prince's army?" he whispered.

Mutely, she shook her head.

"I guess you have plans of your own," he said. "And you want to go home. Wherever that is."

Ilona opened her mouth to explain, but his finger on her lips stopped her.

"Don't tell me." His dark eyes were sad. "It's better for you if I don't know." He slowly released his grip and stepped backward.

"I want you to understand." Ilona laid a hand on his arm. "If I could come with you, if it were anyone else's army . . . if there wasn't something else I need to do . . ." Tears of frustration at her lack of choices blurred Varco's outlines. She blinked them back. *A soldier doesn't cry.* She stomped her foot hard instead.

Varco held her hand. "I do understand," he said quietly. "And if I had a home waiting for me in any world or rath, I wouldn't go with the Captain tonight, either." He smiled and ran a finger along the scar on her cheek. Ilona wished with all her heart she could offer him her own home.

"Good luck tonight." He leaned forward and his warm lips brushed hers, sending a tingle down her back. With quick, determined steps, he left.

Ilona stared at the empty doorway, arms crossed over her chest. She'd never felt so alone in her life. The emotion wrapped around her like a straightjacket.

"There you are." The small, dark shape of Vencel appeared on the threshold, green cat eyes sparkling. "Why are you always so hard to find? Never mind, just hurry. Dinner is almost over. Swallow your glamour and get to work." Without waiting for an answer, he strode back down the corridor.

"Fine." Ilona slapped her troll helmet back on her head, twirled her shield and followed. Bossed around by a cat—did the Hallowed not trust her at all? But when she passed the hidden trolls and entered the banquet hall, she was glad Vencel had rushed her. The candles in the chandelier burned low and only bones and grizzle was left on the silver platters. The fruit baskets that had held the Unhallowed apples stood empty.

The guests' faces were unnaturally red. With their glazed eyes and slow movements, the ladies and gentlemen in evening finery eerily resembled marionettes. The young ladies slumped in their seats with absent smiles, staring at nothing in particular. One older man with receding hair and a thick, yellow mustache had fallen asleep on his half-finished plate. Loud snores escaped his wide-open mouth.

Countess Bathory sat at the end of the table, a satisfied smile playing around her lips. She looked like a cat ready to pounce.

They're all enchanted, Ilona thought, *just like the countess's maidens. I'll need more elderberries.*

Panic rising, her hand slid into her pocket and closed around the glamour. *I've got to act now.* She ducked into the corridor leading toward the kitchen, hoping to find a quiet place where she could swallow the glamour unobserved.

"You should be ashamed of yourself."

Ilona spun around. Gizi glared at Ilona through narrow-slitted eyes and her knuckles tightened on the handles of a delicate china tureen. She stepped so close that Ilona could feel Gizi's hot breath.

"This is your fault." Gizi's chin jerked in the direction of the dinner table, half-visible through the open doorway behind them. "They ate the evil food and drank the wine, and now she'll kill them."

Ilona hesitated. There was a crazed look in Gizi's eyes that warned her to choose her next words carefully.

"Listen, Gizi. I'm sorry about the guests. But—"

"So you say." Gizi snorted. "But then you say many things, don't you?" Her voice lowered into a hiss.

While Ilona mutely shook her head, Gizi continued. "Forgotten your grand promises already, have you? Well, let me refresh your memory. First, you promised to defeat the guard trolls and get us out of here. You also told Dorika you'd reunite her with her family and—just tonight—you said you'd speak to Madame Joo about the broken decanter. Of course that never happened, and now I have an appointment with the torture chamber later tonight." Gizi's voice quivered over the last words and her long nose turned cherry red.

"I don't believe I've ever made such a promise to Dorika," Ilona said, in a rush of defensiveness. "And I can still speak to Madame Joo; it's not too late for that."

Hectic red spots appeared on Gizi's face. Her hands clutched the soup tureen even tighter.

"I know what you are," she said in a rapidly rising tone. "You're one of them. You work for the countess and sleep with her soldiers. You disgust me!"

She lifted the bowl high and brought it down hard on Ilona's head. The attack came so fast and unexpected that she didn't dodge it. The tureen cracked into shards and Ilona stumbled back into the wall. Warm, greasy liquid ran over her face and blurred her vision. Her head pounded. She rubbed a quickly growing lump where the china had hit.

"Gizi!"

Anci's voice rang out over the whooshing noise in Ilona's ears. Using her sleeve, Ilona wiped soup and chunks of vegetables from her face and hair. Anci stood with her hands on her hips, with pursed mouth and an angry glare she directed at Gizi.

Gizi's arms hung limp by her sides, but her eyes still held a defiant sparkle. "I'm not sorry. She deserves worse than I can give her."

Anci untied her apron and dabbed it at Ilona's soaked clothes. "But I told you she had a plan for tonight." Her dark eyes begged Ilona to agree. "Don't you, Ilona?"

Ilona nodded, which hurt her head even more.

"Yes. I have this glamour . . ." Ilona felt her pants, soggy with greasy soup. "Oh, no." Her fingers fumbled with the pocket. *The glamour. It can't get wet.* She pulled out the ball. The sugar coating dripped and ran through her fingers. In several places it had melted so much that rainbows of color glittered through the splotchy coating. Ilona covered the glamour with both hands as if that would prevent the spell from escaping.

"What's wrong?" Anci's eyes grew wide. "What have you got there?"

"It's a glamour." Ilona's voice trembled. *What if it doesn't work now? What will I do then?* "It contains a spell to change my appearance, so that I can approach Countess Bathory without raising her suspicions."

"And kill her?" Anci's face shone with a hopeful glow. Even Gizi stepped closer, the tightness around her mouth softening.

There wasn't any time to explain about the rathstone and her mission—someone might come around the bend any time—so Ilona simply nodded. "But now the soup is dissolving the glamour. I'm not sure it'll work."

Anci gently pried Ilona's fingers apart and peeked at the

glamour. "It's glowing. I think the magic's still inside." She closed Ilona's hand back over it. Her gaze turned intense. "You have to try."

"Of course." Ilona's stomach rolled. The Hallowed had warned her it could melt. Why hadn't she put the glamour into a container?

"Swallow it now," Anci urged.

Gizi eagerly nodded. "Please."

What if there isn't enough magic left to hide me well?

Ilona brought her hand to her mouth and sniffed. The glamour smelled of sweet almonds and vegetable broth. Swirling mist rose from the holes in the melted coating, purple and emerald. It itched her nose and made her sneeze.

"Swallow it." Anci wrung her hands, her gaze darting up and down the corridor. "Before we're discovered."

Ilona closed her eyes. She dropped the glamour into her mouth. Her tongue tingled as the bitter taste of medicine gagged her. *Don't be such a baby.* Ilona swallowed hard. The glamour slipped past her tongue and down her throat, as easily as a melon seed.

"Why are you not in the kitchen?" Madame Joo, pink-faced and out of breath, appeared in the corridor. "What's going on here?"

~ TWENTY-TWO ~

MADAME JOO'S GAZE SLITHERED FROM GIZI AND ANCI, WHO stood wide-eyed and frozen, to Ilona. The skin around her mouth wrinkled as she pursed her thin lips. Her eyes traveled up and down Ilona's body, gleaming bright with interest. She stepped forward and held out her hand.

"And who have we here?" she cooed. "I don't think we've been introduced. I'm Madame Joo, the headmistress of Cachtice School."

Is she insane? Ilona backed into the wall, repulsed by the fake kindness in the woman's voice. Behind Madame Joo, Anci mutely shook her head, mouthing something. Ilona glanced down herself. Instead of her damp, brown soldier's garb, a wide, layered silk dress bobbed over her legs. The tips of two delicate boots made out of soft Florentine atlas peeked out underneath the dress's wide rim.

It worked. Wet or not, the glamour did its job.

Quickly, Ilona thrust out her hand to shake Madame Joo's. To her surprise, her fingers were long and slender, and decked out in golden rings and jeweled bracelets, sparkling in the torchlight. White ruffles drifted over her elbow.

"I'm Anna Fodor," Ilona said, grasping at a common

name. "Of the Budapest Fodors." Even her voice had changed. It rang out as melodious as harp music.

"How charming." Madame Joo curtsied, lifting her severe black dress to show her thick ankles. "Countess Bathory will be delighted to meet you."

Ilona smiled, hoping she looked beautiful and innocent. A laced fan hung from her left wrist where her shield had been, and she fluttered it fashionably in front of her face, as she had seen the girls at Falston do. Ilona had no idea how long the charm would last and thought it best to act immediately.

"Would you introduce me to her? I have a few questions about my classes I would like to ask her in private."

Madame Joo grinned wider, eyes sparkling.

"Of course, my dear," she clucked in her poisonous sugary voice. "I'm sure she has a few minutes to spare for the likes of *you*."

I see. Ilona's heart beat faster. *I'm to be another little appetizer for the countess's blood feast. Like Jeanette.*

Madame Joo took Ilona's arm. Over her shoulder, she said, "As for you two lazy bones, back to the kitchen. The pots won't scrub themselves."

At the end of the corridor, a gilded mirror spanned the length of the wall. Passing it, Ilona glanced at her reflection. And gasped. The girl in the mirror gasping back at her could have been a princess at any court in Europe. The low-cut silk dress in shades of cream and lilac was layered over the confines of a wide crinoline and showed off an ample cleavage. Long, golden hair lay in curls on both sides of her head and twisted into a fancy bun at the nape of her milky white neck. Her troll helmet had turned into an intricate diamond tiara. Her large, dark-lashed eyes, matching the lilac of her dress, held a look of sweet longing, and her rose lips pouted daintily.

Oh my Lord, I'm gorgeous. Ilona stared at her reflection. When Madame Joo gave her a curious look, she quickly tucked an imaginary hair back in place with an embarrassed smile.

Madame Joo motioned Ilona into the banquet hall, where the guests still slouched in their seats like broken dolls. Ilona gracefully glided over the parquet floors, surprised that the glamour apparently not only changed her appearance, but worked wonders on her physical awkwardness as well.

I bet I could even dance a waltz without stumbling. Her thoughts raced to Varco. *If he could see me now.* But she wasn't sure he'd care to see her in a fancy dress. For all she knew, he had no interest in dancing. Besides, he would never even recognize her.

They reached Countess Bathory's table, where the countess twirled a silver goblet between her long fingers. When Madame Joo introduced Ilona as Anna Fodor, the countess's eyes turned dark. Her gaze fastened on Ilona's bare throat, and the tip of her tongue wetted her lips.

"Anna would like to speak to you in private, my lady," Madame Joo said with a wink. "Will you take her up to the emerald parlor?"

The countess rose from her seat and nodded.

"What a perfect idea, Madame Joo."

The emerald parlor. Ilona would never forget her sense of futility as she had pounded the door to the purple dressing room, while Katalin had screamed inside. Ilona's heart hammered faster. *She means to sink her teeth into my neck and drain my blood.* But that could be the ideal chance to reach for the pendant with the blue rathstone.

Ilona followed the countess up the stairs and along the damp and drafty corridor. Goosebumps erupted on her bare arms. Without her sword and shield, Ilona felt naked and vulnerable.

Countess Bathory ushered Ilona into the parlor and gestured to a plush sofa.

Reluctantly, Ilona sank into the cushions. Her hand automatically checked for the nonexistent sword by her side. The glamour had turned it into a wide silk bow.

The countess lit the candles on the walls and on the low table. Then she lifted a pot-bellied decanter from the sideboard and poured herself a glass of dark green liquid. She sniffed it and took a sip.

"Anna Fodor," she said slowly, facing Ilona. "Any relation to Elizabeth Fodor?"

"I don't think so, my lady." Ilona clenched and unclenched her sweaty hands. She hadn't expected to be required to hold up a conversation.

"And how is the weather in Budapest?"

"It's fine." Ilona decided to say as little as possible, even if that made her look taciturn and sullen.

Countess Bathory walked to the crackling fire in the stone hearth. Above the mantle hung a sword for display. Scarlet rubies sparkled in the hilt like scattered drops of blood. The serrated blade was as long as an arm and looked as though sculpted out of white marble. The countess ran a finger along the hilt and sighed.

"Magnificent, isn't it?"

Ilona remained quiet, unsure what a ladylike answer would be.

"It was my late husband's, you know." The countess strode toward Ilona. "Ferencz Nadasdy. He was the chief commander of the Hungarian troops in the war against the Turks. A very brave man. They called him The Black Knight of Hungary."

Countess Bathory sat on the sofa next to Ilona.

Ilona cleared her throat. "I am sorry for your loss, my lady," she said as meekly as possible, eyes cast down on her own flawless fingers.

"Are you? How kind." The countess's white hand stroked Ilona's arm. The touch repulsed Ilona. It took an enormous effort to keep still and not flinch away. "Your skin is so soft." The countess leaned closer and closer, making Ilona feel caged in. "What is your secret?"

"I stay out of the sun?" Ilona fought for control over her squeaking voice.

Countess Bathory guffawed. "Out of the sun! I dare say."

Ilona didn't understand what the joke was, but it didn't matter. She might never get this close to the necklace again. *Take it now.* With a deep breath, Ilona lifted her hand, eyes fastened on the blue stone.

"I suppose sleeping all day and fighting by night will give any skin a pale glow, *Ilona*." The countess's red lips pursed mockingly and her eyes narrowed.

Ilona froze, hand in mid-air.

"You think your pathetic glamour is enough to fool me, Countess Bathory of Castle Cachtice?" Her black eyebrows arched.

Ilona glanced down at herself. She still saw only a slender maiden in an evening gown.

Countess Bathory laughed. "I see your dress as well, and

256

all your splendid finery. But it's too thin a veil. Underneath, you're still ungainly, awkward Ilona, my boy-girl soldier. What are you trying to gain by this masquerade, I wonder? And who gave you the glamour?"

The soup, Ilona thought. *It must have weakened the glamour.* She cleared her throat, trying to grasp at any feeble explanation the countess might believe. Nothing came to mind. With a cry, she lunged forward, aiming for the sparkling pendant.

Countess Bathory caught her wrist in an iron grip.

"Not so fast," she hissed. Her eyes slitted and the dark pupil narrowed vertically, like a cat's. "You betrayed my trust. Now you must pay for it."

Ilona struggled to wrench free, but the countess pulled her ever closer until her hot breath enveloped Ilona like a cloud of poison gas.

"You think you can escape me? Where is your sword now, little girl?" The countess's arms snaked around Ilona's waist, and her intent eyes nailed Ilona in place. She parted her dark red lips in a wide grin. Her eyeteeth elongated and became sharp thorns.

Ilona's vision swirled, then darkened. Her limbs locked in position, arms dangling uselessly by her sides. Her breathing slowed. *I can't move. What kind of magic has she used on me?*

The countess tittered, hugging Ilona to her bosom. With open lips, she licked Ilona's cheek.

Ilona was too paralyzed to even gag. If she couldn't shake off the countess's enchantment, she would certainly die.

Don't look at her. Ilona couldn't close her eyes, but she closed her mind. She thought of Varco, of running together over the autumn-colored fields. Of practicing their sword play. Of him saying good-bye, handing her a small parcel. *My dagger.* She had slipped it into her boot. Her hand was only inches away. If she could only move. She stared into the dark ponds of the countess's eyes that sucked her into a sinister vortex.

Countess Bathory chuckled. "You're not very pretty, and I doubt your blood will be of much use to me." Her voice was as thick and smooth as velvet. "But maybe the glamour will sweeten it a little." With a hiss, her lower jaw dropped. Thorny fangs gleamed below the scarlet lips. A drop of saliva fell onto Ilona's neck. It stung like acid.

A bang on the door made the countess jerk up. A screech rang out, like a small animal in pain, followed by the sound of wood scraping over stone. The door opened and Vencel's little shape appeared.

"Meow."

Looking at Vencel, Ilona realized that the countess's attention must have slipped and her spell had weakened. She rolled out of the countess's arms and dropped to the floor. The countess reached for her, but Ilona scrambled away. Her limbs wobbled as though her muscles had become liquefied.

Vencel raced across the room and jumped into the countess's face. He scratched frantically, his claws digging into her eyes. "Run!" he yelled. "You can't fight her. Run before she enchants you again."

The countess howled. Arms flailing, she knocked a fist into Vencel's head. He fell with a yowl.

Ilona glanced at the door, then back at Vencel. He lay on his side on the Turkish rug, unmoving. Was he dead?

The countess pressed a handkerchief to her right eye. Black circles spread on the white lace.

Ilona darted toward Vencel, scooped him up and ran out of the room. Hurrying down the stairs, she noticed that her dress was fading fast, turning back into trousers. The fan dangling from her wrist kept changing shape, morphing from glimmering shield to lacy fan and back, as though unsure of its true shape. The visor of her troll helmet clanked with every step.

Vencel opened his eyes and moaned. He struggled out of her grasp, jumped to the ground, and tumbled down the remainder of steps. Ilona rushed after him.

"Are you all right? She gave you a wicked blow."

"I think I am." Vencel lifted a furry paw to his head. His eyes still had a glazed look, but he seemed otherwise unharmed.

Ilona rubbed between his ears. "If you hadn't come, I think she would have killed me."

"You're welcome," Vencel pressed himself against her knee. "I saw you leaving the hall with her, and I could see right through your glamour. I thought you might be in trouble. What happened?"

"It got wet." Ilona sighed. How would she ever find another chance to take the rathstone? Now that the countess was suspicious of her, she'd probably throw her into Madame Joo's torture chamber.

No. A bitter ring tightened around Ilona's heart. *I have to leave the rath tonight with the rathstone. And I'll take those poor girls with me. I promised.*

Ilona touched her hip. The silk bow had turned back into her sword. The glamour was gone. Reluctantly, she glanced up the stairs. She was trained to be a soldier. She had a shield and a sword. Why did she feel so small and tired?

She lifted Vencel into an awkward embrace and looked into his deep green eyes.

"Vencel, I have to go back upstairs and fight the countess. And I have to find my friend Jeanette. She must be in one of the countess's chambers." Ilona's breath hitched painfully. She really didn't know where Jeanette was. Perhaps the countess had killed and disposed of her already.

"I'll come with you. I'll help you find your friend." Vencel leaped up the stairs, two or three steps at a time. Hand on her sword's hilt, Ilona followed.

They crept quietly along the corridor. Ilona searched each room while Vencel stood guard on the threshold. In the third parlor, Ilona's heart accelerated. A limp shape lay on a plush chaise lounge, arms spilling to the ground.

"Jeanette." She rushed to her friend's side. Her lacy nightgown was ripped from the neck to her navel, and her white throat bore the twin marks of the Unhallowed. Her breath came in little shallow puffs, and her skin was pale and damp.

"Vencel, I found her," Ilona whispered. She gently stroked Jeanette's soft cheek. "She's still alive!"

Jeanette's eyelids fluttered and opened. She focused on Ilona and her mouth formed a round O. Ilona plucked an elderberry from her pocket and stuffed it in Jeanette's mouth, hoping it would work fast.

"Ilona?" Her voice was a raven's croak. "How . . . ?" She clutched at her wounded neck. "Oh, I'm so thirsty."

"Don't speak now." With one hand under her back and one around her neck, Ilona lifted Jeanette into her arms. "I'm taking you home."

"Shh. Hide!" Vencel jumped from the threshold and slid under the settee.

The countess's tall outline appeared in the doorway. Her right eye was bloodshot and her hair hung in tangles around her furious face. From the folds of her shimmering gown the countess drew a sword, white as marble.

"I thought you had the brains to leave while you could, child." The countess smirked. "But since you're still here, I might as well kill you."

TWENTY-THREE

*I*LONA SWIFTLY SLID JEANETTE BACK ONTO THE CHAISE lounge and pulled her sword out of its sheath. The silver blade's magic threw blue dancing shadows against the damp paneling.

Ilona swung the shield dangling from her wrist into her left hand, wondering how much use it would be. A little shake of her head made the bone visor of her troll helmet slide over her face.

"Don't come any closer," she growled.

Countess Bathory only smiled and shook her tousled dark mane back over her shoulder. A cold glow emanated from her beautiful face. She lifted her marble sword—her husband's sword. A pure white mist blurred its sharp features as the countess slowly sliced the air in a wide arc. "Beautiful, isn't it?"

Yes, but do you know how to use it? Ilona regarded the sword with caution. Instead of glowing like the trolls' and soldiers' bespelled swords, it seemed to inhale the air around it, smudging the colors and spitting them back out as tiny rainbows radiating from its jagged tip.

"It's a fine sword," Ilona said. "Do you miss your husband?"

The countess's eyes became like stones, ungiving. They looked into the middle distance. "Every day."

"Then perhaps you'll be happy to join him tonight." Ilona raised her sword, tightened her hand on the handle of her silver shield. Her blade clanked against the notched white sword. Even though Ilona had put all her muscle into the blow, the countess didn't flinch. She stared at Ilona, a mocking smile spreading over her face. Then, with a slight flick of her wrist, her sword struck Ilona's.

Jeanette screamed, and Vencel hissed under the sofa.

Searing pain shot from the tips of Ilona's fingers to her shoulder. She bit her tongue, stifled an outcry. Her shoulder joint ached as though pulled out of its socket. The ghastly pain drove hot tears into her eyes. She quickly blinked them away. The countess's blade rasped over the back of Ilona's hand. Blood spilled out of the wound and over Ilona's pants. The cut burned like fire. Then the countess struck Ilona's shield, denting it in the center. The shield vibrated at a low, inhuman frequency that wormed its way into Ilona's mind, confusing and unsettling her.

She's stronger than me. Her special powers . . . I can't parry her blows much longer. Dodging the next advance, Ilona lunged forward, striking the countess's wrist. The marble sword dropped from her long fingers and hit the ground with a reverberating thud.

Countess Bathory spread her arms wide and lifted her chin. Her cherry-red lips parted and she muttered words in an ancient dialect Ilona couldn't quite translate. Something about imprisoned souls and blood's dark power.

Now. With a battle yell, Ilona thrust her sword at the

countess's evil heart of stone. It stuck into an invisible shield only inches from the countess's vulnerable ribcage. When Ilona tried to pull it back, it wouldn't budge.

The countess's whispers grew louder and her eyes darkened until both eyeballs had coated over with a silvery black film. Her upraised palms cradled sparkling, sizzling spheres of pure white light. As she spoke, these globes rose and floated in the air above her hands. Countess Bathory lifted her palms and turned them toward Ilona, a menacing snarl etched on her face. The balls of light hit the shield around her and exploded it into a wall of fire.

Ilona's sword burst into flame and she let go of the searing hot hilt. The sword melted as quickly as though it had been fashioned out of candle wax. It dripped onto the wooden floor where it collected into a silvery puddle next to the countess's heavy, jagged marble sword.

Ilona flung her shield aside and darted at the countess's sword with both hands. It took all her strength just to lift it off the ground. The carved marble hilt fit smoothly between her palms. Ilona slashed at the countess's delicate wrist.

The blade sliced through the bone as though it was soft tissue. Yet the countess's wrist remained whole, without any visible injuries.

Deep and contemptuous laughter rang out, echoing from the walls as though a dozen countesses were mocking Ilona.

"Did you really think you could kill me with my own sword?" Countess Bathory showed her growing, glinting eyeteeth. "The sword you are holding embodies the precious relationship I had with my husband. Dead or not, his love protects me still. You can pierce my heart with that sword and I won't feel any pain."

The countess spread her arms again, pushing her heaving bosom toward Ilona, offering herself with a sly smile.

Ilona wavered. Cold sweat glazed the hilt, making it slippery to hold. She glanced behind her. Jeanette had dropped to the floor. Cowering, she hugged her knees and keened softly to herself.

Ilona's gaze flickered back to the countess, tall and imperious in her overbearing brocade dress with the huge frills around her neck and wrists. With a glittering diadem in her hair, and those long, dangling sapphire earrings. And her wedding pendant, sparkling on her proffered chest, featuring the rathstone, liquid blue like the ocean. It beckoned Ilona, winking at her as the light refracted off it in the dancing torchlight.

I'm so close, but this is the wrong weapon.

"All right. I surrender." Ilona slowly bent down and placed the sword onto the ground. Then her hand flew to her boot, reached for her iron dagger. She lunged forward, aiming it at the countess's chest. The countess's smile still mocked her, asking her to *try—try to kill me, foolish girl.* Just before the blade pierced the dress, Ilona flicked the tip sideways, slid it under the silver chain of the necklace and yanked. With a soft snap, the clasp broke and the pendant slithered down the dagger's blade toward Ilona. She flicked her wrist and slid the necklace into her left hand.

Her fist closed around the rathstone.

Countess Bathory's smile faded. Her hands flew to her chest, to her throat, patting the dress frantically for the lost gem.

"My wedding necklace," she groaned. "Give it back."

Jaw dropping, Ilona stared at the countess's outstretched

hand. Wrinkles threaded across the smooth skin. Age spots appeared. Darkened. Blood-red fingernails thickened and curved into claws.

Ilona skittered backward until she hit the sofa, unable to tear her gaze away. Jeanette clutched at her and buried her face in Ilona's pantleg. Vencel stuck his head out from under the couch and meowed.

The countess's face changed rapidly. Lines dug trenches around her eyes and mouth. The soft flesh fell in and the paper-dry skin clung to the high cheekbones underneath. Her neck sagged and creased, her raven hair became white and as brittle as straw. Her eyes turned a demonic golden color and the pupils expanded into vertical lines.

Kill her now. Ilona's hand tightened on her dagger as she sprang forward. She plunged the dagger into the countess's heart, then pushed it in deeper, twisting. Smoke rose where iron met flesh. The stench of burning skin stung Ilona's nostrils. Black blood seeped around the hilt and drenched the brocade dress.

The countess cried out and staggered backward. Only one step, then her legs gave way beneath her. With the hiss of air escaping, the countess fell. When her head crashed to the ground, her white hair fell out and the skin of her face tightened over her skull, cracking and charring. Eyes bubbled out of their sockets, leaving dark holes. Thrashing, her body shrank until it lay curled like an old, withered root. Her clothes crumpled and turned into powdery ashes. Tarry blood poured out of her chest and gathered into a black pool on the wooden floor.

Cautiously, Ilona stepped closer. She nudged the shriveled carcass with the tip of her boot. Tar stuck to it and, with a grimace, she wiped it on a nearby rug. The white-hot iron dagger still stuck firm, surrounded by a cloud of steam.

"Aaaah!" Vencel's outcry made Ilona swivel around. He stood on his hind legs, front paws waving in the air. He began to glow and glitter, as though touched by bright sunshine.

His fur bristled and he swayed like a reed in the breeze. His slim frame began to fill out, became barrel-shaped and chubby, with knobby legs and a short torso. His facial hair turned from black to green, and a long beard grew from his chin to his thick waist. Instead of fur, leaves and twigs grew from his head, and his face was lined with such deep wrinkles, it appeared to be carved from wood.

He shook his little fists in victory, glancing up and down his body. "Thank you, Ilona! Killing the countess removed her hold over me. Finally I look like a proper wood sprite again." Even his voice had changed and deepened into an old man's growl.

Ilona had thought she'd be glad to have the cat that had always gotten underfoot disappear, but it was strange to see Vencel so changed. *I guess I got attached to him after all,* she thought, with a jolt of surprise.

"Don't praise me yet," she said. "We still have to gather all the other girls and sneak them past the soldiers outside."

Vencel shuffled toward the door. "That shall be easy for you. Don't forget, you're still commander."

"I don't even have a weapon." Ilona groaned. "The countess melted mine. How can I be commander without a weapon?"

She turned to Jeanette. The girl still squatted on the ground, making the sign of the cross again and again. Ilona laid a hand on her shoulder.

"It's over, Jeanette. Come on, get up." She helped Jeanette to her feet. It would be slow going to get her out.

Jeanette stopped crying and gave Ilona a look of amazement and wonder out of tired, dark-rimmed eyes.

Vencel leaned over the countess's carcass, sniffing and scowling. "Well done. Where's the rathstone?"

"Safe in my pocket." Ilona patted her pants with a small smile.

An electrifying buzz zoomed in from the corridor and entered the parlor. Ilona held out her hand as the pixie flew closer. Jeanette ducked with a little squeal.

Vanillina spiraled around the smoldering heap of ashes and bones—all that was left of the countess—and squealed. "What have you done?"

"I've killed her. Now you are free."

"I am?" The little fairy landed on Ilona's hand on her tiptoes, twirled around twice and then sat down, her fall-leaf skirts bunched up beneath her. She puckered her rosy lips into a pout. "And what about Madame Joo? She asked me to find you. After all, weren't you supposed to be in charge in the banquet hall tonight?"

Ilona and Vencel exchanged a look. His green wood sprite eyes showed dismay.

"You'd better go with her before Madame Joo comes looking for you," he said. "I can take your friend to the kitchen and hide her for now."

Heart hammering in her chest, Ilona followed Vanillina to the banquet hall.

TWENTY-FOUR

WITH A DEEP BREATH, ILONA PUSHED THE DOOR TO THE banquet hall open. The pixie fluttered in ahead of her and twirled out of sight. A small cry escaped Ilona when she saw the young ladies and their chaperones. They had been roped to their chairs. Their limbs dangled and their heads lolled onto their chests.

Ilona's troop of soldiers had abandoned their posts. Some of them had begun transforming into their animal shapes, becoming grotesque half-creatures with human legs and the sharp facial features of predators. Madame Joo threaded her way through the crowd with a grim smile.

Vanillina sat on Madame Joo's shoulder, whispering into her ear. A chill of foreboding shivered over Ilona's skin. Vanillina hadn't changed at the Countess's defeat like Vencel had. Beware of too much beauty . . . *But she said pixies weren't allies of the Unhallowed.*

"Ilona!" Madame Joo narrowed her beady eyes. "Where have you been? And where's Countess Bathory?"

"I really don't know where she went," Ilona managed with a vague gesture. "Perhaps you should go look for her?"

Vanillina tugged on Madame Joo's earlobe and whispered again. Ilona frowned. What did that fairy whisper?

And why doesn't she fly away now that the Countess is defeated?

Shivering in the drafty hall, Ilona glanced around. She had long known that the castle wasn't as luxurious as the countess made the villagers believe, but now that the countess was gone, the last glamour had fallen away from Castle Cachtice. For the first time, Ilona realized just how decrepit and decaying the castle was. The walls were cracked and crumbling, moss and cobwebs covered every corner, and the ground was filthy.

Madame Joo waved to a group of soldiers huddled in a corner. Two of them had turned into six-foot grizzly bears with deep-set eyes and saliva dripping from their open maws; another was a gigantic black rat. The other three had kept mostly to their human shapes. At Madame Joo's beckoning, they hurried closer.

Madame Joo gave Ilona a long look. "The trolls guarding the maidens' chambers have been killed. I'm stripping you of your command." She nodded at the soldiers. "Put her in shackles."

Ilona opened her mouth to protest, but the six soldiers in front of her raised their swords, and she had no weapon of her own.

"*Commander,* you're outnumbered," the Rat sneered. Then they fell on her, two holding her down by her shoulders, two securing her legs, while the last two wrestled her wrists into the familiar silver shackles.

Ilona groaned and tried to break free. The Rat pulled her up, and the Bears hooked their hairy arms under Ilona's elbows to keep her from running.

"Stop making such a fuss." Madame Joo gave her a look of disapproval. "You cannot get away. Don't you understand?"

Farkas appeared at Madame Joo's shoulder. He bowed to her in a disgustingly subservient manner.

"Do you need any help with this troublesome *girl?*" Pronouncing the last word with a sneer, he glared Ilona's way. Long teeth protruded past his lips and his ears had furry tufts.

His greedy, leering look gave Ilona an uncomfortable feeling deep in her guts. Still, she managed to stare him down.

"Aren't you supposed to guard the gate?"

He chuckled. "Your time to give orders has passed. Madame Joo thinks I'm much more valuable here."

"That's right, Farkas," Madame Joo said. "Accompany us to my chambers and make sure she doesn't escape."

The Bears' hold on her arms tightened as they pulled her along. Farkas poked the tip of his sword into her back, making it dangerous for her to struggle against her bindings. Madame Joo in the lead, they marched her out of the doors at the far end of the banquet hall and toward the tower.

Toward the torture chamber.

I cannot panic, Ilona thought. *I need to keep a clear head to get out of this.* But her palms became clammy with sweat and her heart pounded at a hummingbird's pace against her ribs when she remembered the horrible spiked chair and the crow trained to peck out eyes.

The walk up the spiral staircase was much too short. When the heavy wooden door fell shut behind them, bile rose in Ilona's throat. The Bears shoved her forward and she stumbled straight into Madame Joo's arms.

Madame Joo pointed at a pair of cuffs dangling from the ceiling. "Transfer her to those shackles, Bears."

The Bears dragged Ilona to the indicated spot and

yanked her arms up, while Farkas ran the tip of his sword lazily up and down her torso. One wrong movement on Ilona's part, and he'd impale her. Her breathing became quick and shallow. She tried to keep her focus, weigh her possibilities. But there was nothing she could do. Tears of rage and desperation blurred her vision.

"Look at our lieutenant's pet now." Farkas grinned. "A fat trout caught on a hook. Struggling and gasping for air, where there's none to be had."

Ilona sucked in her cheeks and spat into Farkas's smug, ugly face.

He growled and pushed his sword blade into the soft flesh of her throat. With the back of his other hand, he wiped the spittle off. His eyes flashed dangerously.

Madame Joo pulled on his arm. "Enough. I want to keep her alive for a bit longer. You are not going to ruin my fun by killing her now."

With a sneer, Farkas sheathed his sword. "Yes, ma'am. As you wish."

Madame Joo turned to the tool bench holding her instruments. She ran a gentle hand over one of them, then lifted another to the candlelight, humming softly to herself. When she returned to the group, she held the pincers she had shown Ilona during her last time in the torture chamber. She flicked them open and snapped them shut.

She gave the soldiers a surprised look. "Are you still here? Are you waiting for the show to start?"

Farkas's eyes held a sick gleam. "I wouldn't mind . . ."

Madame Joo's eyebrows furrowed. "I don't think so. You're dismissed. All of you."

With a shooing motion, Madame Joo escorted the soldiers to the door and shut it with a bang behind them.

The crow cawed once, loud and shrill.

Ilona instinctively closed her eyes. *I don't want to be a crow treat.*

Madame Joo went to the hearth, where a merry fire crackled. She held the pincer by its long handles and heated the sharp tips. She was humming again.

Sweat ran down the side of Ilona's face, even though the room wasn't all that warm, despite the fire. She slid her hands around in the shackles, trying to slip free. It was no use.

Oh Lord, I'm going to die here, she thought. *And it's not going to be a quick, easy death, either.* Her stomach rolled and her legs buckled under her. Her body weight pulled on her wrists and ripped on her shoulder joints. The pain returned her senses, and she stood, unsteadily.

Madame Joo approached. She held the red, glowing pincers with a smile. "Your deceit has severely disappointed me. You will now pay for that. Do you remember what I told you about a girl's most sensitive parts?"

Ilona couldn't nod; she just stared at the ominous pincers. Of course she remembered. But how she wished she didn't.

Madame Joo reached forward, undid the first button of Ilona's cotton shirt. A knock on the door stopped her. "What?" She groaned. "Who has the audacity to bother me in the middle of—"

"It's me, Anci," a muffled voice came through the door.

Ilona's head jerked toward it. *Anci.*

"Well, what do you want? I'm busy." Madame Joo rolled her eyes, then put the pincers down and went to the door. When she opened it a crack to peek out, it flew open, and Zador burst through. Anci followed at his heels. She held a heavy frying pan in visibly shaking hands.

Zador shoved Madame Joo into the wall by the fireplace. He pulled his sword and nodded at Anci. "Free her. Hurry."

Anci ran to Ilona, her gaze fluttering over Ilona's body. "Are you all right?" She stood on tiptoe to reach the shackles, clicked the release and freed Ilona's wrist. Then she did the same on the other side.

Ilona rubbed her aching wrists. At least the cut on her hand had stopped bleeding. Her throat was tight with relief and gratitude to have such a brave friend. "You came just in time."

"Varco sent us," Anci whispered.

Varco. Ilona blinked, then shook her head. "No. Varco's gone. He left with the Captain."

Anci gave her a sideways smile. "Then it must be his twin fighting the soldiers in the banquet hall."

Ilona's heart made a strange lurch. *He came back.*

Zador grinned at the girls. "I think he wanted one last kiss good-bye."

Using his momentary inattention, Madame Joo reached behind her and gripped the fire poker. Ilona opened her mouth to yell a warning, but Madame Joo was faster. She rammed the poker into Zador's arm.

He howled and stumbled backward. He dropped his sword and clawed at the poker with hands that had changed into their wolfish shape. Smoke rose from the puncture wound, accompanied by a sizzling sound and the smell of burning skin.

"It's iron." Ilona leaped forward and pulled the tool out of Zador's arm. He doubled over in pain, cradling his injured limb.

Anci ran at Madame Joo, her frying pan lifted high over

her head. "Aa-a-a-a-a-ah-iyah!" she yelled, bringing the pan down hard on Madame Joo's head. The old woman sank to the ground with a soft moan.

"Good job," Ilona said. "Give me your apron."

Anci hurriedly untied her apron strings. Worry flashed in her eyes. "How bad is it?"

Ilona regarded the wound, which oozed a creamy black liquid. "He'll be fine. It's just his arm."

"My sword arm." Zador winced as she tied the apron around the gash. "Never mind, I can fight with my left if I have to."

Anci eyed the door. "We should go. Varco might need us in the banquet hall."

"You're right." Zador straightened up. "Let's hurry."

Ilona found a coil of rope and Anci helped her tie up the unmoving Madame Joo. She brought the fireplace poker that had wounded Zador—who knew if she might need to use the iron on an Unhallowed?

We should kill her, Ilona thought. But after killing the countess, the very idea nauseated Ilona.

Then they sprinted down the corridors. They stopped in front of the closed doors to the banquet hall.

"Here." Zador reached back and pulled his bow off his shoulder. Then he handed her his quiver filled with arrows.

Ilona frowned. It wasn't the same as getting right into the fight, but Zador's instincts were right—if she could pick off a few enemies from across the room, she'd have fewer who could close in on her.

Inside the hall, an uneven battle was in progress. At the far end of the room, Varco defended himself against a group of Ilona's security guards. She recognized Gyala fighting by his side. They usually made a good team, but now they were hopelessly outnumbered.

Ilona counted four soldiers already wounded—or dead?—lying in bleeding heaps on the cool parquet. At the other end of the room, Dorika, Gizi, and Evike, armed with paring knives and other rather ineffective utensils, were fighting a man-sized Bat holding a five-foot sword. Anci hurried past Ilona to join them, and Zador sprinted toward Varco, swerving around fallen chairs and leaping over broken dishes.

Ilona ran to the nearest dinner table and climbed up between two middle-aged gentlemen with glazed eyes and dripping noses. Dropping the iron poker where she could reach it if she needed it, she pushed dirty plates aside with her foot and assumed her shooting stance. Pain paralyzed her fingers for an instant as she pulled back the string. Blood seeped out of the gash on her hand and trickled over her wrist. She sucked in a shaky breath and took careful aim at the soldiers around Varco. In practice she had shot bull's-eyes from farther away, but never at moving targets or into a fighting, squirming group. Varco slid in and out of her aim.

It's impossible. I might hit Varco by accident. She lowered her bow and chewed on her lip.

Then Varco glanced her way. He grinned and winked. Then he slammed his sword against his enemy's.

He's counting on me. He trusts me to help him.

Ilona slowly raised her bow once more. Varco was crossing blades with a soldier who had transformed into a creature with the top half of a man and the lower half of a rat, complete with a thick, undulating tail.

Ilona pulled back, took aim, released the string. The arrow hit the Rat in the chest. He fell with a thud.

The heads of the other soldiers snapped toward her. Their eyes widened. With a lightning-quick thrust, Varco impaled a gaping soldier.

One of the men pointed at Ilona. "Get her!"

The group split in half. Two men and a troll dashed toward her, while three others kept attacking Varco and his friends—Farkas first and foremost among them.

Ilona's heart beat faster. She lifted her bow again and aimed at the fat troll racing toward her table. With a sharp *zip*, her arrow struck his throat. *Zip, zip,* and two more soldiers crashed to the parquet with arrows in their chests.

Ilona exhaled and relaxed her shoulders. *Safe for another moment.* Her gaze slipped from Varco, who seemed to be holding his own, to the maids in the corner. The Bat had his claws on Gizi, yanking at her braids.

Ilona pulled another arrow from her quiver and aimed for the bat's big head. Her first arrow hit the wall behind the creature. He let go of Gizi and spun toward Ilona, glaring at her with large, blood-shot eyes.

Ilona notched the next arrow—her second to last.

It shot through the hall and struck the Bat's left eye. He shrieked, but kept running toward her. Then he suddenly fell and skidded drunkenly across the floor. A long meat cleaver protruded from his spine. Across the room, Evike raised her hand in a gesture of victory.

A shudder ran through the huge Bat and the wings crumbled back into arms, the head reverted to a dark-haired human one, and the legs followed suit last.

The clanking of swords snapped Ilona's attention back to Varco and his men. Gyala was thrusting his sword into his opponent, who went down with a grunt. But Zador and Varco had both lost their swords. A gasp escaped

Ilona as she watched Farkas's blade pierce Zador's chest. Then Farkas grinned wolfishly and raised his sword against Varco.

Without thinking, Ilona grabbed her last arrow. She cursed her shaking hands as she notched it. Her heart pounded so loudly that it seemed to be the only sound echoing through the great hall.

Stay calm. Concentrate.

She willed her hands to be steady, willed the arrow to fly true. It zipped across the room. Farkas's hands shot to his throat. His fingers clawed at the arrow. He stumbled backward, tottering like an old man. Gyala pushed him down, then struck him with his sword for good measure. Farkas's last remaining comrade dropped his weapon and raised his hands in defeat.

"Zador!" Anci broke away from the circle of maids and ran to Zador, who lay in a spreading puddle of his own blood. Varco crouched next to him, already ripping up his shirt for bandages.

Ilona jumped from the table. Dorika, Gizi, and Evike dropped their knives and ran toward her. Red blotches popped up on Gizi's cheeks as she held out her hand to Ilona.

"I'm so sorry I didn't trust you."

Ilona nodded and shook Gizi's proffered hand. She appreciated the maid's direct and honest apology. "It's all right."

Dorika and Evike hugged Ilona tightly, and she let herself relax into the embrace. Across the hall, Varco glanced up from bandaging Zador. His eyes met Ilona's. She smiled, her heart accelerating again. Had he really come back just for a kiss?

"Ilona!" Varco jumped to his feet. "Behind you!"

The girls fell away from her, their faces pale and their eyes large. Ilona spun on her heel. Madame Joo stood before her, holding a leather whip. Vanillina crouched on her shoulder. A wicked smile lit her tiny face.

"You made mistake after mistake, girl." Madame Joo's eyes narrowed and the corners of her mouth drew downward into a cruel sneer. She flicked her whip, and let its tip rasp over Ilona's cheeks.

Ilona leaned back. Her hand slid to her side, to the empty sheath. She had no weapon left.

"I want the rathstone—hand it over." The whip snapped across Ilona's throat. A welt flared with a stinging, blazing pain. Ilona's eyes watered.

"How do you know about the rathstone?" she gasped.

Vanillina giggled. "I overheard you say to Vencel that you put it in your pocket."

"Give it to me," Madame Joo repeated.

"Over my dead body." Ilona tried to grasp the end of the whip, but Madame Joo was faster. The whip parted the air with a whoosh, snapping on Ilona's face. Blood gushed from her forehead and ran down her cheek. Then the strong leather of the whip twisted around her legs, bringing Ilona to her knees. The pain was sudden and unexpected. *It's not a sword. How can it hurt so much?* Ilona raised her hands to ward off the blows, but they came in quick succession, unrelenting. And Madame Joo was humming again.

Ilona closed her eyes and ground her teeth.

When Madame Joo shrieked, Ilona peeked out from under her long bangs. Varco was grabbing the whip handle. He ripped it out of Madame Joo's hands. Then his hand closed around her throat, cutting her off mid-shriek.

Vanillina squealed and fluttered up from Madame Joo's shoulder. Varco threw the whip after her, and the pixie dropped out of the air like a dead fly.

His eyes turned amber and dangerous. His fingers turned into claws and on the back of his hand grew a tuft of black fuzz.

"Don't," Ilona whispered, rising to a crouch. "You promised—remember?"

Varco didn't seem to hear her. He snarled at Madame Joo, lips drawn back from an imposing set of fangs.

Madame Joo whimpered and coughed as the grip on her throat tightened.

Varco shoved her down. Her skull slammed into the stone ground. Varco fell on her, tilted his head back and howled. Then he ripped out her throat.

Madame Joo struggled. Horrible pig-like noises bubbled from her mouth.

"Stop!" Ilona grabbed Varco's shirt and pulled. He elbowed her stomach. Hard. She reeled back, doubling over. She averted her eyes, but her gaze returned to his crouching, brutal shape against her will. Acid bile filled her throat. Her eyes misted over. He had promised not to turn into a wolf in front of her.

Ilona crawled to Vanillina, sprawled a few yards away.

The fairy sat and rubbed her head with a groan.

Ilona scooped her up. "Why did you betray me? I thought you were one of the Hallowed!"

"Shows what you know, doesn't it?" Vanillina fluttered her wings, but Ilona caged her in with her fingers. "Let me go!"

"I don't think so." Ilona's gaze swept the dinner table for a suitable container for her minuscule prisoner. *A teapot.*

That will do. Vanillina squeaked as Ilona stuffed her into the pot.

Ilona glanced back at Varco. He still crouched over Madame Joo, tearing, biting, ripping bloody flesh. Her stomach churned, and she tasted bile.

I have to get out of here. Eyes cast down, Ilona hurried toward the maids, who stood in a frozen, staring huddle.

"Don't watch that," she ordered, throat tight. "I need you to do something for me."

"Yes," Anci said, looking relieved. "What can we do?"

"Untie the guests. Then . . ." Ilona faltered. The guests were still in deep enchantment, unable to walk on their own. "You'll have to gather elderberries for them. Feed one berry to each guest. It's an antidote to the countess's poison and will wake them up soon."

Anci nodded. "We'll do that."

"When the guests are alert, have Gyala lead them into the forest. I'll meet him there, once I collect the countess's maidens."

Anci's eyebrows knitted together. "Gyala? Don't you mean Varco?"

Both glanced over to Varco. He stood over the mutilated carcass of Madame Joo, dripping blood from his muzzle and claws. His amber eyes fastened on Ilona. She backed away a step, shaking her head.

"No," she said quietly. "No."

Vision blurring, Ilona ran out of the banquet hall.

TWENTY-FIVE

*I*LONA RACED THROUGH THE CASTLE TO THE KITCHEN. Tears nearly blinded her, and she kept stumbling into walls at each corner she turned. She tried hard to push the violent and bloody image of the wolfish Varco out of her mind. She was leaving this rath, leaving him behind, and she wanted to remember him in his human form, wanted to remember how he had looked at her when she shot a bull's-eye or managed to parry a particular strong blow with her sword—full of pride and admiration, of kindness and integrity. *That's the Varco I care about,* she thought. *And that creature in the hall—I don't even know who that is.*

In the kitchen, she met Vencel and Jeanette. They rushed toward her with open arms, relief evident in their faces.

"The battle is over. Madame Joo and her loyal soldiers are dead." Ilona didn't want to recount any details, especially not Varco's involvement, so she urged Vencel and Jeanette onward, to the maidens' chambers.

When they entered the guarding trolls' parlor, they found the maidens alert and lively, exchanging their horrid tales of the Unhallowed that had captured them.

Ilona's heart leaped when she spied Katalin. The life had returned to her expressive blue eyes, and a shy smile played around her lips. The countess's powers had evaporated here as well.

"Katalin!" Ilona pulled the younger girl into a tight embrace. "I'm so glad you're better!" She slowly released Katalin and examined her face, then her neck. The two puncture wounds had closed and were now little more than silvery marks. Ilona ran a finger over them, hardly able to feel the small bumps. "Are you ready to go home?"

Katalin nodded, a healthy blush spreading over her cheeks. Ilona turned to the crowd behind her. "All of you, it's time to leave this place."

Chatting in excitement, the girls followed Ilona to the castle's exit in the great hall. Ilona flung the doors wide and stepped outside. To her surprise, the first sliver of dawn smudged the horizon. She slowed as she crossed the yard. The quality of the air had changed in a subtle way. The cool autumn breeze seemed sweeter somehow, and the birds chirped from the trees, calling out in joy.

Her hand slipped into her pocket and closed over the necklace and the rathstone. The countess's power over this rath had ended.

The yard lay quiet in the light of early dawn. Dead soldiers lay in heaps here and there, two of them near the gates. *Varco must have killed them when he returned.* Ilona shuddered as she nudged the bodies aside with the tip of her boot and opened the gates.

She led the girls and Vencel down the path toward the forest. They stopped at the first cluster of poplars.

"Gyala will bring the other girls shortly," Ilona said. At Vencel's astonished look, she added. "Some of the soldiers have joined our side and helped fight Madame Joo. We'll stay right here so they can't miss us."

While they waited, Ilona told Vencel about Vanillina's betrayal and Madame Joo's demise. She handed the teapot with the fairy to Jeanette, who glowered at the lid.

"Good riddance," Vencel grumbled. "And we'll present the traitorous pixie to Edina and Prioska. They'll decide how to punish her."

Ilona glanced down the hill toward the castle. In the warm glow of dawn, a group of people walked through the gate and set out down the rocky slope.

"Here they come," she sighed. She addressed the crowd of girls. "Which of you are from the local villages?"

About a third of the girls lifted their hands, and Ilona separated them from the rest. Gyala could take these girls home, while the others had to travel through the portal with her.

"Are you sure the girls and their families will be safe here, now that the countess is dead?" Ilona asked Vencel. She would have liked to take all of the girls and their families home with her, but realized what a huge undertaking that would be.

"Don't you worry," Vencel said. "With Countess Bathory gone, Edina, Prioska and I will restore peace in this rath and protect the mortals from the Unhallowed. It will be very hard, in our weakened states. We're depending on you, though, to complete your mission and return the rathstone. If we can access Hallowmere again, this rath will be safe forevermore."

When the group crossing the spring meadow came closer, Ilona recognized Varco—in human shape—among them. Her heart jolted with a confusing mix of emotions: simmering anger over how he had broken his promise never to change shape in front of her again, joy over seeing him, frustration about having to say good-bye to him for a second time. Somehow it wasn't getting any easier.

The young ladies and their parents looked unharmed and much improved. However, they glanced about with shock and daze, as though they had awakened from a nightmare in an unfamiliar place. Which wasn't too far from the truth.

Varco and Gyala walked together in the rear. Ilona addressed Gyala, pointedly ignoring Varco.

"How is Zador?"

Gyala pulled on his gray beard. "He is young and strong. I believe he will pull through. Anci is attending to him."

Ilona put the girls who had been stolen from within the countess's rath under his protection and charged him to return them all safely to their respective homes. After swearing an oath to do his very best, Gyala shepherded his girls toward the path leading to the next village.

Then, with Vencel as their guide shuffling ahead on his short legs, the remaining girls and their chaperones set out to meet the Hallowed at the pond. Ilona took up the rear, walking next to Jeanette, who still carried the teapot with Vanillina inside. Varco followed quietly behind them for a while, but then reached forward and grabbed Ilona's arm.

"May I have a word with you?" His beetled eyebrows and low, growling voice turned the request into an order. Ilona glared back at him.

It's the last time you'll see him. Can't you at least make up? The advice of her conscience came in the voice of Miss Brown as clearly as if the teacher had spoken beside her.

"Fine." Ilona motioned at Jeanette to catch up to the other girls.

"What is it?" For all her good intentions, her tone

remained stubbornly hostile. "I thought you were going to join the Captain. What happened?"

"I'll meet up with him later." Varco shrugged. His long, dark hair dripped water onto his shirt.

He washed his hair and face. Ilona's gaze traveled to his hands. They were spotlessly clean. *He must have scrubbed hard to get all that blood off.*

"The Captain and I had traveled as far as the eastern meadows when I decided to head back to the castle." He peered into her face as though trying to read her emotions. "I wanted to be sure you made it home all right."

Ilona hid behind her long bangs, averted her eyes. "I would have been fine."

"Really? It looked to me like Madame Joo had you cornered." He tried to take her hand, but she pulled away. There was a hard edge to his voice. "You're not glad I returned."

I was glad, and then you had to ruin it. Ilona choked back her angry tears. "You broke your promise! Or did you forget already? It was so, so . . ." Her voice broke. She bit her lip and regained composure. "It was hideous."

"I saved your life! What did you want me to do? Let Madame Joo whip you to death?" Incredulity and frustration amplified his voice. He raked his hands through his hair.

"You could have used your sword," Ilona said.

Varco snorted. *"That* would have been better? If I had killed her with my sword? That would have made you happy?"

"Happier," Ilona grumbled. Suddenly she was tired of this argument. He was what he was. There was no point in spending their last minutes together fighting. She took his hand. It was warm, as always. Unhallowed warm.

One last chance to explain, to make him see it my way. She sighed.

"When you shape-shift, you become an instrument of the Prince. Using your fangs and claws to kill puts you on *their* level."

Varco gave her a shocked look, but didn't release her hand. "So you think I'm as dreadful as Madame Joo?"

"You helped the countess for a long time. And now you are going to help the Fey Prince with his army. I don't see how any of that is better than what the countess did to these girls."

Varco was quiet then, thinking it over. "I've become a monster."

"No. I still think you're better than that. You just need to leave this life behind." Ilona's throat threatened to close. What she proposed was outrageous.

"And let the Hallowed save my immortal soul?" Varco gave her a rueful smile. "Why would they?"

Ilona pulled up her shoulders. "They promised they would." Already she was sorry she had brought up the subject. She didn't want Varco to die. He was the only person who had ever seen her true self and liked her anyway. Or even liked her *because* of her strange, unique traits.

She swiped at her useless, blurry eyes.

Varco released her hand to pull her into a tight embrace. "Don't cry," he whispered.

"I'm not. A bug flew in my eye." Ilona fought for self-control with a few gulping, wheezing breaths.

Varco laughed softly. His lips grazed the top of her head. Ilona lifted her mouth for a long kiss. His warmth spread from her lips across her body in a deep, pulsing rhythm.

It's not too late, she thought, dizzy with longing. *We could run together. Away from the Captain and the Hallowed. We'll live in the forests, free and untroubled.* But deep in her heart she knew that Varco was right, that the Fey Prince would never leave them in peace.

Varco let go, his hands slowly slipping off. He wiped her long forelock out of her eyes and smiled at her. Yet his eyes remained serious. "We all do what we must, right?"

She nodded, unsure what he meant.

They walked in silence, hand in hand, through the forest and across the sunny meadows. The trip with a gaggle of tired girls unused to walking took almost twice the time it should have, and when they reached the pond, the sun was already high in a deep blue sky.

Vencel stood on the pebbled bank and called the Hallowed's names. His voice rang out across the soft waves.

Then the two swans appeared, gliding across the water as though pulled by invisible strings. They nodded in unison. When they reached the beach, they transformed into ladies once more, but now their skin was smoother and their silver hair had turned warm shades of brown. The girls shouted in delight and surprise. Some of them clapped.

Varco stepped back into the shadows of the trees.

Vencel jumped around Edina and Prioska, fists in the air. "She's done it! She's done it! Ilona took the rathstone from Countess Bathory!"

Edina said, "We noticed the change in power immediately, as you can see by our transformation. And Vencel—you look much improved!" The Hallowed smiled at Ilona. "I see you freed your friends. Well done."

Vencel hobbled over to Jeanette and took the teapot from her, shaking it with a grim smile. He passed the pot to Prioska. "We also caught a little traitor. A fairy, working for the countess."

Prioska sealed the pot with a wave of her hand. "We shall have to reflect on the right punishment for her. But that can wait. Perhaps until the day we may enter Hallowmere again." She handed the pot back to Vencel and turned to Ilona. "May I see the rathstone?"

Ilona pulled the necklace from her pocket and held it out to Prioska. "Will you be able to make a portal for me and my friends to return home?"

Prioska took the pendant. "Yes, we will. But we won't be able to sustain it for long, so please stay close together and hurry through."

At this, the girls and their chaperones huddled closer.

Edina and Prioska stood face to face. Their tall shapes shone in the bright sunlight and their white robes danced around their ankles. Edina held the rathstone between her palms and raised it toward Prioska, who folded her hands around Edina's. Together, they lifted their arms to form an arc. In a low voice, Edina began a chant, which Prioska echoed. Their voices combined and rose, ringing in Ilona's ears.

The paleness of their arms and shifts intensified into a bright glow, which burst into a rainbow of colors. Underneath the arc of their joined arms, the lake disappeared, and a hazy warm mist swirled into darkness. The two ladies released their grasp and stepped backward. The arc of rainbow light remained. Edina handed Ilona the rathstone.

"Thank you for helping the Hallowed," she said, laying a cool hand on Ilona's cheek. "Have a safe journey home."

Over Edina's shoulder, Ilona caught Varco's eye. She wasn't going to say good-bye to him again. She couldn't bear it. He smiled and nodded toward the portal. *We all do what we must.* Suddenly his meaning became clear. She had to take the rathstone back to Corrine and Father Joseph, as she had promised. She had to guide the girls back home.

"It's our portal." Ilona addressed the crowd in a horse voice. "Everybody step through the arc. One at a time," she cautioned, as the girls rushed closer. She stood next to the portal, making sure the girls and their chaperones walked through in an orderly fashion. Most of them hesitated for a moment, but moved on when Ilona motioned them to go forward. *They trust me with their lives,* she marveled. *I hope they are right.*

The Hallowed stood by a grove of poplars with folded hands and watched them go, one by one. Ilona noted that Varco had crouched next to Vencel and was whispering into his ear. She shifted on her feet, a new worry niggling at the back of her mind.

Jeanette hung back, her face pale and drawn. She waited until everybody else had passed into the mists beyond the portal.

Ilona waved her closer. "You're next. Come on."

Jeanette stepped up to the portal, but then shook her head. "No more magic, Ilona. I don't like it." Tears welled out of her eyes and ran down her cheeks.

"But we have to get home. There's no other way." Frustration seeped into her voice, making her tone abrasive. Ilona had gone through so much to rescue Jeanette, and now she made a fuss?

Jeanette sobbed harder. "I'm scared. Last time . . ."

Ilona blew out a long stream of air, trying to stay calm. "This is different. Don't you want to see Christina again? And Hannah and Abigail?" Speaking of her Falston friends made Ilona's heart ache to be with them again. After her parents had sent her away, her friends had become her home.

Jeanette wiped her tears away and eyed the portal with a dubious look.

"We'll go together," Ilona whispered. "Hand in hand."

Jeanette grasped Ilona's hand and smiled bravely. "All right, Ilona. We'll do it together."

Ilona turned to wave to Varco. *Just one more look at his face.*

He knelt in front of Edina and Prioska, his dark-haired head bowed before them. Edina gripped his sword in both hands. Her usually kind face was severe.

Ilona's heartbeat sped up, galloped in sudden panic. *She's going to fulfill her promise. She's going to kill him.*

Ilona twisted around, yanking on Jeanette's arm. "No! Varco! I changed my mind."

Edina frowned at her. Varco didn't lift his head, but the knuckles on his fists turned white.

Jeanette tugged on her hand and pointed ahead. The portal's arc wavered and flickered, losing its power. "Leave him. We have to hurry."

"I can't. I have to stop them—they're killing him." Ilona tried to shake Jeanette off, but her friend's grip only tightened.

"You promised," Jeanette shrilled. "We'll go through together."

Edina lifted the sword high above Varco's exposed neck. The image blurred in a salty cloud. Ilona pulled free.

Vencel, still unfamiliar in his knobby wood sprite shape, jumped into her path.

"Ilona," he snarled. "You must not interfere." When she tried to push past him, his gnarled fingers closed around her wrist.

"I can't let him do this, just for me. It's not right." She choked on the words. Her tears streamed down her cheeks. "I want him to live."

"It's his choice. He knows exactly what he's doing." Vencel gently turned her around, away from the scene before her. "Your mortal friends need you now. Your work here is done."

Still reluctant, Ilona took Jeanette's outstretched hand. Vencel was right. But it was impossibly hard to leave Varco to his dubious fate. Her lips quivered, sending small shockwaves down her tense body.

Vencel, coming only up to her chest, awkwardly pulled her into a light embrace. "Good-bye, girl. Commander. You did well."

"We have to go." Jeanette tugged at her hand. Ilona tried to cast a last glance back, but Jeanette pulled her forward, into the hazy mists under the portal's arch. Shadows enveloped them, swirled around them. Ilona was sucked into a tight vortex. As she let go, a cool breeze dried her tears.

The girls tumbled through darkness. Ilona's fingers slid into her pocket and tightened around the rathstone. It was warm. And as heavy as her heart. So small and yet so powerful.

I'm going home, she thought. *I hope the other girls were successful as well and the Unhallowed will never be able to take control of Hallowmere.*

But she feared that it might not be quite as easy as this, that another battle lay before her that would call on her fighting skills yet again. She bit down hard on her lip. *If that's so, then I shall be ready.* Whatever lay ahead, she would use the lessons Varco had taught her to the Council's advantage.

And perhaps somehow, somewhere, his immortal soul would be pleased.

AFTERWORD

Although Maiden of the Wolf is a work of fiction, and Ilona and her friends visit the fictional world of Fey raths in *Hallowmere*, the character of Countess Elizabeth Bathory (also sometimes referred to as Erzsebet Bathory, in keeping with the Hungarian form of her name) is based on a historical figure.

The real Erzsebet Bathory lived from 1560 to 1614 in Castle Cachtice in northern Hungary (present day Slovakia). She is considered one of the most notorious serial killers of all time, torturing and killing more than 600 young girls at her castle. This has earned her the nicknames "the Blood Countess" and "Countess Dracula."

If you want to know more about the real Countess Bathory, the following books provide some insight into her life and times. Please be aware that this reading material is intended for a mature audience and is not for the faint of heart, as the countess's deeds were as grotesque as they were disturbing.

Dracula Was a Woman: In Search of the Blood Countess of Transylvania, Raymond T. McNally

Countess Dracula, Tony Thorne

The Trouble with the Pears: An Intimate Portrait of Erzsebet Bathory, Gia Bathory Al Babel

ACKNOWLEDGEMENTS

A big heartfelt thank you to Stacy Whitman, my wonderful editor at Mirrorstone Books, for giving me the opportunity to write in the Hallowmere series, and for Tiffany Trent for creating a fantastic world and letting me play in it. Thanks as well to everybody else at Mirrorstone Books involved in the making of this book.

I'd also like to thank my writing buddy Debi Markee, the Queen of the Strong Verb, for reading my rough drafts and giving helpful, detailed input. You're the best!

Thanks to the members of my writing group, the Blue Dragons, for constant support and for teaching me the art of revision. They are—in random order—Hélène Prévost, Kathleen Bullock, Robin Alberg and Sara Gregory. I wish you all success in your own writing endeavors.

To all my friends at LiveJournal a big virtual hug for sharing their writing journey with me.

Last but not least, thanks to my husband Brent and my son Jeremy for reading and commenting on the manuscript, and to my younger son Tristan for sharing me for a while with an invisible world of Fey.

—Angelika Ranger

Can Christina outsmart the Unhallowed?
The next Hallowmere adventure continues in

Queen of the Masquerade

CHRISTINA WAKES IN A NEW WORLD WITH NO MEMORY OF who she is or where she came from. Tasked with solving a riddle that will save the duke and duchess who take her in as a changeling, Christina seeks to puzzle out just what she's doing here.

But the riddle isn't just a key to saving the duke and duchess—it's Christina's key to something far more dire, a mission she knows she must remember, one that involves the strange young man who keeps appearing in odd places. Is the riddle a prophecy or a warning?